MASTERS OF SHADES AND SHADOWS

Masters of Shades and Shadows

AN ANTHOLOGY OF GREAT
GHOST STORIES ❧ SELECTED
BY SEON MANLEY AND GOGO LEWIS
❧ DOUBLEDAY & COMPANY, INC.
GARDEN CITY, NEW YORK

Library of Congress Cataloging in Publication Data
Main entry under title:

Masters of shades and shadows.

CONTENTS: Classic chillers: Dickens, C. To
be taken with a grain of salt. Stoker, B. The
secret of the growing gold. Collins, W. The dream
woman. [etc.]
1. Ghost stories, English.   2. Ghost stories,
American.   I. Manley, Seon.   II. Lewis, Gogo.
PZ1.M394 [PR1309.G5] 823'.0872
ISBN 0-385-12743-x Trade
0-385-12744-8 Prebound
Library of Congress Catalog Card Number 77–76255

We are grateful to the authors, agents, and publishers who have given us permission to reprint the following selections:

"The Looking-Glass" by Walter de la Mare. Reprinted by permission of The Literary Trustees of Walter de la Mare, and The Society of Authors as their representative.

"The Ghosts" from The Sword of Welleran by Lord Dunsany. Reprinted by permission of Curtis Brown Ltd. and the Estate of Lord Dunsany.

"Rats" from Collected Ghost Stories of M. R. James. Reprinted by permission of Edward Arnold (Publishers) Ltd.

"The Thing in the Moonlight" by H. P. Lovecraft, from Dreams and Fancies, published by Arkham House, © 1962 by August Derleth. Reprinted by permission of the author's Estate and the agents for the Estate, Scott Meredith Literary Agency, Inc., 845 Third Avenue, New York, New York 10022.

"Escort" by Daphne du Maurier. Reprinted by permission of the author and Curtis Brown Ltd. (London).

"The Lake" by Ray Bradbury. Copyright 1944, renewed by the author 1972 Ray Bradbury, reprinted by permission of Harold Matson Co. Inc.

"The Rock" from Come Along with Me by Shirley Jackson. Copyright © 1968 by Stanley Edgar Hyman. Reprinted by permission of The Viking Press.

Our thanks also to Susan Belcher; Betty Shalders; the staff of the Bellport Memorial Library, Bellport, New York; the staff of the Patchogue Library, Patchogue, New York; the staff of the Greenwich Library, Greenwich, Connecticut; our husbands, Robert R. Manley and William W. Lewis; and our daughters, Sara Lewis, Carol Lewis, and Shivaun Manley.

For Rita Wright—still one of the best

Contents

INTRODUCTION

"Any ghost stories for me today?"

With those words Joseph Sheridan Le Fanu approached regularly every old bookseller in the streets of Dublin. When he found an old classic, or an unfamiliar tale, he rejoiced.

Le Fanu was not alone. Since time immemorial, readers and story-tellers have found an exquisitely fearful delight in ghost stories. Charles Dickens first heard them from his nurse; he went on to exorcise them in classic stories. Ghost stories came to Edgar Allan Poe in dreams; to O. Henry who was "haunted," he said, by the people who walked the streets before him, the former inhabitants of rooms he visited. Wilkie Collins fashioned them from a drug-induced world; H. P. Lovecraft from his own addiction to the night; Ray Bradbury from that "secret self" that creates.

All of these great writers kept an open mind as far as "believing" in ghosts, but they nonetheless embellished their hauntings in masterful tales. And why? "For pleasure," said M. R. James. "I write for pleasure, to amuse myself and others." That curious pleasure, as Dickens said, that makes the *flesh creep*.

CLASSIC CHILLERS

(EARLY MASTERS OF THE GHOST STORY)

TO BE TAKEN WITH
A GRAIN OF SALT

BY CHARLES DICKENS

CHARLES DICKENS enjoyed regaling his contemporaries with tales of the "female bard," who, early on, had introduced him to the world of ghosts and goblins. This woman, his nurse before he was six years old, was able to make her ghost stories have a particular immediacy. As she related the tales, she clawed the air with both hands, and uttered long hollow groans. When he was put to bed each night, the infant Dickens was given a dose of ghostly tale, evidently to insure nightmare.

This early influence continued to haunt the mature Dickens, whose overwhelming success as a novelist was matched by his ability in the short story and his sensitivity as an editor. He collaborated with Wilkie Collins and his brother Charles (who had a hand in "To Be Taken With a Grain of Salt") and encouraged extensively the talented men and women of his day to explore the ghost story.

"Ghost stories," he said, "illustrating particular states of mind and processes of the imagination are common property, I always think— except in the matter of relating them, and O, who can rob some people of *that!*"

Certainly not Dickens who, not robbing himself of the pleasure of writing a ghost story, gives us the pleasure of a classic chiller. ॐ

I HAVE always noticed a prevalent want of courage, even among persons of superior intelligence and culture, as to imparting their own psychological experiences when those have been of a strange sort. Almost all men are afraid that what they could relate in such wise would find no parallel or response in a listener's internal life, and might be suspected or laughed at. A truthful traveller who should have seen some extraordinary creature in the likeness of a sea-serpent, would have no fear of mentioning it; but the same traveller having had some singular presentiment, impulse, vagary of thought, vision (so called), dream, or other remarkable mental impression, would hesitate considerably before he would own to it. To this reticence I attribute much of the obscurity in which such subjects are involved. We do not habitually communicate our experiences of these subjective things as we do our experiences of objective creation. The consequence is, that the general stock of experience in this regard appears exceptional, and really is so, in respect of being miserably imperfect.

In what I am going to relate I have no intention of setting up, opposing, or supporting, any theory whatever. I know the history of the Bookseller of Berlin, I have studied the case of the wife of a late Astronomer Royal as related by Sir David Brewster, and I have followed the minutest details of a much more remarkable case of Spectral Illusion occurring within my private circle of friends. It may be necessary to state as to this last that the sufferer (a lady) was in no degree, however distant, related to me. A mistaken assumption on that head, might suggest an explanation of a part of my own case—but only a part—which would be wholly without foundation. It cannot be referred to my inheritance of any developed peculiarity, nor had I ever before any at all similar experience, nor have I ever had any at all similar experience since.

It does not signify how many years ago, or how few, a certain Murder was committed in England, which attracted great attention. We hear more than enough of Murderers as they rise in succession to their atrocious eminence, and I would bury the memory of this particular brute, if I could, as his body was buried, in Newgate Jail. I purposely abstain from giving any direct clue to the criminal's individuality.

When the murder was first discovered, no suspicion fell—or I ought rather to say, for I cannot be too precise in my facts, it was nowhere publicly hinted that any suspicion fell—on the man who was afterwards brought to trial. As no reference was at that time made to him in the newspapers, it is obviously impossible that any description of him can at that time have been given in the newspapers. It is essential that this fact be remembered.

Unfolding at breakfast my morning paper, containing the account of that first discovery, I found it to be deeply interesting, and I read it with close attention. I read it twice, if not three times. The discovery had been made in a bedroom, and, when I laid down the paper, I was aware of a flash—rush—flow—I do not know what to call it—no word I can find is satisfactorily descriptive—in which I seemed to see that bedroom passing through my room, like a picture impossibly painted on a running river. Though almost instantaneous in its passing, it was perfectly clear; so clear that I distinctly, and with a sense of relief, observed the absence of the dead body from the bed.

It was in no romantic place that I had this curious sensation, but in chambers in Piccadilly, very near to the corner of St. James's-street. It was entirely new to me. I was in my easy-chair at the moment, and the sensation was accompanied with a peculiar shiver which started the chair from its position. (But it is to be noted that the chair ran easily on castors.) I went to one of the windows (there are two in the room, and the room is on the second floor) to refresh my eyes with the moving objects down in Piccadilly. It was a bright autumn morning, and the street was sparkling and cheerful. The wind was high. As I looked out, it brought down from the Park a quantity of fallen leaves, which a gust took, and whirled into a spiral pillar. As the pillar fell and the leaves dispersed, I saw two men on the opposite side of the way, going from West to East. They were one behind the other. The foremost man often looked back over his shoulder. The second man followed him, at a distance of some thirty paces, with his right hand menacingly raised. First, the singularity and steadiness of this threatening gesture in so public a thoroughfare attracted my attention; and next, the more remarkable circumstance that nobody heeded it. Both men threaded their way among the other passengers, with a smoothness hardly consistent even with the action of walking on a pavement, and no single creature, that I could see, gave them place, touched them, or looked after them. In passing before my windows, they both stared up at me. I saw their two faces very distinctly, and I knew that I could recognise them anywhere. Not that I had consciously noticed anything very remarkable in either face, except that the man who went first had an unusually lowering appearance, and that the face of the man who followed him was of the colour of impure wax.

I am a bachelor, and my valet and his wife constitute my whole establishment. My occupation is in a certain Branch Bank, and I wish that my duties as head of a Department were as light as they are popularly supposed to be. They kept me in town that autumn, when I stood in need of change. I was not ill, but I was not well. My reader is to make the most that can be reasonably made of my feeling jaded, having a depressing sense upon me of a monotonous life, and being "slightly dyspeptic." I am assured by my renowned doctor that my real state of health at that time justifies no stronger description, and I quote his own from his written answer to my request for it.

As the circumstances of the Murder, gradually unravelling, took stronger and stronger possession of the public mind, I kept them away from mine, by knowing as little about them as was possible in the midst of the universal excitement. But I knew that a verdict of Wilful Murder had been found against the suspected Murderer, and that he had been committed to Newgate for trial. I also knew that his trial had been postponed over one Sessions of the Central Criminal Court, on the ground of general prejudice and want of time for the preparation of the defence. I may further have known, but I believe I did not, when, or about when, the Sessions to which this trial stood postponed would come on.

My sitting-room, bedroom, and dressing-room, are all on one floor. With the last there is no communication but through the bedroom. True, there is a door in it, once communicating with the staircase; but a part of the fitting of my bath has been—and had then been for some years—fixed across it. At the same period, and as a part of the same arrangement, the door had been nailed up and canvased over.

I was standing in my bedroom late one night, giving some directions to my servant before he went to bed. My face was towards the only available door of communication with the dressing-room, and it was closed. My servant's back was towards that door. While I was speaking to him I saw it open, and a man look in, who very earnestly and mysteriously beckoned to me. That man was the man who had gone second of the two along Piccadilly, and whose face was the colour of impure wax.

The figure, having beckoned, drew back and closed the door. With no longer pause than was made by my crossing the bedroom, I opened the dressing-room door, and looked in. I had a lighted candle already in my hand. I felt no inward expectation of seeing the figure in the dressing-room, and I did not see it there.

Conscious that my servant stood amazed, I turned round to him, and said: "Derrick, could you believe that in my cool senses I fancied I saw a——" As I there laid my hand upon his breast, with a sudden start he trembled violently, and said, "O Lord, yes, sir! A dead man beckoning!"

Now, I do not believe that this John Derrick, my trusty and attached servant for more than twenty years, had any impression whatever of having seen any such figure, until I touched him. The change in him was so startling, when I touched him, that I fully believed he derived his impression in some occult manner from me at that instant.

I bade John Derrick bring some brandy, and I gave him a dram, and was glad to take one myself. Of what had proceeded that night's phenomenon, I told him not a single word. Reflecting on it, I was absolutely certain that I had never seen that face before, except on the one occasion in Piccadilly. Comparing its expression when beckoning at the door, with its expression when it had stared up at me as I stood at my window, I came to the conclusion that on the first occasion it had sought to fasten itself upon my memory, and that on the second occasion it had made sure of being immediately remembered.

I was not very comfortable that night, though I felt a certainty, difficult to explain, that the figure would not return. At daylight, I fell into a heavy sleep, from which I was awakened by John Derrick's coming to my bedside with a paper in his hand.

This paper, it appeared, had been the subject of an altercation at the door between its bearer and my servant. It was a summons to me to serve upon a Jury at the forthcoming Sessions of the Central Criminal Court at the Old Bailey. I had never before been summoned on such a Jury, as John Derrick well knew. He believed—I am not certain at this hour whether with reason or otherwise—that the class of Jurors were customarily chosen on a lower qualification than mine, and he had at first refused to accept the summons. The man who served it had taken the matter very coolly. He had said that my attendance or non-attendance was nothing to him; there the summons was; and I should deal with it at my own peril, and not at his.

For a day or two I was undecided whether to respond to this call, or take no notice of it. I was not conscious of the slightest mysterious bias, influence, or attraction, one way or other. Of that I am as strictly sure as of every other statement that I make here. Ultimately I decided, as a break in the monotony of my life, that I would go.

The appointed morning was a raw morning in the month of November. There was a dense brown fog in Piccadilly, and it became positively black and in the last degree oppressive East of Temple Bar. I found the passages and staircases of the Court House flaringly lighted with gas, and the Court itself similarly illuminated. I *think* that until I was conducted by officers into the Old Court and saw its crowded state, I did not know that the Murderer was to be tried that day. I *think* that until I was so helped into the Old Court with considerable difficulty, I did not know into which of the two Courts sitting, my summons would take me. But this must not be received as a positive assertion, for I am not completely satisfied in my mind on either point.

I took my seat in the place appropriated to Jurors in waiting, and I looked about the Court as well as I could through the cloud of fog and breath that was heavy in it. I noticed the black vapour hanging like a murky curtain outside the great windows, and I noticed the stifled sound of wheels on the straw or tan that was littered in the street; also, the hum of the people gathered there, which a shrill whistle, or a louder song or hail than the rest, occasionally pierced. Soon afterwards the Judges, two in number, entered and took their seats. The buzz in the Court was awfully hushed. The direction was given to put the Murderer to the bar. He appeared there. And in that same instant I recognised in him, the first of the two men who had gone down Piccadilly.

If my name had been called then, I doubt if I could have answered to it audibly. But it was called about sixth or eighth in the panel, and I was by that time able to say "Here!" Now, observe. As I stepped into the box, the prisoner, who had been looking on attentively but with no sign of concern, became violently agitated, and beckoned to his attorney. The prisoner's wish to challenge me was so manifest, that it occasioned a pause, during which the attorney, with his hand upon the dock, whispered with his client, and shook his head. I afterwards had it from that gentleman, that the prisoner's first affrighted words to him were, "At all hazards challenge that man!" But, that as he would give no reason for it, and admitted that he had not even known my name until he heard it called and I appeared, it was not done.

Both on the ground already explained, that I wish to avoid reviving the unwholesome memory of that Murderer, and also because a detailed account of his long trial is by no means indispensable to my narrative, I shall confine myself closely to such incidents in the ten days and nights during which we, the Jury, were kept together, as directly bear on my own curious personal experience. It is in that, and not in the Murderer, that I seek to interest my reader. It is to that, and not to a page of the Newgate Calendar, that I beg attention.

I was chosen Foreman of the Jury. On the second morning of the trial, after evidence had been taken for two hours (I heard the church clocks strike), happening to cast my eyes over my brother-jurymen, I found an inexplicable difficulty in counting them. I counted them several times, yet always with the same difficulty. In short, I made them one too many.

I touched the brother-juryman whose place was next me, and I whispered to him, "Oblige me by counting us." He looked surprised by the request, but turned his head and counted. "Why," says he, suddenly, "we are thirt—; but no, it's not possible. No. We are twelve."

According to my counting that day, we were always right in detail, but in the gross we were always one too many. There was no appearance —no figure—to account for it; but I had now an inward foreshadowing of the figure that was surely coming.

The Jury were housed at the London Tavern. We all slept in one large room on separate tables, and we were constantly in the charge and under the eye of the officer sworn to hold us in safe-keeping. I see no reason for suppressing the real name of that officer. He was intelligent, highly polite, and obliging, and (I was glad to hear) much respected in the City. He had an agreeable presence, good eyes, enviable black whiskers, and a fine sonorous voice. His name was Mr. Harker.

When we turned into our twelve beds at night, Mr. Harker's bed was drawn across the door. On the night of the second day, not being disposed to lie down, and seeing Mr. Harker sitting on his bed, I went and sat beside him, and offered him a pinch of snuff. As Mr. Harker's hand touched mine in taking it from my box, a peculiar shiver crossed him, and he said, "Who is this!"

Following Mr. Harker's eyes, and looking along the room, I saw again the figure I expected—the second of the two men who had gone down Piccadilly. I rose, and advanced a few steps; then stopped, and looked round at Mr. Harker. He was quite unconcerned, laughed, and said in a pleasant way, "I thought for a moment we had a thirteenth juryman, without a bed. But I see it is the moonlight."

Making no revelation to Mr. Harker, but inviting him to take a walk with me to the end of the room, I watched what the figure did. It stood for a few moments by the bedside of each of my eleven brother-jurymen, close to the pillow. It always went to the right-hand side of the bed, and always passed out crossing the foot of the next bed. It seemed from the action of the head, merely to look down pensively at each recumbent figure. It took no notice of me, or of my bed, which was that nearest to Mr. Harker's. It seemed to go out where the moonlight came in, through a high window, as by an aërial flight of stairs.

Next morning at breakfast, it appeared that everybody present had dreamed of the murdered man last night, except myself and Mr. Harker.

I now felt as convinced that the second man who had gone down Piccadilly was the murdered man (so to speak), as if it had been borne into my comprehension by his immediate testimony. But even this took place, and in a manner for which I was not at all prepared.

On the fifth day of the trial, when the case for the prosecution was drawing to a close, a miniature of the murdered man, missing from his bedroom upon the discovery of the deed, and afterwards found in a hiding-place where the Murderer had been seen digging, was put in evidence. Having been identified by the witness under examination, it was handed up to the Bench, and thence handed down to be inspected by the Jury. As an officer in a black gown was making his way with it across to me, the figure of the second man who had gone down Piccadilly impetuously started from the crowd, caught the miniature from the officer, and gave it to me with its own hands, at the same time saying in a low and hollow tone—before I saw the miniature, which was in a locket—"I was younger then, and my face was not then drained of blood." It also came between me and the brother-juryman to whom I would have given the miniature, and between him and the brother-juryman to whom he would have given it, and so passed it on through the whole of our number, and back into my possession. Not one of them, however, detected this.

At table, and generally when we were shut up together in Mr. Harker's custody, we had from the first naturally discussed the day's proceedings a good deal. On that fifth day, the case for the prosecution being closed, and we having that side of the question in a completed shape before us, our discussion was more animated and serious. Among our number was a vestryman—the densest idiot I have ever seen at large —who met the plainest evidence with the most preposterous objections, and who was sided with by two flabby parochial parasites; all the three empanelled from a district so delivered over to Fever that they ought to have been upon their own trial, for five hundred Murders. When these mischievous blockheads were at their loudest, which was towards midnight while some of us were already preparing for bed, I again saw the murdered man. He stood grimly behind them, beckoning to me. On my going towards them and striking into the conversation, he immediately retired. This was the beginning of a separate series of appearances, confined to that long room in which *we* were confined. Whenever a knot of my brother-jurymen laid their heads together, I saw the head of the murdered man among theirs. Whenever their comparison of notes was going against him, he would solemnly and irresistibly beckon to me.

It will be borne in mind that down to the production of the miniature on the fifth day of the trial, I had never seen the Appearance in Court. Three changes occurred, now that we entered on the case for the defence. Two of them I will mention together, first. The figure was now in Court continually, and it never there addressed itself to me, but always to the person who was speaking at the time. For instance. The throat of the murdered man had been cut straight across. In the opening speech for the defence, it was suggested that the deceased might have cut his own throat. At that very moment, the figure with its throat in the dreadful condition referred to (this it had concealed before) stood at the speaker's elbow, motioning across and across its wind-pipe, now with the right hand, now with the left, vigorously suggesting to the speaker himself, the impossibility of such a wound having been self-inflicted by either hand. For another instance. A witness to character, a woman, deposed to the prisoner's being the most amiable of mankind. The figure at that instant stood on the floor before her, looking her full in the face, and pointing out the prisoner's evil countenance with an extended arm and an outstretched finger.

The third change now to be added, impressed me strongly, as the most marked and striking of all. I do not theorise upon it; I accurately state it, and there leave it. Although the Appearance was not itself perceived by those whom it addressed, its coming close to such persons was

invariably attended by some trepidation or disturbance on their part. It
seemed to me as if it were prevented by laws to which I was not amena-
ble, from fully revealing itself to others, and yet as if it could, invisibly,
dumbly, and darkly, overshadow their minds. When the leading counsel
for the defence suggested that hypothesis of suicide and the figure stood
at the learned gentleman's elbow, frightfully sawing at its severed
throat, it is undeniable that the counsel faltered in his speech, lost for a
few seconds the thread of his ingenious discourse, wiped his forehead
with his hankerchief, and turned extremely pale. When the witness to
character was confronted by the Appearance, her eyes most certainly did
follow the direction of its pointed finger, and rest in great hesitation and
trouble upon the prisoner's face. Two additional illustrations will
suffice. On the eighth day of the trial, after the pause which was every
day made early in the afternoon for a few minutes' rest and refresh-
ment, I came back into court with the rest of the Jury, some little time
before the return of the Judges. Standing up in the box and looking
about me, I thought the figure was not there, until, chancing to raise my
eyes to the gallery, I saw it bending forward and leaning over a very decent woman, as if to assure itself whether the Judges had resumed their
seats or not. Immediately afterwards that woman screamed, fainted, and
was carried out. So with the venerable, sagacious, and patient Judge who
conducted the trial. When the case was over, and he settled himself and
his papers to sum up, the murdered man entering by the Judges' door,
advanced to his Lordship's desk, and looked eagerly over his shoulder at
the pages of his notes which he was turning. A change came over his
Lordship's face; his hand stopped; the peculiar shiver that I knew so well,
passed over him; he faltered, "Excuse me, gentlemen, for a few moments. I am somewhat oppressed by the vitiated air"; and did not
recover until he had drunk a glass of water.

Through all the monotony of six of these interminable ten days—the
same Judges and others on the bench, the same Murderer in the dock,
the same lawyers at the table, the same tones of question and answer rising to the roof of the Court, the same scratching of the Judge's pen, the
same ushers going in and out, the same lights kindled at the same hour
when there had been any natural light of day, the same foggy curtain
outside the great windows when it was foggy, the same rain pattering
and dripping when it was rainy, the same footmarks of turnkeys and
prisoner day after day on the same sawdust, the same keys locking and

unlocking the same heavy doors—through all the wearisome monotony which made me feel as if I had been Foreman of the Jury for a vast period of time, and Piccadilly had flourished coevally with Babylon, the murdered man never lost one trace of his distinctness in my eyes, nor was he at any moment less distinct than anybody else. I must not omit, as a matter of fact, that I never once saw the Appearance which I call by the name of the murdered man, look at the Murderer. Again and again I wondered, "Why does he not?" But he never did.

Nor did he look at me, after the production of the miniature, until the last closing minutes of the trial arrived. We retired to consider, at seven minutes before ten at night. The idiotic vestryman and his two parochial parasites gave us so much trouble, that we twice returned into Court, to beg to have certain extracts from the Judge's notes re-read. Nine of us had not the smallest doubt about those passages, neither, I believe, had any one in Court; the dunderheaded triumvirate however, having no idea but obstruction, disputed them for that very reason. At length we prevailed, and finally the Jury returned into Court at ten minutes past twelve.

The murdered man at that time stood directly opposite the Jury-box, on the other side of the Court. As I took my place, his eyes rested on me, with great attention; he seemed satisfied, and slowly shook a great grey veil, which he carried on his arm for the first time, over his head and whole form. As I gave in our verdict, "Guilty," the veil collapsed, all was gone, and his place was empty.

The Murderer being asked by the Judge, according to usage, whether he had anything to say before sentence of Death should be passed upon him, indistinctly muttered something which was described in the leading newspapers of the following day as "a few rambling, incoherent, and half-audible words, in which he was understood to complain that he had not had a fair trial, because the Foreman of the Jury was prepossessed against him." The remarkable declaration that he really made was this: "*My Lord, I knew I was a doomed man when the Foreman of my Jury came into the box. My Lord, I knew he would never let me off, because, before I was taken, he somehow got to my bedside in the night, woke me, and put a rope round my neck.*"

THE SECRET OF
THE GROWING GOLD

BY BRAM STOKER

M Y DEAR, *Dracula* is splendid, . . . and I feel certain it
will place you very high in the writers of the day. No
book since Mrs. Shelley's *Frankenstein*, or indeed any other at all
has come near yours in originality or terror."

In this congratulatory letter to her son Bram, Mrs. Charlotte
Stoker was just one of the thousands of his contemporary readers
who felt the same. Mrs. Stoker's sickly child Abraham, the third
of seven children, had grown up to be the Athletic Champion of
Dublin University, and his own gift for macabre storytelling
astounded him. A lusty red-haired Irishman who thrived in the
theater world of London, Bram Stoker, his friends said, was a whirl
of energy.

Stoker published some dozen books, and a handful of short stories
that have escaped being overfamiliar to today's readers. "The Secret
of the Growing Gold" was inspired by a trip to the ghostly, isolated
great houses of Scotland. ৡৣ

W HEN MARGARET DELANDRE went to live at Brent's Rock the
whole neighbourhood awoke to the pleasure of an entirely new scandal.
Scandals in connection with either the Delandre family or the Brents of
Brent's Rock, were not few; and if the secret history of the county had
been written in full both names would have been found well repre-

sented. It is true that the status of each was so different that they might have belonged to different continents—or to different worlds for the matter of that—for hitherto their orbits had never crossed. The Brents were accorded by the whole section of the country a unique social dominance, and had ever held themselves as high above the yeoman class to which Margaret Delandre belonged, as a blue-blooded Spanish hidalgo-out-tops his peasant tenantry.

The Delandres had an ancient record and were as proud of it in their way as the Brents were of theirs. But the family had never risen above yeomanry and although they had been once well-to-do in the good old times of foreign wars and protection, their fortunes had withered under the scorching of the free trade sun and the "piping times of peace." They had, as the elder members used to assert, "stuck to the land," with the result that they had taken root in it, body and soul. In fact, they, having chosen the life of vegetables, had flourished as vegetation does—blossomed and thrived in the good season and suffered in the bad. Their holding, Dander's Croft, seemed to have been worked out, and to be typical of the family which had inhabited it. The latter had declined generation after generation, sending out now and again some abortive shoot of unsatisfied energy in the shape of a soldier or sailor, who had worked his way to the minor grades of the services and had there stopped, cut short either from unheeding gallantry in action or from that destroying cause to me without breeding or youthful care—the recognition of a position above them which they feel unfitted to fill. So, little by little, the family dropped lower and lower, the men brooding and dissatisfied, and drinking themselves into the grave, the women drudging at home, or marrying beneath them—or worse. In process of time all disappeared, leaving only two in the Croft, Wykham Delandre and his sister Margaret. The man and woman seemed to have inherited in masculine and feminine form respectively the evil tendency of their race, sharing in common the principles, though manifesting them in different ways, of sullen passion, voluptuousness and recklessness.

The history of the Brents had been something similar, but showing the causes of decadence in their aristocratic and not their plebeian forms. They, too, had sent their shoots to the wars; but their positions had been different and they had often attained honour—for without flaw they were gallant, and brave deeds were done by them before the selfish dissipation which marked them had sapped their vigour.

The present head of the family—if family it could now be called when one remained of the direct line—was Geoffrey Brent. He was almost a type of worn out race, manifesting in some ways its most brilliant qualities, and in others its utter degradation. He might be fairly compared with some of those antique Italian nobles whom the painters have preserved to us with their courage, their unscrupulousness, their refinement of lust and cruelty—the voluptuary actual with the fiend potential. He was certainly handsome, with that dark, aquiline, commanding beauty which women so generally recognise as dominant. With men he was distant and cold; but such a bearing never deters womankind. The inscrutable laws of sex have so arranged that even a timid woman is not afraid of a fierce and haughty man. And so it was that there was hardly a woman of any kind or degree, who lived within view of Brent's Rock, who did not cherish some form of secret admiration for the handsome wastrel. The category was a wide one, for Brent's Rock rose up steeply from the midst of a level region and for a circuit of a hundred miles it lay on the horizon, with its high old towers and steep roofs cutting the level edge of wood and hamlet, and far-scattered mansions.

So long as Geoffrey Brent confined his dissipations to London and Paris and Vienna—anywhere out of sight and sound of his home—opinion was silent. It is easy to listen to far off echoes unmoved, and we can treat them with disbelief, or scorn, or disdain, or whatever attitude of coldness may suit our purpose. But when the scandal came close home it was another matter; and the feelings of independence and integrity which is in people of every community which is not utterly spoiled, asserted itself and demanded that condemnation should be expressed. Still there was a certain reticence in all, and no more notice was taken of the existing facts than was absolutely necessary. Margaret Delandre bore herself so fearlessly and so openly—she accepted her position as the justified companion of Geoffrey Brent so naturally that people came to believe that she was secretly married to him, and therefore thought it wiser to hold their tongues lest time should justify her and also make her an active enemy.

The one person who, by his interference, could have settled all doubts was debarred by circumstances from interfering in the matter. Wykham Delandre had quarrelled with his sister—or perhaps it was that she had quarrelled with him—and they were on terms not merely of armed neutrality but of bitter hatred. The quarrel had been antecedent to Mar-

garet going to Brent's Rock. She and Wykham had almost come to
blows. There had certainly been threats on one side and on the other;
and in the end Wykham, overcome with passion, had ordered his sister
to leave his house. She had risen straightway, and, without waiting to
pack up even her own personal belongings, had walked out of the house.
On the threshold she had paused for a moment to hurl a bitter threat at
Wykham that he would rue in shame and despair to the last hour of his
life his act of that day. Some weeks had since passed; and it was understood in the neighbourhood that Margaret had gone to London, when
she suddenly appeared driving out with Geoffrey Brent, and the entire
neighbourhood knew before nightfall that she had taken up her abode
at the Rock. It was no subject of surprise that Brent had come back unexpectedly, for such was his usual custom. Even his own servants never
knew when to expect him, for there was a private door, of which he
alone had the key, by which he sometimes entered without anyone in
the house being aware of his coming. This was his usual method of appearing after a long absence.

Wykham Delandre was furious at the news. He vowed vengeance—
and to keep his mind level with his passion drank deeper than ever. He
tried several times to see his sister, but she contemptuously refused to
meet him. He tried to have an interview with Brent and was refused by
him also. Then he tried to stop him in the road, but without avail, for
Geoffrey was not a man to be stopped against his will. Several actual en-
counters took place between the two men, and many more were threat-
ened and avoided. At last Wykham Delandre settled down to a morose,
vengeful acceptance of the situation.

Neither Margaret nor Geoffrey was of a pacific temperament, and it
was not long before there began to be quarrels between them. One
thing would lead to another, and wine flowed freely at Brent's Rock.
Now and again the quarrels would assume a bitter aspect, and threats
would be exchanged in uncompromising language that fairly awed the
listening servants. But such quarrels generally ended where domestic al-
tercations do, in reconciliation, and in a mutual respect for the fighting
qualities proportionate to their manifestation. Fighting for its own sake
is found by a certain class of persons, all the world over, to be a matter
of absorbing interest, and there is no reason to believe that domestic
conditions minimise its potency. Geoffrey and Margaret made occasional absences from Brent's Rock, and on each of these occasions

Wykham Delandre also absented himself; but as he generally heard of the absence too late to be of any service, he returned home each time in a more bitter and discontented frame of mind than before.

At last there came a time when the absence from Brent's Rock became longer than before. Only a few days earlier there had been a quarrel, exceeding in bitterness anything which had gone before; but this, too, had been made up, and a trip on the Continent had been mentioned before the servants. After a few days Wykham Delandre also went away, and it was some weeks before he returned. It was noticed that he was full of some new importance—satisfaction, exaltation—they hardly knew how to call it. He went straightaway to Brent's Rock, and demanded to see Geoffrey Brent, and on being told that he had not yet returned, said, with a grim decision which the servants noted:

"I shall come again. My news is solid—it can wait!" and turned away. Week after week went by, and month after month; and then there came a rumour, certified later on, that an accident had occurred in the Zermatt valley. Whilst crossing a dangerous pass the carriage containing an English lady and the driver had fallen over a precipice, the gentleman of the party, Mr. Geoffrey Brent, having been fortunately saved as he had been walking up the hill to ease the horses. He gave information, and search was made. The broken rail, the excoriated roadway, the marks where the horses had struggled on the decline before finally pitching over into the torrent—all told the sad tale. It was a wet season, and there had been much snow in the winter, so that the river was swollen beyond its usual volume, and the eddies of the stream were packed with ice. All search was made, and finally the wreck of the carriage and the body of one horse were found in an eddy of the river. Later on the body of the driver was found on the sandy, torrent-swept waste near Täsch; but the body of the lady, like that of the other horse, had quite disappeared, and was—what was left of it by that time—whirling amongst the eddies of the Rhone on its way down to the Lake of Geneva.

Wykham Delandre made all the enquiries possible, but could not find any trace of the missing woman. He found, however, in the books of the various hotels the name of "Mr. and Mrs. Geoffrey Brent." And he had a stone erected at Zermatt to his sister's memory, under her married name, and a tablet put up in the church at Bretten, the parish in which both Brent's Rock and Dander's Croft were situated.

There was a lapse of nearly a year, after the excitement of the matter had worn away, and the whole neighbourhood had gone on its accustomed way. Brent was still absent, and Delandre more drunken, more morose, and more revengeful than before.

Then there was a new excitement. Brent's Rock was being made ready for a new mistress. It was officially announced by Geoffrey himself in a letter to the Vicar, that he had been married some months before to an Italian lady, and that they were then on their way home. Then a small army of workmen invaded the house; and hammer and plane sounded, and a general air of size and paint pervaded the atmosphere. One wing of the old house, the south, was entirely re-done; and then the great body of the workmen departed, leaving only materials for the doing of the old hall when Geoffrey Brent should have returned, for he had directed that the decoration was only to be done under his own eyes. He had brought with him accurate drawings of a hall in the house of his bride's father, for he wished to reproduce for her the place to which she had been accustomed. As the moulding had all to be re-done, some scaffolding poles and boards were brought in and laid on one side of the great hall, and also a great wooden tank or box for mixing the lime, which was laid in bags beside it.

When the new mistress of Brent's Rock arrived the bells of the church rang out, and there was a general jubilation. She was a beautiful creature, full of the poetry and fire and passion of the South; and the few English words which she had learned were spoken in such a sweet and pretty broken way that she won the hearts of the people almost as much by the music of her voice as by the melting beauty of her dark eyes.

Geoffrey Brent seemed more happy than he had ever before appeared; but there was a dark, anxious look on his face that was new to those who knew him of old, and he started at times as though at some noise that was unheard by others.

And so months passed and the whisper grew that at last Brent's Rock was to have an heir. Geoffrey was very tender to his wife, and the new bond between them seemed to soften him. He took more interest in his tenants and their needs than he had ever done; and works of charity on his part as well as on his sweet young wife's were not lacking. He seemed to have set all his hopes on the child that was coming, and as he looked deeper into the future the dark shadow that had come over his face seemed to die gradually away.

All the time Wykham Delandre nursed his revenge. Deep in his heart had grown up a purpose of vengeance which only waited an opportunity to crystallise and take a definite shape. His vague idea was somehow centred in the wife of Brent, for he knew that he could strike him best through those he loved, and the coming time seemed to hold in its womb the opportunity for which he longed. One night he sat alone in the living-room of his house. It had once been a handsome room in its way, but time and neglect had done their work and it was now little better than a ruin, without dignity or picturesqueness of any kind. He had been drinking heavily for some time and was more than half stupefied. He thought he heard a noise as of someone at the door and looked up. Then he called half savagely to come in; but there was no response. With a muttered blasphemy he renewed his potations. Presently he forgot all around him, sank into a daze, but suddenly awoke to see standing before him someone or something like a battered, ghostly edition of his sister. For a few moments there came upon him a sort of fear. The woman before him, with distorted features and burning eyes seemed hardly human, and the only thing that seemed a reality of his sister, as she had been, was her wealth of golden hair, and this was now streaked with grey. She eyed her brother with a long, cold stare; and he, too, as he looked and began to realise the actuality of her presence, found the hatred of her which he had had, once again surging up in his heart. All the brooding passion of the past year seemed to find a voice at once as he asked her:

"Why are you here? You're dead and buried."

"I am here, Wykham Delandre, for no love of you, but because I hate another even more than I do you!" A great passion blazed in her eyes.

"Him?" he asked, in so fierce a whisper that even the woman was for an instant startled till she regained her calm.

"Yes, him!" she answered. "But make no mistake, my revenge is my own; and I merely use you to help me to it." Wykham asked suddenly;

"Did he marry you?"

The woman's distorted face broadened out in a ghastly attempt at a smile. It was a hideous mockery, for the broken features and seamed scars took strange shapes and strange colours, and queer lines of white showed out as the straining muscles pressed on the old cicatrices.

"So you would like to know! It would please your pride to feel that your sister was truly married! Well, you shall not know. That was my revenge on you, and I do not mean to change it by a hair's breadth. I have come here tonight simply to let you know that I am alive, so that if any violence be done me where I am going there may be a witness."

"Where are you going?" demanded her brother.

"That is my affair! and I have not the least intention of letting you know!" Wykham stood up, but the drink was on him and he reeled and fell. As he lay on the floor he announced his intention of following his sister; and with an outburst of splenetic humour told her that he would follow her through the darkness by the light of her hair, and of her beauty. At this she turned on him, and said that there were others beside him that would rue her hair and her beauty too. "As he will," she hissed; "for the hair remains though the beauty be gone. When he withdrew the lynch-pin and sent us over the precipice into the torrent, he had little thought of my beauty. Perhaps his beauty would be scarred like mine were he whirled, as I was, among the rocks of the Visp, and frozen on the ice pack in the drift of the river. But let him beware! His time is coming!" and with a fierce gesture she flung open the door and passed out into the night.

Later on that night, Mrs. Brent, who was but half-asleep, became suddenly awake and spoke to her husband:

"Geoffrey, was not that the click of a lock somewhere below our window?"

But Geoffrey—though she thought that he, too, had started at the noise—seemed sound asleep, and breathed heavily. Again Mrs. Brent dozed; but this time awoke to the fact that her husband had arisen and was partially dressed. He was deadly pale, and when the light of the lamp which he had in his hand fell on his face, she was frightened at the look in his eyes.

"What is it, Geoffrey? What dost thou?" she asked.

"Hush! little one," he answered, in a strange, hoarse voice. "Go to sleep. I am restless, and wish to finish some work I left undone."

"Bring it here, my husband," she said; "I am lonely and I fear when thou art away."

For reply he merely kissed her and went out, closing the door behind him. She lay awake for awhile, and then nature asserted itself, and she slept.

Suddenly she started broad awake with the memory in her ears of a smothered cry from somewhere not far off. She jumped up and ran to the door and listened, but there was no sound. She grew alarmed for her husband, and called out: "Geoffrey! Geoffrey!"

After a few moments the door of the great hall opened, and Geoffrey appeared at it, but without his lamp.

"Hush!" he said, in a sort of whisper, and his voice was harsh and stern. "Hush! Get to bed! I am working, and must not be disturbed. Go to sleep, and do not wake the house!"

With a chill in her heart—for the harshness of her husband's voice was new to her—she crept back to bed and lay there trembling, too frightened to cry, and listened to every sound. There was a long pause of silence, and then the sound of some iron implement striking muffled blows! Then there came a clang of a heavy stone falling, followed by a muffled curse. Then a dragging sound, and then more noise of stone on stone. She lay all the while in an agony of fear, and her heart beat dreadfully. She heard a curious sort of scraping sound; and then there was silence. Presently the door opened gently, and Geoffrey appeared. His wife pretended to be asleep; but through her eyelashes she saw him wash from his hands something white that looked like lime.

In the morning he made no allusion to the previous night, and she was afraid to ask any question.

From that day there seemed some shadow over Geoffrey Brent. He neither ate nor slept as he had been accustomed, and his former habit of turning suddenly as though someone were speaking from behind him revived. The old hall seemed to have some kind of fascination for him. He used to go there many times in the day, but grew impatient if anyone, even his wife, entered it. When the builder's foreman came to inquire about continuing his work Geoffrey was out driving; the man went into the hall, and when Geoffrey returned the servant told him of his arrival and where he was. With a frightful oath he pushed the servant aside and hurried up to the old hall. The workman met him almost at the door; and as Geoffrey burst into the room he ran against him. The man apologised:

"Beg pardon, sir, but I was just going out to make some enquiries. I directed twelve sacks of lime to be sent here, but I see there are only ten."

"Damn the ten sacks and the twelve too!" was the ungracious and incomprehensible rejoinder.

The workman looked surprised, and tried to turn the conversation.

"I see, sir, there is a little matter which our people must have done; but the governor will of course see it set right at his own cost."

"What do you mean?"

"That 'ere 'arth-stone, sir: Some idiot must have put a scaffold pole on it and cracked it right down the middle, and it's thick enough you'd think to stand hanythink." Geoffrey was silent for quite a minute, and then said in a constrained voice and with much gentler manner:

"Tell your people that I am not going on with the work in the hall at present. I want to leave it as it is for a while longer."

"All right sir. I'll send up a few of our chaps to take away these poles and lime bags and tidy the place up a bit."

"No! No!" said Geoffrey, "leave them where they are. I shall send and tell you when you are to get on with the work." So the foreman went away, and his comment to his master was:

"I'd send in the bill, sir, for the work already done. 'Pears to me that money's a little shaky in that quarter."

Once or twice Delandre tried to stop Brent on the road, and, at last, finding that he could not attain his object rode after the carriage, calling out:

"What has become of my sister, your wife?" Geoffrey lashed his horses into a gallop, and the other, seeing from his white face and from his wife's collapse almost into a faint that his object was attained, rode away with a scowl and a laugh.

That night when Geoffrey went into the hall he passed over to the great fireplace, and all at once started back with a smothered cry. Then with an effort he pulled himself together and went away, returning with a light. He bent down over the broken hearth-stone to see if the moonlight falling through the storied window had in any way deceived him. Then with a groan of anguish he sank to his knees.

There, sure enough, through the crack in the broken stone were protruding a multitude of threads of golden hair just tinged with grey!

He was disturbed by a noise at the door, and looking round, saw his wife standing in the doorway. In the desperation of the moment he took action to prevent discovery, and lighting a match at the lamp, stooped down and burned away the hair that rose through the broken stone. Then rising nonchalantly as he could, he pretended surprise at seeing his wife beside him.

For the next week he lived in an agony; for, whether by accident or design, he could not find himself alone in the hall for any length of time. At each visit the hair had grown afresh through the crack, and he had to watch it carefully lest his terrible secret should be discovered. He tried to find a receptacle for the body of the murdered woman outside the house, but someone always interrupted him; and once, when he was coming out of the private doorway, he was met by his wife, who began to question him about it, and manifested surprise that she should not have before noticed the key which he now reluctantly showed her. Geoffrey dearly and passionately loved his wife, so that any possibility of her discovering his dread secrets, or even of doubting him, filled him with anguish; and after a couple of days had passed, he could not help coming to the conclusion that, at least, she suspected something.

That very evening she came into the hall after her drive and found him there sitting moodily by the deserted fireplace. She spoke to him directly.

"Geoffrey, I have been spoken to by that fellow Delandre, and he says horrible things. He tells to me that a week ago his sister returned to this house, the wreck and ruin of her former self, with only her golden hair as of old, and announced some fell intention. He asked me where she is —and oh, Geoffrey, she is dead, she is dead! So how can she have returned? Oh! I am in dread, and I know not where to turn!"

For answer, Geoffrey burst into a torrent of blasphemy which made her shudder. He cursed Delandre and his sister and all their kind, and in especial he hurled curse after curse on her golden hair.

"Oh, hush! hush!" she said, and was then silent, for she feared her husband when she saw the evil effect of his humour. Geoffrey in the torrent of his anger stood up and moved away from the hearth; but suddenly stopped as he saw a new look of terror in his wife's eyes. He followed their glance, and then he too, shuddered—for there on the broken hearth-stone lay a golden streak as the point of the hair rose through the crack.

"Look, look!" she shrieked. "It is some ghost of the dead! Come away —come away!" and seizing her husband by the wrist with the frenzy of madness, she pulled him from the room.

That night she was in a raging fever. The doctor of the district attended her at once, and special aid was telegraphed for to London. Geoffrey was in despair, and in his anguish at the danger to his young wife almost forgot his own crime and its consequences. In the evening the doctor had to leave to attend to others; but he left Geoffrey in charge of his wife. His last words were:

"Remember, you must humour her till I come in the morning, or till some other doctor has her case in hand. What you have to dread is another attack of emotion. See that she is kept warm. Nothing more can be done."

Late in the evening, when the rest of the household had retired, Geoffrey's wife got up from her bed and called to her husband.

"Come!" she said. "Come to the old hall! I know where the gold comes from! I want to see it grow!"

Geoffrey would fain have stopped her, but he feared for her life or reason on the one hand, and lest in a paroxysm she should shriek out her terrible suspicion, and seeing that it was useless to try to prevent her, wrapped a warm rug around her and went with her to the old hall. When they entered, she turned and shut the door and locked it.

"We want no strangers amongst us three tonight!" she whispered with a wan smile.

"We three! nay we are but two," said Geoffrey with a shudder; he feared to say more.

"Sit here," said his wife as she put out the light. "Sit here by the hearth and watch the gold growing. The silver moonlight is jealous! See, it steals along the floor towards the gold—our gold!" Geoffrey looked with growing horror, and saw that during the hours that had passed the golden hair had protruded further through the broken hearth-stone. He tried to hide it by placing his feet over the broken place; and his wife, drawing her chair beside him, leant over and laid her head on his shoulder.

"Now do not stir, dear," she said; "let us sit still and watch. We shall find the secret of the growing gold!" He passed his arm round her and sat silent; and as the moonlight stole along the floor she sank to sleep.

He feared to wake her; and so sat silent and miserable as the hours stole away.

Before his horror-struck eyes the golden hair from the broken stone grew and grew; and as it increased, so his heart got colder and colder, till at last he had not power to stir, and sat with eyes full of terror watching his doom.

In the morning when the London doctor came, neither Geoffrey nor his wife could be found. Search was made in all the rooms, but without avail. As a last resource the great door of the old hall was broken open, and those who entered saw a grim and sorry sight.

There by the deserted hearth Geoffrey Brent and his young wife sat cold and white and dead. Her face was peaceful, and her eyes were closed in sleep; but his face was a sight that made all who saw shudder, for there was on it a look of unutterable horror. The eyes were open and stared glassily at his feet, which were twined with tresses of golden hair, streaked with grey, which came through the broken hearth-stone.

THE DREAM WOMAN

BY WILKIE COLLINS

WILKIE COLLINS, twelve years younger than Charles Dickens, became the latter's intimate friend after he was first introduced to him in 1851. Dickens' although he admired and published Collins' work, including the best-selling *Woman in White* and *The Moonstone*, always looked on Collins with a wry eye. Collins had been trained as a painter, and he lectured Dickens on the characteristics of color until Dickens was in a frenzy; he was equally oracular about music. Often under the influence of laudanum he expanded upon the nature of time.

Dickens laughed at Collins' extravagance in speech and appearance (he grew a beard that overshadowed Dickens', drenched himself in snuff, and cared nothing for nineteenth-century propriety). There was never, however, any doubt in Dickens' mind that Collins was a superb storyteller.

Collins confided that his storytelling skill came from the oppression of a bully he had met in his boarding school, who forced him to tell a story every night. "The tyrant," he said, "made for himself a cat-o'-nine-tails, and as often as my voice died away he leaned across the bed and gave me a cut or two with it which started me afresh. But I owe him a debt of gratitude, for it was this brute who first awakened in me a power of which, but for him, I might never have been aware. When I left school I still continued storytelling for my own pleasure."

That pleasure extended to others—in "The Dream Woman" Collins was at the top of his storytelling form. 〰

I

I HAD not been settled much more than six weeks in my country practice, when I was sent for to a neighbouring town, to consult with the resident medical man there, on a case of very dangerous illness.

My horse had come down with me, at the end of a long ride the night before, and had hurt himself, luckily much more than he had hurt his master. Being deprived of the animal's services, I started for my destination by the coach (there were no railways at that time); and I hoped to get back again, towards the afternoon, in the same way.

After the consultation was over I went to the principal inn of the town to wait for the coach. When it came up, it was full inside and out. There was no resource left me but to get home as cheaply as I could, by hiring a gig. The price asked for this accommodation struck me as being so extortionate, that I determined to look out for an inn of inferior pretensions, and to try if I could not make a better bargain with a less prosperous establishment.

I soon found a likely-looking house, dingy and quiet, with an old-fashioned sign, that had evidently not been repainted for many years past. The landlord, in this case, was not above making a small profit; and as soon as we came to terms, he rang the yard bell to order the gig.

"Has Robert not come back from that errand?" asked the landlord, appealing to the waiter, who answered the bell.

"No, sir, he hasn't."

"Well, then, you must wake up Isaac."

"Wake up Isaac?" I repeated; "that sounds rather odd. Do your ostlers go to bed in the day-time?"

"This one does," said the landlord, smiling to himself in rather a strange way.

"And dreams, too," added the waiter.

"Never you mind about that," retorted his master; "you go and rouse Isaac up. The gentleman's waiting for his gig."

The landlord's manner and the waiter's manner expressed a great deal more than they either of them said. I began to suspect that I might be on the trace of something professionally interesting to me, as a medical man; and I thought I should like to look at the ostler, before the waiter awakened him.

"Stop a minute," I interposed; "I have rather a fancy for seeing this man before you wake him up. I am a doctor; and if this queer sleeping and dreaming of his comes from anything wrong in his brain, I may be able to tell you what to do with him."

"I rather think you will find his complaint past all doctoring, sir," said the landlord. "But if you would like to see him, you're welcome, I'm sure."

He led the way across a yard and down a passage to the stables; opened one of the doors; and waiting outside himself, told me to look in.

I found myself in a two-stall stable. In one of the stalls a horse was munching his corn. In the other, an old man was lying asleep on the litter.

I stooped and looked at him attentively. It was a withered, woebegone face. The eyebrows were painfully contracted; the mouth was set fast, and drawn down at the corners. The hollow, wrinkled cheeks, and the scanty grizzled hair, told their own tale of past sorrow or suffering. He was drawing his breath convulsively when I first looked at him; and in a moment more he began to talk in his sleep.

"Wake up!" I heard him say in a quick whisper, through his clenched teeth. "Wake up, there! Murder!"

He moved one lean arm slowly till it rested over his throat, shuddered a little, and turned on the straw. Then the arm left his throat, the hand stretched itself out, and clutched at the side towards which he had turned, as if he fancied himself to be grasping at the edge of something. I saw his lips move, and bent lower over him. He was still talking in his sleep.

"Light grey eyes," he murmured, "and a droop in the left eyelid—flaxen hair, with a gold-yellow streak in it—all right, mother—fair white arms, with a down on them—little lady's hand, with a reddish look under the fingernails. The knife—always the cursed knife—first on one side, then on the other. Aha! you she-devil, where's the knife?"

At the last word his voice rose, and he grew restless on a sudden. I saw him shudder on the straw; his withered face became distorted, and he threw up both his hands with a quick, hysterical gasp. They struck against the bottom of the manger under which he lay, and the blow awakened him. I had just time to slip through the door, and close it, before his eyes were fairly open, and his senses his own again.

"Do you know anything about that man's past life?" I said to the landlord.

"Yes, sir. I know pretty well all about it," was the answer, "and an uncommon queer story it is. Most people don't believe it. It's true, though, for all that. Why, just look at him," continued the landlord, opening the stable door again. "Poor devil! he's so worn out with his restless nights that he's dropped back into his sleep already."

"Don't wake him," I said; "I'm in no hurry for the gig. Wait till the other man comes back from his errand. And, in the meantime, suppose I have some lunch, and a bottle of sherry; and suppose you come and help me to get through it."

The heart of mine host, as I had anticipated, warmed to me over his own wine. He soon became communicative on the subject of the man asleep in the stable; and by little and little, I drew the whole story out of him. Extravagant and incredible as the events must appear to everybody, they are related here just as I heard them, and just as they happened.

II

Some years ago there lived in the suburbs of a large seaport town, on the west coast of England, a man in humble circumstances, by name Isaac Scatchard. His means of subsistence were derived from any employment he could get as an ostler, and occasionally, when times went well with him, from temporary engagements in service as stable-helper in private houses. Though a faithful, steady, and honest man, he got on badly in his calling. His ill-luck was proverbial among his neighbours. He was always missing good opportunities by no fault of his own; and always living longest in service with amiable people who were not punctual payers of wages. "Unlucky Isaac" was his nickname in his own neighbourhood—and no-one could say that he did not richly deserve it.

With far more than one man's fair share of adversity to endure, Isaac had but one consolation to support him—and that was of the dreariest and most negative kind. He had no wife and children to increase his anxieties and add to the bitterness of his various failures in life. It might have been from mere insensibility, or it might have been from generous unwillingness to involve another in his own unlucky destiny—but the fact undoubtedly was, that he had arrived at the middle term of life without marrying; and, what is much more remarkable, without once exposing himself from eighteen to eight-and-thirty, to the genial imputation of ever having had a sweetheart.

When he was out of service, he lived alone with his widowed mother. Mrs. Scatchard was a woman above the average in her lowly station, as to capacity and manners. She had seen better days, as the phrase is; but she never referred to them in the presence of curious visitors; and, though perfectly polite to everyone who approached her, never cultivated any intimacies among her neighbours. She contrived to provide, hardly enough for her simple wants, by doing rough work for the tailors; and always managed to keep a decent home for her son to return to, whenever his ill-luck drove him out helpless into the world.

One bleak Autumn, when Isaac was getting fast towards forty, and when he was, as usual, out of place through no fault of his own, he set forth from his mother's cottage on a long walk inland to a gentleman's seat, where he had heard that a stable-helper was required.

It wanted then but two days of his birthday; and Mrs. Scatchard, with her usual fondness, made him promise before he started, that he would be back in time to keep that anniversary with her in as festive a way as their poor means would allow. It was easy for him to comply with her request, even supposing he slept a night each way on the road.

He was to start from home on Monday morning; and whether he got the new place or not, he was to be back for his birthday dinner on Wednesday at two o'clock.

Arriving at his destination too late on the Monday night to make application for the stable-helper's place, he slept at the village inn, and, in good time on the Tuesday morning, presented himself at the gentleman's house to fill the vacant situation. Here, again, his ill-luck pursued him as inexorably as ever. The excellent written testimonials to his character which he was able to produce, availed him nothing; his long walk had been taken in vain—only the day before, the stable-helper's place had been given to another man.

Isaac accepted this new disappointment resignedly, and as a matter of course. Naturally slow in capacity, he had the bluntness of sensibility and phlegmatic patience of disposition which frequently distinguish men with sluggishly-working mental powers. He thanked the gentleman's steward with his usual quiet civility, for granting him an interview, and took his departure with no appearance of unusual depression in his face or manner.

Before starting on his homeward walk, he made some inquiries at the inn, and ascertained that he might save a few miles, on his return, by following a new road. Furnished with full instructions, several times repeated, as to the various turnings he was to take, he set forth on his homeward journey, and walked on all day with only one stoppage for bread and cheese. Just as it was getting towards dark, the rain came on and the wind began to rise; and he found himself, to make matters worse, in a part of the country with which he was entirely unacquainted, though he knew himself to be some fifteen miles from home. The first house he found to inquire at was a lonely roadside inn, standing on the outskirts of a thick wood. Solitary as the place looked, it was welcome to a lost man who was also hungry, thirsty, footsore, and wet. The landlord was civil and respectable-looking; and the price he asked for a bed was reasonable enough. Isaac, therefore, decided on stopping comfortably at the inn for that night.

He was constitutionally a temperate man. His supper simply consisted of two rashers of bacon, a slice of homemade bread, and a pint of ale. He did not go to bed immediately after this moderate meal, but sat up with the landlord, talking about his bad prospects and his long run of ill-luck, and diverging from these topics to the subjects of horse-flesh and racing. Nothing was said, either by himself, his host, or the few labourers who strayed into the taproom, which could, in the slightest degree, excite the very small and very dull imaginative faculty which Isaac Scatchard possessed.

At a little after eleven the house was closed. Isaac went round with the landlord, and held the candle while the doors and lower windows were being secured. He noticed, with surprise, the strength of the bolts, bars, and iron-sheathed shutters.

"You see, we are rather lonely here," said the landlord. "We never have had any attempts made to break in yet, but it's always as well to be on the safe side. When nobody is sleeping here I am the only man in the house. My wife and daughter are timid, and the servant-girl takes after her missuses. Another glass of ale before you turn in?—No!—Well, how such a sober man as you comes to be out of a place is more than I can make out, for one. . . . Here's where you're to sleep. You're the only lodger to-night, and I think you'll say my missus has done her best to make you comfortable. You're quite sure you won't have another glass of ale?—Very well. Good night."

It was half-past eleven by the clock in the passage as they went upstairs to the bedroom, the window of which looked on to the wood at the back of the house.

Isaac locked the door, set his candle on the chest of drawers, and wearily got ready for bed. The bleak autumn wind was still blowing, and the solemn, surging moan of it in the wood was dreary and awful to hear through the night-silence. Isaac felt strangely wakeful. He resolved, as he lay down in bed, to keep the candle alight until he began to grow sleepy; for there was something unendurably depressing in the bare idea of lying awake in the darkness, listening to the dismal, ceaseless moan of the wind in the wood.

Sleep stole on him before he was aware of it. His eyes closed, and he fell off insensibly to rest, without having so much as thought of extinguishing the candle.

The first sensation of which he was conscious, after sinking into slumber, was a strange shivering that ran through him suddenly from head to foot, and a dreadful sinking pain at the heart, such as he had never felt before. The shivering only disturbed his slumbers—the pain woke him instantly. In one moment he passed from a state of sleep to a state of wakefulness—his eyes wide open—his mental perceptions cleared on a sudden as if by a miracle.

The candle had burnt down nearly to the last morsel of tallow, but the top of the unsnuffed wick had just fallen off, and the light in the little room was, for the moment, fair and full.

Between the foot of his bed and the closed door, there stood a woman with a knife in her hand, looking at him.

He was stricken speechless with terror, but he did not lose the preternatural clearness of his faculties; and he never took his eyes off the woman. She said not a word as they stared each other in the face; but she began to move slowly towards the left hand side of the bed.

His eyes followed her. She was a fair, fine woman, with yellowish flaxen hair, and light grey eyes, with a droop in the left eyelid. He noticed these things, and fixed them on his mind, before she was round at the side of the bed. Speechless, with no expression in her face, with no noise following her footfall, she came closer and closer—stopped—and slowly raised the knife. He laid his right arm over his throat to save it;

but, as he saw the knife coming down, threw his hand across the bed to the right side, and jerked his body over that way, just as the knife descended on the mattress within an inch of his shoulder.

His eyes fixed on her arm and hand, as she slowly drew her knife out of the bed. A white, well-shaped arm, with a pretty down lying lightly over the fair skin. A delicate, lady's hand, with the crowning beauty of a pink flush under and round the finger-nails.

She drew the knife out, and passed back again slowly to the foot of the bed; stopped there for a moment looking at him; then came on—still speechless, still with no expression on the beautiful face, still with no sound following the stealthy footfalls—came on to the right side of the bed where he now lay.

As she approached, she raised the knife again, and he drew himself away to the left side. She struck, as before, right into the mattress, with a deliberate, perpendicularly downward action of the arm. This time his eyes wandered from her to the knife. It was like the large clasp-knives which he had often seen labouring men use to cut their bread and bacon with. Her delicate little fingers did not conceal more than two-thirds of the handle; he noticed that it was made of buckhorn, clean and shining as the blade was, and looking like new.

For the second time she drew the knife out, concealed it in the wide sleeve of her gown, then stopped by the bedside, watching him. For an instant he saw her standing in that position—then the wick of the spent candle fell over into the socket. The flame diminished to a little blue point, and the room grew dark.

A moment, or less if possible, passed so—and then the wick flamed up, smokily, for the last time. His eyes were still looking eagerly over the right-hand side of the bed when the final flash of light came, but they discerned nothing. The fair woman with the knife was gone.

The conviction that he was alone again, weakened the hold of the terror that had struck him dumb up to this time. The preternatural sharpness which the very intensity of his panic had mysteriously imparted to his faculties, left them suddenly. His brain grew confused—his heart beat wildly—his ears opened, for the first time since the appearance of the woman, to a sense of the woeful, ceaseless moaning of the wind among the trees. With the dreadful conviction of the reality of what he had seen still strong within him, he leapt out of bed, and screaming—"Murder!—Wake up there, wake up!"—dashed headlong through the darkness to the door.

It was fast locked, exactly as he had left it on going to bed.

His cries, on starting up, had alarmed the house. He heard the terrified, confused exclamations of women; he saw the master of the house approaching along the passage, with his burning rush-candle in one hand and his gun in the other.

"What is it?" asked the landlord, breathlessly.

Isaac could only answer in a whisper. "A woman, with a knife in her hand," he gasped out. "In my room—a fair, yellow-haired woman; she jabbed at me with the knife twice over."

The landlord's pale cheek grew paler. He looked at Isaac eagerly by the flickering light of his candle; and his face began to get red again—his voice altered, too, as well as his complexion.

"She seems to have missed you twice," he said.

"I dodged the knife as it came down," Isaac went on, in the same scared whisper. "It struck the bed each time."

The landlord took his candle into the bedroom immediately. In less than a minute he came out again into the passage in a violent passion.

"The devil fly away with you and your woman with the knife! There isn't a mark in the bed-clothes anywhere. What do you mean by coming into a man's place and frightening his family out of their wits by a dream?"

"I'll leave your house," said Isaac, faintly. "Better out on the road, in rain and dark, on my way home, than back again in that room, after what I've seen in it. Lend me a light to get my clothes by, and tell me what I'm to pay."

"Pay!" cried the landlord, leading the way with his light sulkily into the bedroom. "You'll find your score on the slate when you go downstairs. I wouldn't have taken you in for all the money you've got about you, if I'd known your dreaming, screeching ways beforehand. Look at the bed. Where's the cut of a knife in it? Look at the window—is the lock bursted? Look at the door (which I heard you fasten yourself) is it broke in? A murdering woman with a knife in my house! You ought to be ashamed of yourself!"

Isaac answered not a word. He huddled on his clothes; and then they went downstairs together.

"Nigh on twenty minutes past two!" said the landlord, as they passed the clock. "A nice time in the morning to frighten honest people out of their wits!"

Isaac paid his bill, and the landlord let him out at the front door, asking, with a grin of contempt, as he undid the strong fastenings, whether "the murdering woman got in that way?"

They parted without a word on either side. The rain had ceased; but the night was dark, and the wind bleaker than ever. Little did the darkness, or the cold, or the uncertainty about the way home matter to Isaac. If he had been turned out into a wilderness in a thunderstorm, it would have been a relief, after what he had suffered in the bedroom of the inn.

What was the fair woman with the knife? The creature of a dream, or that other creature from the unknown world, called among men by the name of ghost? He could make nothing of the mystery—had made nothing of it, even when it was midday on Wednesday, and when he stood, at last, after many times missing his road, once more on the doorstep of home.

III

His mother came out eagerly to receive him. His face told her in a moment that something was wrong.

"I've lost the place; but that's my luck. I dreamed an ill dream last night, mother—or, maybe, I saw a ghost. Take it either way, it scared me out of my senses, and I'm not my own man again yet."

"Isaac! your face frightens me. Come in to the fire. Come in, and tell mother all about it."

He was as anxious to tell as she was to hear; for it had been his hope, all the way home, that his mother, with her quicker capacity and superior knowledge, might be able to throw some light on the mystery which he could not clear up for himself. His memory of the dream was still mechanically vivid, though his thoughts were entirely confused by it.

His mother's face grew paler and paler as he went on. She never interrupted him by so much as a single word; but when he had done, she moved her chair close to his, put her arm round his neck, and said to him:

"Isaac, you dreamed your ill dream on this Wednesday morning.

What time was it when you saw the fair woman with the knife in her hand?"

Isaac reflected on what the landlord had said when they had passed by the clock on his leaving the inn—allowed as nearly as he could for the time that must have elapsed between the unlocking of his bedroom door and the paying of his bill just before going away, and answered:

"Somewhere about two o'clock in the morning."

His mother suddenly quitted her hold of his neck, and struck her hands together with a gesture of despair.

"This Wednesday is your birthday, Isaac; and two o'clock in the morning is the time when you were born!"

Isaac's capacities were not quick enough to catch the infection of his mother's superstitious dread. He was amazed, and a little startled also, when she suddenly rose from her chair, opened her old writing-desk, took pen, ink and paper, and then said to him:

"Your memory is but a poor one, Isaac, and now I'm an old woman, mine's not much better. I want all about this dream of yours to be as well known to both of us, years hence, as it is now. Tell me over again all you told me a minute ago, when you spoke of what the woman with the knife looked like."

Isaac obeyed, and marvelled much as he saw his mother carefully set down on paper the very words that he was saying.

"Light grey eyes," she wrote as they came to the descriptive part, "with a droop in the left eyelid. Flaxen hair, with a gold-yellow streak in it. White arms, with a down upon them. Little lady's hand, with a reddish look about the finger-nails. Clasp-knife with a buckhorn handle, that seemed as good as new." To these particulars, Mrs. Scatchard added the year, month, day of the week, and time in the morning, when the woman of the dream appeared to her son. She then locked up the paper carefully in her writing-desk.

Neither on that day, nor on any day after, could her son induce her to return to the matter of the dream. She obstinately kept her thoughts about it to herself, and even refused to refer again to the paper in her writing-desk. Ere long, Isaac grew weary of attempting to make her break her resolute silence; and time, which sooner or later wears out all things, gradually wore out the impression produced on him by the dream. He began by thinking of it carelessly, and he ended by not thinking of it at all.

This result was the more easily brought about by the advent of some important changes for the better in his prospects, which commenced not long after his terrible night's experience at the inn. He reaped at last the reward of his long and patient suffering under adversity, by getting an excellent place, keeping it for seven years, and leaving it, on the death of his master, not only with an excellent character, but also with a comfortable annuity bequeathed to him as a reward for saving his mistress's life in a carriage accident. Thus it happened that Isaac Scatchard returned to his old mother, seven years after the time of the dream at the inn, with an annual sum of money at his disposal, sufficient to keep them both in ease and independence for the rest of their lives.

The mother, whose health had been bad of late years, profited so much by the care bestowed on her and by freedom from money anxieties, that when Isaac's birthday came round she was able to sit up comfortably at table and dine with him.

On that day, as the evening drew on, Mrs. Scatchard discovered that a bottle of tonic medicine—which she was accustomed to take, and in which she had fancied that a dose or more was still left—happened to be empty. Isaac immediately volunteered to go to the chemist's, and get it filled again. It was as rainy and bleak an autumn night as on the memorable past occasion when he lost his way and slept at the roadside inn.

On going into the chemist's shop, he was passed hurriedly by a poorly-dressed woman coming out of it. The glimpse he had of her face struck him, and he looked back after her as she descended the doorsteps.

"You're noticing that woman?" said the chemist's apprentice behind the counter. "It's my opinion there's something wrong with her. She's been asking for laudanum to put to a bad tooth. Master's out for half an hour; and I told her I wasn't allowed to sell poison to strangers in his absence. She laughed in a queer way, and said she would come back in half an hour. If she expects master to serve her, I think she'll be disappointed. It's a case of suicide, sir, if ever there was one yet."

These words added immeasurably to the sudden interest in the woman which Isaac had felt at the first sight of her face. After he had got the medicine bottle filled, he looked about anxiously for her, as soon as he was out in the street. She was walking slowly up and down on the opposite side of the road. With his heart, very much to his own surprise, beating fast, Isaac crossed over and spoke to her.

He asked if she was in any distress. She pointed to her torn shawl, her scanty dress, her crushed, dirty bonnet—then moved under a lamp so as to let the light fall on her stern, pale, but still most beautiful face.

"I look like a comfortable, happy woman—don't I?" she said, with a bitter laugh.

She spoke with a purity of intonation which Isaac had never heard before from other than ladies' lips. Her slightest actions seemed to have the easy, negligent grace of a thorough-bred woman. Her skin, for all its poverty-stricken paleness, was as delicate as if her life had been passed in the enjoyment of every social comfort that wealth can purchase. Even her small, finely-shaped hands, gloveless as they were, had not lost their whiteness.

Little by little, in answer to his questions, the sad story of the woman came out. There is no need to relate it here; it is told over and over again in police reports and paragraphs descriptive of Attempted Suicides.

"My name is Rebecca Murdoch," said the woman, as she ended. "I have ninepence left, and I thought of spending it at the chemist's over the way in securing a passage to the other world. Whatever it is, it can't be worse to me than this—so why should I stop here?"

Besides the natural compassion and sadness moved in his heart by what he heard, Isaac felt within him some mysterious influence at work all the time the woman was speaking, which utterly confused his ideas and almost deprived him of his powers of speech. All that he could say in answer to her last reckless words was, that he would prevent her from attempting her own life, if he followed her about all night to do it. His rough, trembling earnestness seemed to impress her.

"I won't occasion you that trouble," she answered, when he repeated his threat. "You have given me a fancy for living by speaking kindly to me. No need for the mockery of protestations and promises. You may believe me without them. Come to Fuller's Meadow to-morrow at twelve, and you will find me alive, to answer for myself. No!—no money. My ninepence will do to get me as good a night's lodgings as I want."

She nodded and left him. He made no attempt to follow—he felt no suspicion that she was deceiving him.

"It's strange, but I can't help believing her," he said to himself, and walked away bewildered towards home.

On entering the house, his mind was still so completely absorbed by its new subject of interest, that he took no notice of what his mother was doing when he came in with the bottle of medicine. She had opened her old writing-desk in his absence, and was now reading a paper attentively that lay inside it. On every birthday of Isaac's since she had written down the particulars of his dream from his own lips, she had been accustomed to read that same paper, and ponder over it in private.

The next day he went to Fuller's Meadow.

He had done only right in believing her so implicitly—she was there, punctual to a minute, to answer for herself. The last-left faint defences in Isaac's heart, again the fascination which a word or look from her began inscrutably to exercise over him, sank down and vanished before her for ever on that memorable morning.

When a man, previously insensible to the influence of women, forms an attachment in middle life, the instances are rare indeed, let the warning circumstances be what they may, in which he is found capable of freeing himself from the tyranny of the new ruling passion. The charm of being spoken to familiarly, fondly, and gratefully by a woman whose language and manners still retained enough of their early refinement to hint at the high social station that she had lost, would have been a dangerous luxury to a man of Isaac's rank at the age of twenty. But it was far more than that—it was certain ruin to him—now that his heart was opening unworthily to a new influence at that middle time of life when strong feelings of all kinds, once implanted, strike root most stubbornly in a man's moral nature. A few more stolen interviews after that first morning in Fuller's Meadow completed his infatuation. In less than a month from the time when he first met her, Isaac Scatchard had consented to give Rebecca Murdoch a new interest in existence, and a chance of recovering the character she had lost, by promising to make her his wife.

She had taken possession not of his passions only, but of his faculties as well. All the mind he had he put into her keeping. She directed him on every point, even instructing him how to break the news of his approaching marriage in the safest manner to his mother.

"If you tell her how you met me, and who I am at first," said the cunning woman, "she will move heaven and earth to prevent our marriage. Say I am the sister of one of your fellow-servants—ask her to see me before you go into any more particulars—and leave it to me to do the rest. I mean to make her love me next best to you, Isaac, before she knows anything of who I really am."

The motive of the deceit was sufficient to sanctify it to Isaac. The stratagem proposed relieved him of his one great anxiety, and quieted his uneasy conscience on the subject of his mother. Still, there was something wanting to perfect his happiness, something that he could not realize, something mysteriously untraceable, and yet something that perpetually made itself felt—not when he was absent from Rebecca Murdoch, but, strange to say, when he was actually in her presence! She was kindness itself with him; she never made him feel his inferior capacities and inferior manners—she showed the sweetest anxiety to please him in the smallest trifles; but, in spite of all these attractions, he never could feel quite at his ease with her. At their first meeting, there had mingled with his admiration, when he looked in her face, a faint, involuntary feeling of doubt whether that face was entirely strange to him. No after-familiarity had the slightest effect on this inexplicable, wearisome uncertainty.

Concealing the truth, as he had been directed, he announced his marriage engagement precipitately and confusedly to his mother, on the day when he contracted it. Poor Mrs. Scatchard showed her perfect confidence in her son by flinging her arms round his neck, and giving him joy of having found at last, in the sister of one of his fellow-servants, a woman to comfort and care for him after his mother was gone. She was all eagerness to see the woman of her son's choice, and the next day was fixed for the introduction.

It was a bright, sunny morning, and the little cottage parlour was full of light, as Mrs. Scatchard, happy and expectant, dressed for the occasion in her Sunday gown, sat waiting for her son and her future daughter-in-law.

Punctual to the appointed time, Isaac hurriedly and nervously led his promised wife into the room. His mother rose to receive her—advanced a few steps, smiling—looked Rebecca full in the eyes—and suddenly stopped. Her face, which had been flushed the moment before, turned white in an instant—her eyes lost their expression of softness and kindness, and assumed a blank look of terror—her outstretched hands fell to her sides, and she staggered back a few steps with a low cry to her son.

"Isaac!" she whispered, clutching him fast by the arm, when he asked, alarmedly, if she was taken ill. "Isaac! does that woman's face remind you of nothing?"

Before he could answer, before he could look round to where Rebecca stood, astonished and angered by her reception, at the lower end of the room, his mother pointed impatiently to her writing-desk and gave him the key.

"Open it," she said, in a quick, breathless whisper.

"What does this mean? Why am I treated as if I had no business here? Does your mother want to insult me?" asked Rebecca, angrily.

"Open it, and give me the paper in the left-hand drawer. Quick! quick! for heaven's sake!" said Mrs. Scatchard, shrinking further back in terror.

Isaac gave her the paper. She looked it over eagerly for a moment—then followed Rebecca, who was now turning away haughtily to leave the room, and caught her by the shoulder—abruptly raised the long, loose sleeve of her gown—and glanced at her hand and arm. Something like fear began to steal over the angry expression of Rebecca's face, as she shook herself free from the old woman's grasp. "Mad!" she said to herself, "and Isaac never told me." With those few words she left the room.

Isaac was hastening after her, when his mother turned and stopped his further progress. It wrung his heart to see the misery and terror in her face as she looked at him.

"Light grey eyes," she said, in low, mournful, awestruck tones, pointing towards the open door. "A droop in the left eyelid; flaxen hair, with a gold-yellow streak in it; white arms with a down on them; little, lady's hand, with a reddish look under the finger-nails. *The Dream Woman!* Isaac, the Dream Woman!"

That faint cleaving doubt which he had never been able to shake off in Rebecca Murdoch's presence, was fatally set at rest for ever. He *had* seen her face, then, before—seven years before, on his birthday, in the bedroom of the lonely inn.

"Be warned! Oh, my son, be warned! Isaac! Isaac! let her go, and do you stop with me!"

Something darkened the parlour window as those words were said. A sudden chill ran through him, and he glanced sidelong at the shadow. Rebecca Murdoch had come back. She was peering in curiously at them over the low window blind.

"I have promised to marry, mother," he said, "and marry I must."

The tears came into his eyes as he spoke, and dimmed his sight; but he could just discern the fatal face outside, moving away again from the window.

His mother's head sank lower.

"Are you faint?" he whispered.

"Broken-hearted, Isaac."

He stooped down and kissed her. The shadow, as he did so, returned to the window; and the fatal face peered in curiously once more.

IV

Three weeks after that day Isaac and Rebecca were man and wife. All that was hopelessly dogged and stubborn in the man's moral nature seemed to have closed round his fatal passion, and to have fixed it unassailably in his heart.

After that first interview in the cottage parlour, no consideration could induce Mrs. Scatchard to see her son's wife again, or even to talk of her when Isaac tried hard to plead her cause after their marriage.

This course of conduct was not in any degree occasioned by a discovery of the degradation in which Rebecca had lived. There was no question of that between mother and son. There was no question of anything but the fearfully exact resemblance between the living, breathing woman, and the spectre-woman of Isaac's dream.

Rebecca, on her side, neither felt nor expressed the slightest sorrow at the estrangement between herself and her mother-in-law. Isaac, for the sake of peace, had never contradicted her first idea that age and long illness had affected Mrs. Scatchard's mind. He even allowed his wife to upbraid him for not having confessed this to her at the time of their marriage engagement, rather than risk anything by hinting at the truth. The sacrifice of his integrity before his one all-mastering delusion, seemed but a small thing, and cost his conscience but little, after the sacrifices he had already made.

The time of waking from his delusion—the cruel and the rueful time —was not far off. After some quiet months of married life, as the summer was ending, and the year was getting on towards the month of his birthday, Isaac found his wife altering towards him. She grew sullen and contemptuous; she formed acquaintances of the most dangerous kind, in defiance of his objections, his entreaties, and his commands; and, worst of all, she learnt, ere long, after every fresh difference with her husband, to seek the deadly self-oblivion of drink. Little by little, after the first miserable discovery that his wife was keeping company with drunkards, the shocking certainty forced itself on Isaac that she had grown to be a drunkard herself.

He had been in a sadly desponding state for some time before the occurrence of these domestic calamities. His mother's health, as he could but too plainly discern every time he went to see her at the cottage, was failing fast; and he upbraided himself in secret as the cause of the bodily and mental suffering she endured. When to his remorse on his mother's account was added the shame and misery occasioned by the discovery of his wife's degradation, he sank under the double trial, his face began to alter fast, and he looked, what he was, a spirit-broken man.

His mother, still struggling bravely against the illness that was hurrying her to her grave, was the first to notice the sad alteration in him, and the first to hear of his last, worst trouble with his wife. She could only weep bitterly, on the day when he made his humiliating confession; but on the next occasion when he went to see her, she had taken a resolution, in reference to his domestic afflictions, which astonished, and even alarmed him. He found her dressed to go out, and on asking the reason, received this answer:

"I am not long for this world, Isaac," she said; "and I shall not feel easy on my death-bed, unless I have done my best to the last to make my son happy. I mean to put my own fears and my own feelings out of the question, and to go with you to your wife, and try what I can do to reclaim her. Give me your arm, Isaac; and let me do the last thing I can in this world to help my son, before it is too late."

He could not disobey her; and they walked together slowly towards his miserable home.

It was only one o'clock in the afternoon when they reached the cottage where he lived. It was their dinner hour, and Rebecca was in the kitchen. He was thus able to take his mother quietly into the parlour and then prepare his wife for the interview. She had fortunately drunk but little at that early hour, and she was less sullen and capricious than usual.

He returned to his mother, with his mind tolerably at ease. His wife soon followed him into the parlour, and the meeting between her and

WILKIE COLLINS 55

Mrs. Scatchard passed off better than he had ventured to anticipate; though he observed, with secret apprehension, that his mother, resolutely as she controlled herself in other respects, could not look his wife in the face when she spoke to her. It was a relief to him, therefore, when Rebecca began to lay the cloth.

She laid the cloth, brought in the bread-tray, and cut a slice from the loaf for her husband, then returned to the kitchen. At that moment, Isaac, still anxiously watching his mother, was startled by seeing the same ghastly change pass over her face which had altered it so awfully on the morning when Rebecca and she first met. Before he could say a word, she whispered with a look of horror:

"Take me back!—home, home, again, Isaac! Come with me and never go back again!"

He was afraid to ask for an explanation; he could only sign to her to be silent, and help her quickly to the door. As they passed the bread-tray on the table, she stopped and pointed to it.

"Did you see what your wife cut your bread with?" she asked in a low whisper.

"No, mother; I was not noticing. What was it?"

"Look!"

He did look. A new clasp-knife, with a buckhorn handle, lay with the loaf in the bread-tray. He stretched out his hand, shudderingly, to possess himself of it; but at the same time there was a noise in the kitchen, and his mother caught at his arm.

"The knife of the dream! Isaac, I'm faint with fear—take me away, before she comes back!"

He was hardly able to support her. The visible, tangible reality of the knife struck him with a panic, and utterly destroyed any faint doubts he might have entertained up to this time, in relation to the mysterious dream-warning of nearly eight years before. By a last desperate effort, he summoned self-possession enough to help his mother out of the house— so quietly, that the "Dream Woman" (he thought of her by that name now) did not hear their departure.

"Don't go back, Isaac, don't go back!" implored Mrs. Scatchard, as he turned to go away, after seeing her safely seated again in her own room.

"I must get the knife," he answered under his breath. His mother tried to stop him again; but he hurried out without another word.

On his return, he found that his wife had discovered their secret departure from the house. She had been drinking, and was in a fury of passion. The dinner in the kitchen was flung under the grate; the cloth was off the parlour table. Where was the knife?

Unwisely, he asked for it. She was only too glad of the opportunity of irritating him, which the request afforded her. "He wanted the knife, did he? Could he give her a reason why?—No? Then he should not have it—not if he went down on his knees to ask for it." Further recriminations elicited the fact that she had bought it as a bargain, and that she considered it her own especial property. Isaac saw the uselessness of attempting to get the knife by fair means, and determined to search for it, later in the day, in secret. The search was unsuccessful. Night came on, and he left the house to walk about the streets. He was afraid, now, to sleep in the same room with her.

Three weeks passed. Still sullenly enraged with him, she would not give up the knife; and still that fear of sleeping in the same room with her possessed him. He walked about at night, or dozed in the parlour, or sat watching by his mother's bedside. Before the expiration of the first week in the new month his mother died. It wanted then but ten days of her son's birthday. She had longed to live till that anniversary. Isaac was present at her death; and her last words in this world were addressed to him:

"Don't go back, my son—don't go back!"

He was obliged to go back, if it were only to watch his wife. Exasperated to the last degree by his distrust of her, she had revengefully sought to add a sting to his grief, during the last days of his mother's illness, by declaring that she would assert her right to attend the funeral. In spite of all that he could do or say, she held with wicked pertinacity to her word; and on the day appointed for the burial, forced herself—inflamed and shameless with drink—into her husband's presence, and declared that she would walk in the funeral procession to his mother's grave.

This last, worst outrage, accompanied by all that was most insulting in word and look, maddened him for the moment. He struck her.

The instant the blow was dealt he repented it. She crouched down, silent, in a corner of the room, and eyed him steadily; it was a look that cooled his hot blood and made him tremble. But there was no time now to think of a means of making atonement. Nothing remained but to risk the worst till the funeral was over. There was but one way of making sure of her. He locked her into her bedroom.

When he came back, some hours after, he found her sitting, very much altered in look and bearing, by the bedside, with a bundle on her lap. She rose and faced him quietly, and spoke with a strange stillness in her voice, a strange repose in her eyes, a strange composure in her manner.

"No man has ever struck me twice," she said; "and my husband shall have no second opportunity. Set the door open and let me go. From this day forth we see each other no more."

Before he could answer she passed him, and left the room. He saw her walk away up the street.

Would she return?

All that night he watched and waited; but no footstep came near the house. The next night, overcome by fatigue, he lay down in bed in his clothes, with the door locked, the key on the table, and the candle burning. His slumber was not disturbed. The third night, the fourth, the fifth, the sixth passed, and nothing happened. He lay down on the seventh, still in his clothes, still with the door locked, the key on the table, and the candle burning; but easier in his mind.

Easier in his mind, and in perfect health of body, when he fell off to sleep. But his rest was disturbed. He woke twice, without any sensation of uneasiness. But the third time it was that never-to-be-forgotten shivering of the night at the lonely inn, that dreadful sinking pain at the heart, which once more aroused him in an instant.

His eyes opened towards the left-hand side of the bed, and there stood . . .

The Dream Woman again? No! His wife; the living reality, with the dream-spectre's face—in the dream-spectre's attitude; the fair arm up; the knife clasped in the delicate, white hand.

He sprang upon her almost at the instant of seeing her, and yet not quickly enough to prevent her from hiding the knife. Without a word from him, without a cry from her, he pinioned her in a chair. With one hand he felt up her sleeve; and there, where the Dream Woman had hidden the knife, his wife had hidden it—the knife with the buckhorn handle, that looked like new.

In the despair of that fearful moment his brain was steady, his heart was calm. He looked at her fixedly, with the knife in his hand, and said these last words:

"You told me we should see each other no more, and you have come back. It is my turn now to go, and to go for ever. I say that we shall see each other no more; and my word shall not be broken."

He left her, and set forth into the night. There was a bleak wind abroad, and the smell of recent rain was in the air. The distant church clocks chimed the quarter as he walked rapidly beyond the last houses in the suburb. He asked the first policeman he met, what hour that was, of which the quarter past had just struck.

The man referred sleepily to his watch, and answered, "Two o'clock." Two in the morning. What day of the month was this day that had just begun? He reckoned it up from the date of his mother's funeral. The fatal parallel was complete—it was his birthday!

Had he escaped the mortal peril which his dream foretold? or had he only received a second warning?

As this ominous doubt forced itself on his mind, he stopped, reflected, and turned back again towards the city. He was still resolute to hold his word, and never to let her see him more; but there was a thought now in his mind of having her watched and followed. The knife was in his possession; the world was before him; but a new distrust of her—a vague, unspeakable, superstitious dread—had overcome him.

"I must know where she goes, now she thinks I have left her," he said to himself, as he stole back wearily to the precincts of his house.

It was still dark. He had left the candle burning in the bedchamber, but when he looked up to the window of the room now, there was no light in it. He crept cautiously to the house door. On going away, he remembered to have closed it; on trying it now, he found it open.

He waited outside, never losing sight of the house till daylight. Then he ventured indoors—listened, and heard nothing—looked into kitchen, scullery, parlour; and found nothing: went up at last into the bedroom —it was empty. A picklock lay on the floor, betraying how she had gained entrance in the night, and that was the only trace of her.

Whither had she gone? No mortal tongue could tell him. The darkness had covered her flight; and when the day broke no man could say where the light found her.

Before leaving the house and the town for ever, he gave instructions to a friend and neighbour to sell his furniture for anything that it would fetch, and to apply the proceeds towards employing the police to trace her. The directions were honestly followed, and the money was all spent; but the enquiries led to nothing. The picklock on the bedroom floor remained the last useless trace of the Dream Woman.

At this part of the narrative the landlord paused; and, turning towards the window of the room in which we were sitting, looked in the direction of the stable-yard.

"So far," he said, "I tell you what was told to me. The little that remains to be added lies within my own experience. Between two and three months after the events I have just been relating, Isaac Scatchard came to me, withered and old-looking before his time, just as you saw him to-day. He had his testimonials to character with him, and he asked me for employment here. Knowing that my wife and he were distantly related, I gave him a trial in consideration of that relationship, and liked him in spite of his queer habits. He is as sober, honest, and willing a man as there is in England. As for his restlessness at night, and his sleeping away his leisure time in the day, who can wonder at it after hearing his story? Besides, he never objects to being roused up, when he's wanted, so there's not much inconvenience to complain of, after all."

"I suppose he is afraid of a return of that dreadful dream, and of waking out of it in the dark?"

"No," returned the landlord. "The dream comes back to him so often, that he has got to bear with it by this time resignedly enough. It's his wife keeps him waking at night, as he has often told me."

"What! Has she never been heard of yet?"

"Never. Isaac himself has the one perpetual thought, that she is alive and looking for him. I believe he wouldn't let himself drop off to sleep towards two in the morning for a king's ransom. Two in the morning, he says, is the time she will find him, one of these days. Two in the morning is the time, all the year round, when he likes to be most certain that he has got the clasp-knife safe about him. He does not mind being alone, as long as he is awake, except on the night before his birthday, when he firmly believes himself to be in peril of his life. The birthday has only come round once since he has been here, and then he sat up along with the night-porter. 'She's looking for me,' is all he says, when anybody speaks to him about the one anxiety of his life; 'she's looking for me.' He may be right. She *may* be looking for him. Who can tell?"

"Who can tell?" said I.

LIGEIA

BY EDGAR ALLAN POE

NO WRITER has ever explored the strange webs that make up the dark side of the human psyche more than that great American writer, Edgar Allan Poe. Master of the science fiction story, the detective, the ghost story, he was acclaimed and attacked during his lifetime.

Genius and charlatan, Henry James called him, despite, or because of, the range of his talent. Cryptograms, ciphers, puzzles, labyrinths, wonders of nature and the supernatural, all these he mastered. A servant to terror only, Poe knew the ghost stories that lurk within all of us.

"Ligeia" is one of his finest stories. Tinged with vampirism, touched with the popular transmigration of soul theories of Poe's day, "Ligeia" is a richly tapestried tale composed by Poe when he was living in a hovel, nearly destitute.

Drink, drugs, personal drama all seemed in pursuit of Poe; he fought back with words, spectral sentences, strange stories of ghostly guilt. ?

And the will therein lieth, which dieth not. Who knoweth the mysteries of the will, with its vigor? For God is but a great will pervading all things by nature of its intentness. Man doth not yield himself to the angels, nor unto death utterly, save only through the weakness of his feeble will.—*Joseph Glanvill*

I CANNOT, for my soul, remember how, when, or even precisely where, I first became acquainted with the lady Ligeia. Long years have since elapsed, and my memory is feeble through much suffering. Or, perhaps, I cannot *now* bring these points to mind, because, in truth, the character of my beloved, her rare learning, her singular yet placid cast of beauty, and the thrilling and enthralling eloquence of her low musical language, made their way into my heart by paces so steadily and stealthily progressive, that they have been unnoticed and unknown. Yet I believe that I met her first and most frequently in some large, old, decaying city near the Rhine. Of her family—I have surely heard her speak. That it is of a remotely ancient date cannot be doubted. Ligeia! Ligeia! Buried in studies of a nature more than all else adapted to deaden impressions of the outward world, it is by that sweet word alone—by Ligeia—that I bring before mine eyes in fancy the image of her who is no more. And now, while I write, a recollection flashes upon me that I have *never known* the paternal name of her who was my friend and my betrothed, and who became the partner of my studies, and finally the wife of my bosom. Was it a playful charge on the part of my Ligeia? or was it a test of my strength of affection, that I should institute no inquiries upon this point? or was it rather a caprice of my own—a wildly romantic offering on the shrine of the most passionate devotion? I but indistinctly recall the fact itself—what wonder that I have utterly forgotten the circumstances which originated or attended it? And, indeed, if ever that spirit which is entitled *Romance*—if ever she, the wan and the misty-winged *Ashtophet* of idolatrous Egypt, presided, as they tell, over marriages ill-omened, then most surely she presided over mine.

There is one dear topic, however, on which my memory fails me not. It is the *person* of Ligeia. In stature she was tall, somewhat slender, and, in her latter days, even emaciated. I would in vain attempt to portray the majesty, the quiet ease of her demeanor, or the incomprehensible lightness and elasticity of her footfall. She came and departed as a shadow. I was never made aware of her entrance into my closed study, save by the dear music of her low sweet voice, as she placed her marble hand upon my shoulder. In beauty of face no maiden ever equalled her. It was the radiance of an opium-dream—an airy and spirit-lifting vision more wildly divine than the phantasies which hovered about the slumbering souls of the daughters of Delos. Yet her features were not of that regular mould which we have been falsely taught to worship in the classical labors of the heathen. "There is no exquisite beauty," says Bacon, Lord Verulam, speaking truly of all the forms and *genera* of beauty, "without some *strangeness* in the proportion." Yet, although I saw that the features of Ligeia were not of a classic regularity—although I perceived that her loveliness was indeed "exquisite," and felt that there was much of "strangeness" pervading it, yet I have tried in vain to detect the irregularity and to trace home my own perception of "the strange." I examined the contour of the lofty and pale forehead—it was faultless—how cold indeed that word when applied to a majesty so divine!—the skin rivalling the purest ivory, the commanding extent and repose, the gentle prominence of the regions above the temples; and then the raven-black, the glossy, the luxuriant, and naturally-curling tresses, setting forth the full force of the Homeric epithet, "hyacinthine!" I looked at the delicate outlines of the nose—and nowhere but in the graceful medallions of the Hebrews had I beheld a similar perfection. There were the same luxurious smoothness of surface, the same scarcely perceptible tendency to the aquiline, the same harmoniously curved nostrils speaking the free spirit. I regarded the sweet mouth. Here was indeed the triumph of all things heavenly—the magnificent turn of the short upper lip—the soft, voluptuous slumber of the under—the dimples which sported, and the color which spoke—the teeth glancing back, with a brilliancy almost startling, every ray of the holy light which fell upon them in her serene and placid yet most exultingly radiant of all smiles. I scrutinized the formation of the chin—and, here too, I found the gentleness of breadth, the softness and the majesty, the fulness and the spirituality, of the Greek—the contour which the god Apollo revealed but in a dream, to Cleomenes, the son of the Athenian. And then I peered into the large eyes of Ligeia.

For eyes we have no models in the remotely antique. It might have been, too, that in these eyes of my beloved lay the secret to which Lord Verulam alludes. They were, I must believe, far larger than the ordinary eyes of our own race. They were even fuller than the fullest of the gazelle eyes of the tribe of the valley of Nourjahad. Yet it was only at intervals—in moments of intense excitement—that this peculiarity became more than slightly noticeable in Ligeia. And at such moments was her beauty—in my heated fancy thus it appeared perhaps—the beauty of beings either above or apart from the earth—the beauty of the fabulous Houri of the Turk. The hue of the orbs was the most brilliant of black, and, far over them, hung jetty lashes of great length. The brows, slightly irregular in outline, had the same tint. The "strangeness," however, which I found in the eyes was of a nature distinct from the formation, or the color, or the brilliancy of the features, and must, after all, be referred to the *expression*. Ah, word of no meaning! behind whose vast latitude of mere sound we intrench our ignorance of so much of the spiritual. The expression of the eyes of Ligeia! How for long hours have I pondered upon it! How have I, through the whole of a midsummer night, struggled to fathom it! What was it—that something more profound than the well of Democritus—which lay far within the pupils of my beloved? What *was* it? I was possessed with a passion to discover. Those eyes! those large, those shining, those divine orbs! they became to me twin stairs of Leda, and I to them devoutest of astrologers.

There is no point, among the many incomprehensible anomalies of the science of mind, more thrillingly exciting than the fact—never, I believe, noticed in the schools—that in our endeavors to recall to memory something long forgotten, we often find ourselves *upon the very verge* of remembrance, without being able, in the end, to remember. And thus how frequently, in my intense scrutiny of Ligeia's eyes, have I felt approaching the full knowledge of their expression—felt it approaching —yet not quite be mine—and so at length entirely depart! And (strange, oh, strangest mystery of all!) I found, in the commonest objects of the universe, a circle of analogies to that expression. I mean to say that, subsequently to the period when Ligeia's beauty passed into my spirit, there dwelling as in a shrine, I derived, from many existences in the material world, a sentiment such as I felt always around, within me, by her large and luminous orbs. Yet not the more could I define that sentiment, or analyze, or even steadily view it. I recognized it, let me repeat, sometimes in the survey of a rapidly growing vine—in the contemplation of a moth, a butterfly, a chrysalis, a stream of running water. I have felt it in the ocean—in the falling of a meteor. I have felt it in the glances of unusually aged people. And there are one or two stars in heaven (one especially, a star of the sixth magnitude, double and changeable, to be found near the large star in Lyra) in a telescopic scrutiny of which I have been made aware of the feeling. I have been filled with it by certain sounds from stringed instruments, and not unfrequently by passages from books. Among innumerable other instances, I well remember something in a volume of Joseph Glanvill, which (perhaps merely from its quaintness—who shall say?) never failed to inspire me with the sentiment: "And the will therein lieth, which dieth not. Who knoweth the mysteries of the will, with its vigor? For God is but a great will pervading all things by nature of its intentness. Man doth not yield him to the angels, nor unto death utterly, save only through the weakness of his feeble will."

Length of years and subsequent reflection have enabled me to trace, indeed, some remote connection between this passage in the English moralist and a portion of the character of Ligeia. An *intensity* in thought, action, or speech was possibly, in her, a result, or at least an index, of that gigantic volition which, during our long intercourse, failed to give other and more immediate evidence of its existence. Of all the women whom I have ever known, she, the outwardly calm, the ever-placid Ligeia, was the most violently a prey to the tumultuous vultures of stern passion. And of such passion I could form no estimate, save by the miraculous expansion of those eyes which at once so delighted and appalled me,—by the almost magical melody, modulation, distinctness, and placidity of her very low voice,—and by the fierce energy (rendered doubly effective by contrast with her manner of utterance) of the wild words which she habitually uttered.

I have spoken of the learning of Ligeia: it was immense—such as I have never known in woman. In the classical tongues was she deeply proficient, and as far as my own acquaintance extended in regard to the modern dialects of Europe, I have never known her at fault. Indeed upon any theme of the most admired because simply the most abstruse of the boasted erudition of the Academy, have I *ever* found Ligeia at fault? How singularly—how thrillingly, this one point in the nature of my wife has forced itself, at this late period only, upon my attention! I said her knowledge was such as I have never known in woman—but where breathes the man who has traversed, and successfully, *all* the wide areas of moral, physical, and mathematical science? I saw not then what I now clearly perceive, that the acquisitions of Ligeia were gigantic, were astounding; yet I was sufficiently aware of her infinite supremacy to resign myself, with a child-like confidence, to her guidance through the chaotic world of metaphysical investigation at which I was most busily occupied during the earlier years of our marriage. With how vast a triumph—with how vivid a delight—with how much of all that is ethereal in hope did I *feel*, as she bent over me in studies but little sought—but less known,—that delicious vista by slow degrees expanding before me, down whose long, gorgeous, and all untrodden path, I might at length pass onward to the goal of a wisdom too divinely precious not to be forbidden!

How poignant, then, must have been the grief with which, after some years, I beheld my well-grounded expectations take wings to themselves and fly away! Without Ligeia I was but as a child groping benighted. Her presence, her readings alone, rendered vividly luminous the many mysteries of the transcendentalism in which we were immersed. Wanting the radiant lustre of her eyes, letters, lambent and golden, grew duller than Saturnian lead. And now those eyes shone less and less frequently upon the pages over which I pored. Ligeia grew ill. The wild eyes blazed with a too—too glorious effulgence; the pale fingers became of the transparent waxen hue of the grave; and the blue veins upon the lofty forehead swelled and sank impetuously with the tides of the most gentle emotion. I saw that she must die—and I struggled desperately in spirit with the grim Azrael. And the struggles of the passionate wife were to my astonishment, even more energetic than my own. There had been much in her stern nature to impress me with the belief that, to her, death would have come without its terrors; but not so. Words are impotent to convey any just idea of the fierceness of resistance with which she wrestled with the Shadow. I groaned in anguish at the pitiable spectacle. I would have soothed—I would have reasoned; but in the intensity of her wild desire for life—for life—*but* for life—solace and reason were alike the uttermost of folly. Yet not until the last instance, amid the most convulsive writhings of her fierce spirit, was shaken the external placidity of her demeanor. Her voice grew more gentle—grew more low—yet I would not wish to dwell upon the wild meaning of the quietly uttered words. My brain reeled as I hearkened, entranced to a melody more than mortal—to assumptions and aspirations which mortality had never before known.

That she loved me I should not have doubted; and I might have been easily aware that, in a bosom such as hers, love would have reigned no ordinary passion. But in death only was I fully impressed with the strength of her affection. For long hours, detaining my hand, would she pour out before me the overflowing of a heart whose more than passionate devotion amounted to idolatry. How had I deserved to be so blessed by such confessions?—how had I deserved to be so cursed with the removal of my beloved in the hour of my making them? But upon this subject I cannot bear to dilate. Let me say only, that in Ligeia's more

than womanly abandonment to a love, alas! all unmerited, all unworthily bestowed, I at length recognized the principle of her longing,
with so wildly earnest a desire, for the life which was now fleeing so rapidly away. It is this wild longing—it is this eager vehemence of desire for
life—*but* for life—that I have no power to portray—no utterance capable
of expressing.

At high noon of the night in which she departed, beckoning me, peremptorily, to her side, she bade me repeat certain verses composed by
herself not many days before. I obeyed her. They were these:—

> Lo! 'tis a gala night
>   Within the lonesome latter years!
> An angel throng, bewinged, bedight
>   In veils, and drowned in tears,
> Sit in a theatre, to see
>   A play of hopes and fears,
> While the orchestra breathes fitfully
>   The music of the spheres.
>
> Mimes, in the form of God on high,
>   Mutter and mumble low,
> And hither and thither fly;
>   Mere puppets they, who come and go
> At bidding of vast formless things
>   That shift the scenery to and fro,
> Flapping from out their condor wings
>   Invisible Woe!
>
> That motley drama!—oh, be sure
>   It shall not be forgot!
> With its Phantom chased for evermore,
>   By a crowd that seize it not,
> Through a circle that ever returneth in
>   To the self-same spot;
> And much of Madness, and more of Sin
>   And Horror, the soul of the plot!
>
> But see, amid the mimic rout
>   A crawling shape intrude!
> A blood-red thing that writhes from out

The scenic solitude!
It writhes!—it writhes!—with mortal pangs
The mimes become its food,
And the seraphs sob at vermin fangs
In human gore imbued.

Out—out are the lights—out all!
And over each quivering form,
The curtain, a funeral pall,
Comes down with the rush of a storm—
And the angels, all pallid and wan,
Uprising, unveiling, affirm
That the play is the tragedy, "Man,"
And its hero, the conqueror Worm.

"O God!" half shrieked Ligeia, leaping to her feet and extending her arms aloft with a spasmodic movement, as I made an end of these lines —"O God! O Divine Father!—shall these things be undeviatingly so?— shall this conqueror be not once conquered? Are we not part and parcel in Thee? Who—who knoweth the mysteries of the will with its vigor? Man doth not yield him to the angels, *nor unto death utterly*, save only through the weakness of his feeble will."

And now, as if exhausted with emotion, she suffered her white arms to fall, and returned solemnly to her bed of death. And as she breathed her last sighs, there came mingled with them a low murmur from her lips. I bent to them my ear, and distinguished, again, the concluding words of the passage in Glanvill: *"Man doth not yield him to the angels, nor unto death utterly, save only through the weakness of his feeble will."*

She died: and I, crushed into the very dust with sorrow, could no longer endure the lonely desolation of my dwelling in the dim and decaying city by the Rhine. I had no lack of what the world calls wealth. Ligeia had brought me far more, very far more, than ordinarily falls to the lot of mortals. After a few months, therefore, of weary and aimless wandering, I purchased and put in some repair, an abbey, which I shall not name, in one of the wildest and least frequented portions of fair England. The gloomy and dreary grandeur of the building, the al- most savage aspect of the domain, the many melancholy and time-honored memories connected with both, had much in unison with the feelings of utter abandonment which had driven me into that remote and unsocial region of the country. Yet although the external abbey, with its verdant decay hanging about it, suffered but little alteration, I gave way, with a child-like perversity, and perchance with a faint hope of alleviating my sorrows, to a display of more than regal magnificence within. For such follies, even in childhood, I had imbibed a taste, and now they came back to me as if in the dotage of grief. Alas, I feel how much even of incipient madness might have been discovered in the gorgeous and fantastic draperies, in the solemn carvings of Egypt, in the wild cornices and furniture, in the Bedlam patterns of the carpets of tufted gold! I had become a bounden slave in the trammels of opium, and my labors and my orders had taken a coloring from my dreams. But these absurdities I must not pause to detail. Let me speak only of that one chamber, ever accursed, whither, in a moment of mental alienation, I led from the altar as my bride—as the successor of the unforgotten Ligeia—the fair-haired and blue-eyed Lady Rowena Trevanion, of Tremaine.

There is no individual portion of the architecture and decoration of that bridal chamber which is not now visibly before me. Where were the souls of the haughty family of the bride, when, through thirst of gold, they permitted to pass the threshold of an apartment so bedecked, a maiden and a daughter so beloved? I have said, that I minutely remember the details of the chamber—yet I am sadly forgetful on topics of deep moment; and here there was no system, no keeping, in the fantastic display, to take hold upon the memory. The room lay in a high turret of the castellated abbey, was pentagonal in shape, and of capacious size. Occupying the whole southern face of the pentagon was the sole window—an immense sheet of unbroken glass from Venice—a single pane, and tinted of a leaden hue, so that the rays of either the sun or moon passing through it, fell with a ghastly lustre on the objects within. Over the upper portion of this huge window, extended the trellis-work of an aged vine, which clambered up the massy walls of the turret. The ceiling, of gloomy-looking oak, was excessively lofty, vaulted, and elaborately fretted with the wildest and most grotesque specimens of a semi-Gothic, semi-Druidical device. From out the most central recess of this melancholy vaulting, depended, by a single chain of gold with long links, a huge censer of the same metal, Saracenic in pattern, and with many perforations so contrived that there writhed in and out of them, as if endued with a serpent vitality, a continual succession of parti-colored fires.

Some few ottomans and golden candelabra, of Eastern figure, were in various stations about; and there was the couch, too—the bridal couch—of an Indian model, and low, and sculptured of solid ebony, with a pall-like canopy above. In each of the angles of the chamber stood on end a gigantic sarcophagus of black granite, from the tombs of the kings over against Luxor, with their aged lids full of immemorial sculpture. But in the draping of the apartment lay, alas! the chief phantasy of all. The lofty walls, gigantic in height—even unproportionably so—were hung from summit to foot, in vast folds, with a heavy and massive-looking tapestry—tapestry of a material which was found alike as a carpet on the floor, as a covering for the ottomans and the ebony bed, as a canopy for the bed and as the gorgeous volutes of the curtains which partially shaded the window. The material was the richest cloth of gold. It was spotted all over, at irregular intervals, with arabesque figures, about a foot in diameter, and wrought upon the cloth in patterns of the most jetty black. But these figures partook of the true character of the arabesque only when regarded from a single point of view. By a con-trivance now common, and indeed traceable to a very remote period of antiquity, they were made changeable in aspect. To one entering the room, they bore the appearance of simple monstrosities; but upon a far-ther advance, this appearance gradually departed; and, step by step, as the visitor moved his station in the chamber, he saw himself surrounded by an endless succession of the ghastly forms which belong to the super-stition of the Norman, or arise in the guilty slumbers of the monk. The phantasmagoric effect was vastly heightened by the artificial intro-duction of a strong continual current of wind behind the draperies—giv-ing a hideous and uneasy animation to the whole.

In halls such as these—in a bridal chamber such as this—I passed, with the Lady of Tremaine, the unhallowed hours of the first month of our marriage—passed them with but little disquietude. That my wife dreaded the fierce moodiness of my temper—that she shunned me, and loved me but little—I could not help perceiving; but it gave me rather pleasure than otherwise. I loathed her with a hatred belonging more to demon than to man. My memory flew back (oh, with what intensity of regret!) to Ligeia, the beloved, the august, the beautiful, the entombed.

I revelled in recollections of her purity, of her wisdom, of her lofty—her ethereal nature, of her passionate, her idolatrous love. Now, then, did my spirit fully and freely burn with more than all the fires of her own. In the excitement of my opium dreams (for I was habitually fettered in the shackles of the drug), I would call aloud upon her name, during the silence of the night, or among the sheltered recesses of the glens by day, as if, through the wild eagerness, the solemn passion, the consuming ardor of my longing for the departed, I could restore her to the pathways she had abandoned—ah, *could* it be for ever?—upon the earth.

About the commencement of the second month of the marriage, the Lady Rowena was attacked with sudden illness, from which her recovery was slow. The fever which consumed her rendered her nights uneasy; and in her perturbed state of half-slumber, she spoke of sounds, and of motions, in and about the chamber of the turret, which I concluded had no origin save in the distemper of her fancy, or perhaps in the phantas-magoric influences of the chamber itself. She became at length convales-cent—finally, well. Yet but a brief period elapsed, ere a second more vio-lent disorder again threw her upon a bed of suffering; and from this attack her frame, at all times feeble, never altogether recovered. Her illnesses were, after this epoch, of alarming character, and of more alarming recurrence, defying alike the knowledge and the great exertions of her physicians. With the increase of the chronic disease, which had thus, apparently, taken too sure hold upon her constitution to be eradi-cated by human means, I could not fail to observe a similar increase in the nervous irritation of her temperament, and in her excitability by trivial causes of fear. She spoke again, and now more frequently and per-tinaciously, of the sounds—of the slight sounds—and of the unusual mo-tions among the tapestries, to which she had formerly alluded.

One night, near the closing in of September, she pressed this distress-ing subject with more than usual emphasis upon my attention. She had just awakened from an unquiet slumber, and I had been watching, with feelings half of anxiety, half of vague terror, the workings of her emaciated countenance. I sat by the side of her ebony bed, upon one of the ottomans of India. She partly arose, and spoke, in an earnest low whisper, of sounds which she *then* heard, but which I could not hear— of motions which she *then* saw, but which I could not perceive. The wind was rushing hurriedly behind the tapestries, and I wished to show her (what, let me confess it, I could not *all* believe) that those almost inarticulate breathings, and those very gentle variations of the figures upon the wall, were but the natural effects of that customary rushing of the wind. But a deadly pallor, overspreading her face, had proved to me that my exertions to reassure her would be fruitless. She appreared to be fainting, and no attendants were within call. I remembered where was deposited a decanter of light wine which had been ordered by her physicians, and hastened across the chamber to procure it. But, as I stepped beneath the light of the censer, two circumstances of a startling nature attracted my attention. I had felt that some palpable although invisible object had passed lightly by my person; and I saw that there lay upon the golden carpet, in the very middle of the rich lustre thrown from the censer, a shadow—a faint, indefinite shadow of angelic aspect—such as might be fancied for the shadow of a shade. But I was wild with the excitement of an immoderate dose of opium, and heeded these things but little, nor spoke of them to Rowena. Having found the wine, I recrossed the chamber, and poured out a gobletful, which I held to the lips of the fainting lady. She had now partially recovered, however, and took the vessel herself, while I sank upon an ottoman near me, with my eyes fastened upon her person. It was then that I became distinctly aware of a gentle foot-fall upon the carpet, and near the couch; and in a second thereafter, as Rowena was in the act of raising the wine to her lips, I saw, or may have dreamed that I saw, fall within the goblet, as if from some invisible spring in the atmosphere of the room, three or four large drops of a brilliant and ruby colored fluid. If this I saw—not so Rowena. She swallowed the wine unhesitatingly, and I forbore to speak to her of a circumstance which must, after all, I considered, have been but the suggestion of a vivid imagination, rendered morbidly active by the terror of the lady, by the opium, and by the hour.

Yet I cannot conceal it from my own perception that, immediately subsequent to the fall of the ruby-drops, a rapid change for the worse took place in the disorder of my wife; so that, on the third subsequent night, the hands of her menials prepared her for the tomb, and on the fourth, I sat alone, with her shrouded body, in that fantastic chamber which had received her as my bride. Wild visions, opium-engendered, flitted, shadow-like, before me. I gazed with unquiet eye upon the sarcophagi in the angles of the room, upon the varying figures of the drapery, and upon the writhing of the parti-colored fires in the censer overhead. My eyes then fell, as I called to mind the circumstances of a

former night, to the spot beneath the glare of the censer where I had
seen the faint traces of the shadow. It was there, however, no longer;
and breathing with greater freedom, I turned my glances to the pallid
and rigid figure upon the bed. Then rushed upon me a thousand memories of Ligeia—and then came back upon my heart, with the turbulent
violence of a flood, the whole of that unutterable woe with which I had
regarded *her* thus enshrouded. The night waned; and still, with a bosom
full of bitter thoughts of the one only and supremely beloved, I
remained gazing upon the body of Rowena.

It might have been midnight, or perhaps earlier, or later, for I had
taken no note of time, when a sob, low, gentle, but very distinct, startled me from my revery. I *felt* that it came from the bed of ebony—the
bed of death. I listened in an agony of superstitious terror—but there
was no repetition of the sound. I strained my vision to detect any motion in the corpse—but there was not the slightest perceptible. Yet I
could not have been deceived. I *had* heard the noise, however faint, and
my soul was awakened within me. I resolutely and perseveringly kept
my attention riveted upon the body. Many minutes elapsed before any
circumstance occurred tending to throw light upon the mystery. At
length it became evident that a slight, a very feeble, and barely noticeable tinge of color had flushed up within the cheeks, and along the
sunken small veins of the eyelids. Through a species of unutterable horror and awe, for which the language of mortality has no sufficiently energetic expression, I felt my heart cease to beat, my limbs grow rigid
where I sat. Yet a sense of duty finally operated to restore my self-
possession. I could no longer doubt that we had been precipitate in our
preparations—that Rowena still lived. It was necessary that some immediate exertion be made; yet the turret was altogether apart from the portion of the abbey tenanted by the servants—there were none within call
—I had no means of summoning them to my aid without leaving the
room for many minutes—and this I could not venture to do. I therefore
struggled alone in my endeavors to call back the spirit still hovering. In
a short period it was certain, however, that a relapse had taken place;
the color disappeared from both eyelid and cheek, leaving a wanness
even more than that of marble; the lips became doubly shrivelled and
pinched up in the ghastly expression of death; a repulsive clamminess
and coldness overspread rapidly the surface of the body; and all the
usual rigorous stiffness immediately supervened. I fell back with a shud-

der upon the couch from which I had been so startlingly aroused, and again gave myself up to passionate waking visions of Ligeia.

An hour thus elapsed, when (could it be possible?) I was a second time aware of some vague sound issuing from the region of the bed. I listened—in extremity of horror. The sound came again—it was a sigh. Rushing to the corpse, I saw—distinctly saw—a tremor upon the lips. In a minute afterward they relaxed, disclosing a bright line of the pearly teeth. Amazement now struggled in my bosom with the profound awe which had hitherto reigned there alone. I felt that my vision grew dim, that my reason wandered; and it was only by a violent effort that I at length succeeded in nerving myself to the task which duty thus once more had pointed out. There was now a partial glow upon the forehead and upon the cheek and throat; a perceptible warmth pervaded the whole frame; there was even a slight pulsation at the heart. The lady *lived*; and with redoubled ardor I betook myself to the task of restoration. I chafed and bathed the temples and the hands, and used every exertion which experience, and no little medical reading, could suggest. But in vain. Suddenly, the color fled, the pulsation ceased, the lips resumed the expression of the dead, and, in an instant afterward, the whole body took upon itself the icy chilliness, the livid hue, the intense rigidity, the sunken outline, and all the loathsome peculiarities of that which has been, for many days, a tenant of the tomb.

And again I sunk into visions of Ligeia—and again (what marvel that I shudder while I write?), *again* there reached my ears a low sob from the region of the ebony bed. But why shall I minutely detail the unspeakable horrors of that night? Why shall I pause to relate how, time after time, until near the period of the gray dawn, this hideous drama of revivification was repeated; how each terrific relapse was only into a sterner and apparently more irredeemable death; how each agony wore the aspect of a struggle with some invisible foe; and how each struggle was succeeded by I know not what of wild change in the personal appearance of the corpse? Let me hurry to a conclusion.

The greater part of the fearful night had worn away, and she who had been dead once again stirred—and now more vigorously than hitherto, although arousing from a dissolution more appalling in its utter hopelessness than any. I had long ceased to struggle or to move, and remained sitting rigidly upon the ottoman, a helpless prey to a whirl of violent emotions, of which extreme awe was perhaps the least terrible, the least consuming. The corpse, I repeat, stirred, and now more vigorously than before. The hues of life flushed up with unwonted energy into the countenance—the limbs relaxed—and, save that the eyelids were yet pressed heavily together, and that the bandages and draperies of the grave still imparted their charnel character to the figure, I might have dreamed that Rowena had indeed shaken off, utterly, the fetters of Death. But if this idea was not, even then, altogether adopted, I could at least doubt no longer, when, arising from the bed, tottering, with feeble steps, with closed eyes, and with the manner of one bewildered in a dream, the thing that was enshrouded advanced boldly and palpably into the middle of the apartment.

I trembled not—I stirred not—for a crowd of unutterable fancies connected with the air, the stature, the demeanor, of the figure, rushing hurriedly through my brain, had paralyzed—had chilled me into stone. I stirred not—but gazed upon the apparition. There was a mad disorder in my thoughts—a tumult unappeasable. Could it, indeed, be the *living* Rowena who confronted me? Could it, indeed, be Rowena *at all*—the fair-haired, the blue-eyed Lady Rowena Trevanion of Tremaine? Why, *why* should I doubt it? The bandage lay heavily about the mouth—but then might it not be the mouth of the breathing Lady of Tremaine? And the cheeks—there were the roses as in her noon of life—yes, these might indeed be the fair cheeks of the living Lady of Tremaine. And the chin, with its dimples, as in health, might it not be hers?—but *had she then grown taller since her malady*? What inexpressible madness seized me with that thought? One bound, and I had reached her feet! Shrinking from my touch, she let fall from her head, unloosened, the ghastly cerements which had confined it, and there streamed forth into the rushing atmosphere of the chamber huge masses of long and dishevelled hair; *it was blacker than the raven wings of midnight!* And now slowly opened *the eyes* of the figure which stood before me. "Here then, at least," I shrieked aloud, "can I never—can I never be mistaken— these are the full, and the black, and the wild eyes—of my lost love— of the Lady—of the LADY LIGEIA."

THE WHITE CAT

BY SHERIDAN LE FANU

JOSEPH SHERIDAN LE FANU was a Dubliner, descended from the dramatist Richard Brinsley Sheridan. He was a Victorian favorite of the terror set whose popularity underwent a decline until M. R. James, a master ghost writer of the twentieth century, revived his work and declared that Le Fanu was "absolutely in the front rank as a writer of ghost stories."

Le Fanu trained to be a lawyer but turned instead to journalism; he edited newspapers during the day and wrote his tales at night by the light of two wax candles. His friends and family thought he never lived up to his promise as a lawyer; he did not seem to care. He became more and more a recluse while he turned out fourteen novels and innumerable short stories, some based on Irish folklore of the period, as witnessed by "The White Cat."

"Every home," said Henry James, "should have upon the bed table a Le Fanu story for those hours on the other side of midnight." ह⁀

THERE IS a famous story of a white cat, with which we all become acquainted in the nursery. I am going to tell a story of a white cat very different from the amiable and enchanted princess who took that disguise for a season. The white cat of which I speak was a more sinister animal.

The traveller from Limerick towards Dublin, after passing the hills of Killaloe upon the left, as Keeper Mountain rises high in view, finds himself gradually hemmed in, up the right, by a range of lower hills. An undulating plain that dips gradually to a lower level than that of the road interposes, and some scattered hedgerows relieve its somewhat wild and melancholy character.

One of the few human habitations that send up their films of turf-smoke from that lonely plain, is the loosely thatched, earth-built dwelling of a "strong farmer," as the more prosperous of the tenant-farming classes are termed in Munster. It stands in a clump of trees near the edge of a wandering stream, about half-way between the mountains and the Dublin road, and had been for generations tenanted by people named Donovan.

In a distant place, desirous of studying some Irish records which had fallen into my hands, and inquiring for a teacher capable of instructing me in the Irish language, a Mr. Donovan, dreamy, harmless, and learned, was recommended to me for the purpose.

I found that he had been educated as a Sizar in Trinity College, Dublin. He now supported himself by teaching, and the special direction of my studies, I suppose, flattered his national partialities, for he unbosomed himself of much of his long-reserved thoughts, and recollections about his country and his early days. It was he who told me this story, and I mean to repeat it, as nearly as I can, in his own words.

I have myself seen the old farmhouse, with its orchard of huge moss-grown apple trees. I have looked round on the peculiar landscape; the roofless, ivied tower, that two hundred years before had afforded a refuge from raid and rapparee, and which still occupies its old place in the angle of the haggard; the bush-grown "liss," that scarcely a hundred and fifty steps away records the labours of a bygone race; the dark and towering outline of old Keeper in the background; and the lonely range of furze and heath-clad hills that form a nearer barrier, with many a line of grey rock and clump of dwarf oak or birch. The pervading sense of loneliness made it a scene not unsuited for a wild and unearthly story. And I could quite fancy how, seen in the grey of a wintry morning, shrouded far and wide in snow, or in the melancholy glory of an autumnal sunset, or in the chill splendour of a moonlight night, it might have helped to tone a dreamy mind like honest Dan Donovan's to superstition and a proneness to the illusion of fancy. It is certain, however, that I never anywhere met with a more simple-minded creature, or one on whose good faith I could more entirely rely.

When I was a boy, said he, living at home at Drumgunniol, I used to take my Goldsmith's *Roman History* in my hand and go down to my favourite seat, the flat stone, sheltered by a hawthorn tree beside the little lough, a large and deep pool, such as I have heard called a tarn in England. It lay in the gentle hollow of a field that is overhung towards the north by the old orchard, and being a deserted place was favourable to my studious quietude.

One day reading here, as usual, I wearied at last, and began to look about me, thinking of the heroic scenes I had just been reading of. I was as wide awake as I am at this moment, and I saw a woman appear at the corner of the orchard and walk down the slope. She wore a long, light grey dress, so long that it seemed to sweep the grass behind her, and so singular was her appearance in a part of the world where female attire is so inflexibly fixed by custom, that I could not take my eyes off her. Her course lay diagonally from corner to corner of the field, which was a large one, and she pursued it without swerving.

When she came near I could see that her feet were bare, and that she seemed to be looking steadfastly upon some remote object for guidance. Her route would have crossed me—had the tarn not interposed—about ten or twelve yards below the point at which I was sitting. But instead of arresting her course at the margin of the lough, as I had expected, she went on without seeming conscious of its existence, and I saw her, as plainly as I see you, sir, walk across the surface of the water, and pass, without seeming to see me, at about the distance I had calculated.

I was ready to faint from sheer terror. I was only thirteen years old then, and I remember every particular as if it had happened this hour.

The figure passed through the gap at the far corner of the field, and there I lost sight of it. I had hardly strength to walk home, and was so nervous, and ultimately so ill, that for three weeks I was confined to the house, and could not bear to be alone for a moment. I never entered that field again such was the horror with which from that moment every object in it was clothed. Even at this distance of time I should not like to pass through it.

This apparition I connected with a mysterious event; and, also, with a singular liability, that has for nearly eighty years distinguished, or rather afflicted, our family. It is no fancy. Everybody in that part of the country knows all about it. Everybody connected what I had seen with it.

I will tell it all to you as well as I can.

When I was about fourteen years old—that is about a year after the sight I had seen in the lough field—we were one night expecting my father home from the fair of Killoloe. My mother sat up to welcome him home, and I was with her, for I liked nothing better than such a vigil. My brothers and sisters, and the farm servants, except the men who were driving home the cattle from the fair, were asleep in their beds. My mother and I were sitting in the chimney corner chatting together, and watching my father's supper, which was kept hot over the fire. We knew that he would return before the men who were driving home the cattle, for he was riding, and told us that he would only wait to see them fairly on the road, and then push homeward.

At length we heard his voice and the knocking of his loaded whip at the door, and my mother let him in. I don't think I ever saw my father drunk, which is more than most men of my age, from the same part of the country, could say of theirs. But he could drink his glass of whiskey as well as another, and he usually came home from fair or market a little merry and mellow, and with a jolly flush in his cheeks.

Tonight he looked sunken, pale, and sad. He entered with the saddle and bridle in his hand, and he dropped them against the wall, near the door, and put his arms round his wife's neck, and kissed her kindly.

"Welcome home, Meehal," said she, kissing him heartily.

"God bless you, mavourneen," he answered.

And hugging her again, he turned to me, who was plucking him by the hand, jealous of his notice. I was little, and light of my age, and he lifted me up in his arms, and kissed me, and my arms being about his neck, he said to my mother:

"Draw the bolt, acuishla."

She did so, and setting me down very dejectedly, he walked to the fire and sat down on a stool, and stretched his feet towards the glowing turf, leaning with his hands on his knees.

"Rouse up, Mick, darlin'," said my mother, who was growing anxious, "and tell me how did the cattle sell, and did everything go lucky at the fair, or is there anything wrong with the landlord, or what in the world is it that ails you, Mick, jewel?"

"Nothin', Molly. The cows sould well, thank God, and there's nothin' fell out between me an' the landlord, an' everything's the same way. There's no fault to find anywhere."

"Well, then, Mickey, since so it is, turn round to your hot supper, and ate it, and tell us is there anything new."

"I got my supper, Molly, on the way, and I can't ate a bit," he answered.

"Got your supper on the way, an' you knowin' 'twas waiting for you at home, an' your wife sittin' up an' all!" cried my mother, reproachfully.

"You're takin' a wrong meanin' out of what I say," said my father. "There's something happened that leaves me that I can't eat a mouthful, and I'll not be dark with you, Molly, for, maybe, it ain't very long I have to be here, an' I'll tell you what it was. It's what I've seen, the white cat."

"The Lord between us and harm!" exclaimed my mother, in a moment as pale and as chap-fallen as my father; and then, trying to rally, with a laugh, she said: "Ha! 'tis only funnin' me you are. Sure a white rabbit was snared a Sunday last, in Grady's wood; an' Teigue seen a big white rat in the haggard yesterday."

"'Twas neither rat nor rabbit was in it. Don't ye think but I'd know a rat or a rabbit from a big white cat, with green eyes as big as halfpennies, and its back riz up like a bridge, trottin' on and across me, and ready, if I dar' stop, to rub its sides against my shins and maybe to make a jump and seize my throat, if that it's a cat at all, an' not something worse?"

As he ended his description in a low tone, looking straight at the fire my father drew his big hand across his forehead once or twice, his face being damp and shining with the moisture of fear, and he sighed, or rather groaned, heavily.

My mother had relapsed into panic, and was praying again in her fear. I, too, was terribly frightened, and on the point of crying, for I knew all about the white cat.

Clapping my father on the shoulder, by way of encouragement, my mother leaned over him, kissing him, and at last began to cry. He was wringing her hands in his, and seemed in great trouble.

"There was nothin' came into the house with me?" he asked, in a very low tone, turning to me.

"There was nothin', father," I said, "but the saddle and bridle that was in your hand."

"Nothin' white kem in at the doore wid me," he repeated.

"Nothin' at all," I answered.

"So best," said my father, and making the sign of the cross, he began mumbling to himself, and I knew he was saying his prayers.

Waiting for a while, to give him time for this exercise, my mother asked him where he first saw it.

"When I was riding up the bohereen"—the Irish term meaning a little road, such as leads up to a farmhouse—"I bethought myself that the men was on the road with the cattle, and no one to look to the horse barrin' myself, so I thought I might as well leave him in the crooked field below, an' I tuck him there, he bein' cool, and not a hair turned, for I rode him aisy all the way. It was when I turned, after lettin' him go —the saddle and bridle bein' in my hand—that I saw it, pushin' out o' the long grass at the side o' the path, an' it walked across it, in front of me, an' then back again, before me, the same way, an' sometimes at one side, an' then at the other, lookin' at me wid them shinin' eyes; and I consayted I heard it growlin' as it kep' beside me—as close as ever you see—till I kem up to the doore, here, an' knocked an' called, as ye heered me."

Now, what was it, in so simple an incident, that agitated my father, my mother, myself, and finally every member of this rustic household, with a terrible foreboding? It was this that we, one and all, believed that my father had received, in thus encountering the white cat, a warning of his approaching death.

The omen had never failed hitherto. It did not fail now. In a week after my father took the fever that was going, and before a month he was dead.

My honest friend, Dan Donovan, paused here; I could perceive that he was praying, for his lips were busy, and I concluded that it was for the repose of that departed soul.

In a little while he resumed.

It is eighty years now since that omen first attached to my family. Eighty years? Ay, is it. Ninety is nearer the mark. And I have spoken to many old people, in those earlier times, who had a distinct recollection of everything connected with it.

It happened in this way.

My grand-uncle, Connor Donovan, had the old farm of Drumgunniol in his day. He was richer than ever my father was, or my father's father either, for he took a short lease of Balraghan, and made money out of it. But money won't soften a hard heart, and I'm afraid my grand-uncle was a cruel man—a profligate man he was, surely, and that is mostly a cruel man at heart. He drank his share, too, and cursed and swore, when he was vexed, more than was good for his soul, I'm afraid.

At that time there was a beautiful girl of the Colemans, up in the mountains, not far from Capper Cullen. I'm told that there are no Colemans there now at all, and that family has passed away. The famine years made great changes.

Ellen Coleman was her name. The Colemans were not rich. But, being such a beauty, she might have made a good match. Worse than she did for herself, poor thing, she could not.

Con Donovan—my grand-uncle, God forgive him!—sometimes in his rambles saw her at fairs or patterns, and he fell in love with her, as who might not?

He used her ill. He promised her marriage, and persuaded her to come away with him; and, after all, he broke his word. It was just the old story. He tired of her, and he wanted to push himself in the world; and he married a girl of the Collopys, that had a great fortune—twenty-four cows, seventy sheep, and a hundred and twenty goats.

He married this Mary Collopy, and grew richer than before; and Ellen Coleman died broken-hearted. But that did not trouble the strong farmer much.

He would have liked to have children, but he had none, and this was the only cross he had to bear, for everything else went much as he wished.

One night he was returning from the fair of Nenagh. A shallow stream at that time crossed the road—they have thrown a bridge over it, I am told, some time since—and its channel was often dry in summer weather. When it was so, as it passes close by the old farmhouse of Drumgunniol, without a great deal of winding, it makes a sort of road, which people then used as a short cut to reach the house by. Into this dry channel, as there was plenty of light from the moon, my grand-uncle turned his horse, and when he had reached the two ash trees at the meering of the farm he turned his horse short into the river field, intending to ride through the gap at the other end, under the oak tree, and so he would have been within a few hundred yards of his door.

As he approached the "gap" he saw, or thought he saw, with a slow motion, gliding along the ground towards the same point, and now and then with a soft bound, a white object, which he described as being no bigger than his hat, but what it was he could not see, as it moved along the hedge and disappeared at the point to which he was himself tending.

When he reached the gap the horse stopped short. He urged and coaxed it in vain. He got down to lead it through, but it recoiled, snorted, and fell into a wild trembling fit. He mounted it again. But its terror continued, and it obstinately resisted his caresses and his whip. It was bright moonlight, and my grand-uncle was chafed by the horse's resistance, and, seeing nothing to account for it, and being so near home, what little patience he possessed forsook him, and, plying his whip and spur in earnest, he broke into oaths and curses.

All of a sudden the horse sprang through, and Con Donovan, as he passed under the broad branch of the oak, saw clearly a woman standing on the bank beside him, her arm extended, with the hand of which, as he flew by, she struck him a blow upon the shoulders. It threw him forward upon the neck of the horse, which, in wild terror, reached the door at a gallop, and stood there quivering and steaming all over.

Less alive than dead, my grand-uncle got in. He told his story, at least, so much as he chose. His wife did not quite know what to think. But that something very bad had happened she could not doubt. He was very faint and ill, and begged that the priest should be sent for forthwith. When they were getting him to his bed they saw distinctly the marks of five fingerprints on the flesh of his shoulder, where the spectral blow had fallen. These singular marks—which they said resembled in tint the hue of a body struck by lightning—remained imprinted on his flesh, and were buried with him.

When he had recovered sufficiently to talk with the people about him —speaking, like a man at his last hour, from a burdened heart, and troubled conscience—he repeated his story, but said he did not see, or, at all events, know, the face of the figure that stood in the gap. No one believed him. He told more about it to the priest than to others. He certainly had a secret to tell. He might as well have divulged it frankly, for the neighbours all knew well enough that it was the face of dead Ellen Coleman that he had seen.

From that moment my grand-uncle never raised his head. He was a scared, silent, broken-spirited man. It was early summer then, and at the fall of the leaf in the same year he died.

Of course there was a wake, such as beseemed a strong farmer so rich as he. For some reason the arrangements of this ceremonial were a little different from the usual routine.

The usual practice is to place the body in the great room, or kitchen, as it is called, of the house. In this particular case there was as I told you, for some reason, an unusual arrangement. The body was placed in a small room that opened upon the greater one. The door of this, during the wake, stood open. There were candles about the bed, and pipes and tobacco on the table, and stools for such guests as chose to enter, the door standing open for their reception.

The body, having been laid out, was left alone, in this smaller room, during the preparations for the wake. After nightfall one of the women, approaching the bed to get a chair which she had left near it, rushed from the room with a scream, and, having recovered her speech at the farther end of the "kitchen," and surrounded by a gaping audience, she said, at last:

"May I never sin, if his face bain't riz up again the back o' the bed, and he starin' down to the doore, wid eyes as big as pewter plates, that id be shinin' in the moon!"

"Arra, woman! Is it cracked you are?" said one of the farm boys as they are termed, being men of any age you please.

"Ahg, Molly, don't be talkin', woman! 'Tis what ye consayted it, goin' into the dark room, out o' the light. Why didn't ye take a candle in your fingers, ye aumadhaun?" said one of her female companions.

"Candle, or no candle; I seen it," insisted Molly. "An' what's more, I could a'most tak' my oath I seen his arum, too, stretchin' out o' the bed along the flure, three times as long as it should be, to take hould o' me be the fut."

"Nansinse, ye fool, what id he want o' yer fut?" exclaimed one scornfully.

"Gi' me the candle, some o' yez—in the name o' God," said old Sal Doolan, that was straight and lean, and a woman that could pray like a priest almost.

"Give her a candle," agreed all.

But whatever they might say, there wasn't one among them that did not look pale and stern enough as they followed Mrs. Doolan, who was praying as fast as her lips could patter, and leading the van with a tallow candle, held like a taper, in her fingers.

The door was half open, as the panic-stricken girl had left it; and holding the candle on high the better to examine the room, she made a step or so into it.

If my grand-uncle's hand had been stretched along the floor, in the unnatural way described, he had drawn it back again under the sheet that covered him. And tall Mrs. Doolan was in no danger of tripping over his arm as she entered. But she had not gone more than a step or two with her candle aloft, when, with a drowning face, she suddenly stopped short, staring at the bed which was now fully in view.

"Lord, bless us, Mrs. Doolan, ma'am, come back," said the woman next her, who had fast hold of her dress, or her "coat," as they call it, and drawing her backward with a frightened pluck, while a general recoil among her followers betokened the alarm which her hesitation had inspired.

"Whisht, will yez?" said the leader, peremptorily, "I can't hear my own ears wid the noise ye're makin', an' which iv yez let the cat here, an' whose cat is it?" she asked, peering suspiciously at a white cat that was sitting on the breast of the corpse.

"Put it away, will yez?" she resumed, with horror at the profanation. "Many a corpse as I sthretched and crossed in the bed, the likes o' that I never seen yet. The man o' the house, wid a brute baste like that mounted on him, like a phooka, Lord forgi' me for namin' the like in this room. Dhrive it away, some o' yez! out o' that, this minute, I tell ye."

Each repeated the order, but no one seemed inclined to execute it. They were crossing themselves, and whispering their conjectures and misgivings as to the nature of the beast, which was no cat of that house, nor one that they had ever seen before. On a sudden, the white cat placed itself on the pillow over the head of the body, and having from that place glared for a time at them over the features of the corpse, it crept softly along the body towards them, growling low and fiercely as it drew near.

Out of the room they bounced, in dreadful confusion, shutting the door fast after them, and not for a good while did the hardiest venture to peep in again.

The white cat was sitting in its old place, on the dead man's breast, but this time it crept quietly down the side of the bed, and disappeared under it, the sheet which was spread like a coverlet, and hung down nearly to the floor, concealed it from view.

Praying, crossing themselves, and not forgetting a sprinkling of holy water, they peeped, and finally searched, poking spades, "wattles," pitchforks and such implements under the bed. But the cat was not to be found, and they concluded that it had made its escape among their feet as they stood near the threshold. So they secured the door carefully, with hasp and padlock.

But when the door was opened next morning they found the white cat sitting, as if it had never been disturbed, upon the breast of the dead man.

Again occurred very nearly the same scene with a like result, only that some said they saw the cat afterwards lurking under a big box in a corner of the outer room, where my grand-uncle kept his leases and papers, and his prayer-book and beads.

Mrs. Doolan heard it growling at her heels wherever she went; and although she could not see it, she could hear it spring on the back of her chair when she sat down, and growl in her ear, so that she would bounce up with a scream and a prayer, fancying that it was on the point of taking her by the throat.

And the priest's boy, looking round the corner, under the branches of the old orchard, saw a white cat sitting under the little window of the room where my grand-uncle was laid out and looking up at the four small panes of glass as a cat will watch a bird.

The end of it was that the cat was found on the corpse again, when the room was visited, and do what they might, whenever the body was left alone, the cat was found again in the same ill-omened contiguity with the dead man. And this continued, to the scandal and fear of the neighbourhood, until the door was opened finally for the wake.

My grand-uncle being dead, and, with all due solemnities, buried, I have done with him. But not quite yet with the white cat. No banshee ever yet was more inalienably attached to a family than this apparition is to mine. But there is this difference. The banshee seems to be animated with an affectionate sympathy with the bereaved family to whom it is hereditarily attached, whereas this thing has about it a suspicion of malice. It is the messenger simply of death. And its taking the shape of a cat—the coldest, and they say, the most vindictive of brutes— is indicative of the spirit of its visit.

When my grandfather's death was near, although he seemed quite well at the time, it appeared not exactly, but very nearly in the same way in which I told you it showed itself to my father.

The day before my Uncle Teigue was killed by the bursting of his gun, it appeared to him in the evening, at twilight, by the lough, in the field where I saw the woman who walked across the water, as I told you. My uncle was washing the barrel of his gun in the lough. The grass is short there, and there is no cover near it. He did not know how it approached but the first he saw of it, the white cat was walking close round his feet, in the twilight, with an angry twist of its tail, and a green glare in its eyes, and do what he would, it continued walking round and round him, in larger or smaller circles, till he reached the orchard, and there he lost it.

My poor Aunt Peg—she married one of the O'Brians, near Oolah— came to Drumgunniol to go to the funeral of a cousin who died about a mile away. She died herself, poor woman, only a month after.

Coming from the wake, at two or three o'clock in the morning, as she got over the stile into the farm of Drumgunniol, she saw the white cat at her side, and it kept close beside her, she ready to faint all the time, till she reached the door of the house, where it made a spring up into the white-thorn tree that grows close by, and so it parted from her. And my little brother Jim saw it also, just three weeks before he died. Every member of our family who dies, or takes his death-sickness, at Drum-gunniol, is sure to see the white cat, and no one of us who sees it need hope for long life after.

Horror at the Hearthside

(VICTORIAN WOMEN GHOST WRITERS)

NOTHING BUT THE TRUTH

BY RHODA BROUGHTON

YOU WILL succeed, and when you do, remember that I prophesied it." Those were the words spoken to Rhoda Broughton by her uncle, Joseph Sheridan Le Fanu when she first brought him her work during her girlhood.

In those days Le Fanu had not become the recluse of Dublin, but instead kept a small literary salon in Ireland. Rhoda Broughton would often read her apprentice work aloud in front of the large open fire that graced the dining room. The magnificent Sheridan family portraits seemed to come alive with that firelight in the room, and Le Fanu, too, seemed to sparkle with excitement. His encouragement extended to help in the publication of her early work.

The Victorian world of England and Ireland produced some remarkable ghost stories. Many of them were written by women, who found publication easy in the various periodicals that were emerging. They had, said Dickens, a particular gift for writing about a spectral world.

Authorities in the ghost story consider Rhoda Broughton one of the major writers of her period. In the days of candle, firelight, and gaslight, she introduced an innovative personal style; she discarded Victorian verbiage and wrote briskly. Her style was electric long before electricity revolutionized the ghost story.

Her subjects, however, were often traditional. She left Ireland when young but could not leave behind its haunted houses. In a contemporary setting in England, she invaded the world of the haunted house to write her engrossing "Nothing But the Truth." ॐ

MRS. DE WYNT TO MRS. MONTRESOR.

"18, ECCLESTON SQUARE,
"*May 5th.*

"MY DEAREST CECILIA,

"I had no idea till yesterday how closely we were packed in this great smoky beehive, as tightly as herrings in a barrel. Don't be frightened, however. By dint of squeezing and crowding, we have managed to make room for two more herrings in our barrel, and those two are yourself and your husband. Let me begin at the beginning. After having looked over, I verily believe, every undesirable residence in West London; after having seen nothing intermediate between what was suited to the means of a duke, and what was suited to the needs of a chimney-sweep; after having felt bed-ticking, and explored kitchen-ranges till my brain reeled under my accumulated experience, I arrived at about half-past five yesterday afternoon at 32, —— Street, Mayfair.

"'Failure No. 253, I don't doubt,' I said to myself, as I toiled up the steps, feeling as ill-tempered as you please. So much for my spirit of prophecy. Once inside, I thought I had got into a small compartment of Heaven by mistake. Fresh as a daisy, clean as a cherry, bright as a seraph's face, it is all these, and a hundred more. Two drawing-rooms, marvellously, *immorally* becoming, my dear, as I ascertained entirely for your benefit, Persian mats, easy chairs, and lounges suited to every possible physical conformation, and a thousand of the important trivialities that make up the sum of a woman's life: peacock fans, Japanese screens, naked boys and *décolletée* shepherdesses; not to speak of a family of china pugs, with blue ribbons round their necks, which ought of themselves to have added fifty pounds a year to the rent. Apropos, I asked, in fear and trembling, what the rent might be—'Three hundred pounds a year.' A feather would have knocked me down. I could hardly believe my ears, and made the woman repeat it several times, that there might be no mistake. To this hour it is a mystery to me.

"With that suspiciousness which is so characteristic of you, you will immediately begin to think that there must be some terrible unaccountable smell, or some odious inexplicable noise haunting the reception-rooms. Nothing of the kind, the woman assured me, and she did not look as if she were telling stories. Its last occupant was an elderly and unexceptionable Indian officer, with a most lawful wife. They did not stay long, it is true, but then, as the housekeeper told me, he was a deplorable old hypochondriac, who never could bear to stay a fortnight in any one place. So lay aside that scepticism, which is your besetting sin, and give unfeigned thanks to your tutelar saint, for having provided you with a palace at the cost of a hovel, and for having sent you such an invaluable friend as

"Your attached
"Elizabeth De Wynt.

"P.S.—I am so sorry I shall not be in town to witness your first raptures, but dear Artie looks so pale and thin and tall after hooping-cough, that I am sending him off at once to the sea, and as I cannot bear the child out of my sight, I am going into banishment likewise."

MRS. MONTRESOR TO MRS. DE WYNT.

"32,——Street, Mayfair,
"May 14th.

"Dearest Bessy,

"Why did not dear little Artie defer his hooping-cough convalescence &c., till August? It is very odd, to me, the perverse way in which children always fix upon the most inconvenient times and seasons for their diseases. Here we are installed in our Paradise, and have searched high and low, in every hole and corner, for the serpent, without succeeding in catching a glimpse of his spotted tail. Most things in this world are disappointing, but 32, —— Street, Mayfair, is not. The mystery of the rent is still a mystery. I have been for my first ride in the Row this morning; my horse was a little fidgety; I am half afraid that my nerve is not what it was. Adela comes to us next week; I am so glad. It is dull driving by oneself of an afternoon; and I always think that one young woman alone in a brougham or with only a dog beside her, does not look *good*. We sent round our cards a fortnight before we came up, and have been already deluged with callers. Considering that we have been two years exiled from civilized life, and that London memories are not generally of the longest, we shall do pretty well, I think. Ralph Gordon came to see me on Sunday; he is in the Hussars now. He has grown up such a *dear* fellow, and so good-looking! Just my style, large and fair and whiskerless! I intend to be quite a *mother* to him. I hear a knock at the door! Peace is a word that might as well be expunged from one's London dictionary.

> "Yours affectionately,
> "CECILIA MONTRESOR."

MRS. DE WYNT TO MRS. MONTRESOR.

> "THE LORD WARDEN, DOVER,
> "*May 18th.*

"DEAREST CECILIA,

"You will perceive that I am about to devote only one small sheet of note-paper to you. This is from no dearth of time, Heaven knows! time is a drug in the market here, but from a total dearth of ideas. My life here is not an eminently suggestive one. It is spent in digging with a wooden spade, and eating prawns. Those are my employments at least; my relaxation is going down to the Pier, to see the Calais boat come in. When one is miserable oneself, it is decidedly consolatory to see some-one more miserable still; and wretched and bored, and reluctant vegetable as I am, I am not *sea-sick*. I always feel my spirits rise after having seen that peevish, draggled procession of blue, green and yellow fellow-Christians file past me. There is a wind here *always*. There are heights to climb which require more daring perseverance than ever Wolfe displayed, with his paltry heights of Abraham. There are glaring white houses, glaring white roads, glaring white cliffs. If any one knew how unpatriotically I detest the chalk-cliffs of Albion! Having grumbled through my two little pages—I have actually been reduced to writing very large in order to fill even them—I will send off my dreary little billet. How I wish I could get into the envelope myself too, and whirl up with it to dear, beautiful, filthy London. Not more heavily could

Madame de Staël have sighed for Paris from among the shades of Coppet.

"Your disconsolate,
"BESSY."

MRS. MONTRESOR TO MRS. DE WYNT.

"32——STREET, MAYFAIR,
"*May 27th.*

"Oh, my dearest Bessy, how I wish we were out of this dreadful, dreadful house! Please don't think me very ungrateful for saying this, after your taking such pains to provide us with a Heaven upon earth, as you thought.

"What has happened could, of course, have been neither foretold, nor guarded against, by any human being. About ten days ago, Benson (my maid) came to me with a very long face, and said, 'If you please, ma'am, did you know that this house was *haunted?*' I was *so* startled: you know what a coward I am. I said, 'Good Heavens! No! is it?' 'Well, I'm pretty nigh sure it is,' she said, and the expression of her countenance was about as lively as an undertaker's; and then she told me that cook had been that morning to order in groceries from a shop in the neighbourhood, and on her giving the man the direction where to send the things to, he had said, with a very peculiar smile, 'No. 32,—— Street, eh? h'm? I wonder how long *you'll* stand it; last lot held out just a fortnight.' He looked so odd that she asked him what he meant, but he only said, 'Oh! nothing! only that parties never *do* stay long at 32.' He had known parties go in one day, and out the next, and during the last four years he had never known any remain over the month. Feeling a good deal alarmed by this information, she naturally inquired the reason; but he declined to give it, saying that if she had not found it out for herself, she had much better leave it alone, as it would only frighten her out of her wits; and on her insisting and urging him, she could only extract from him, that the house had such a villainously bad name, that the owners were glad to let it for a mere song. You know how firmly I believe in apparitions, and what an unutterable fear I have of them; anything material, tangible, that I can lay hold of—anything of the same fibre, blood, and bone as myself, I could, I think, confront bravely enough; but the mere thought of being brought face to face with the 'bodiless dead,' makes my brain unsteady. The moment Henry came in, I ran to him, and told him; but he pooh-poohed the whole story, laughed at me, and asked whether we should turn out of the prettiest house in London, at the very height of the season, because a grocer said it had a bad name. He derided my 'babyish fears,' as he called them, to such an extent that I felt half ashamed, and yet not quite comfortable, either; and then came the usual rush of London engagements, during which one has no time to think of anything. Adela was to arrive yesterday, and in the morning our weekly hamper of flowers, fruit and vegetables arrived from home. I always dress the flower vases myself, servants are so tasteless, and as I was arranging them, it occurred to me—you know Adela's passion for flowers—to carry up one particular cornucopia of roses and mignonette and set it on her toilet-table, as a pleasant surprise for her. As I came downstairs, I had seen the housemaid—a fresh, round-faced country girl—go into the room, which was being prepared for Adela, with a pair of sheets that she had been airing over her arm. I went upstairs very slowly, as my cornucopia was full of water, and I was afraid of spilling some. I turned the handle of the bedroom-door and entered, keeping my eyes fixed on my flowers, to see whether any of them had fallen out. Suddenly a sort of shiver passed over me; and feeling frightened—I did not know why—I looked up quickly. The girl was standing by the bed, leaning forward a little with her hands clenched rigid, every nerve tense, her eyes, wide open, starting out of her head, and a look of unutterable horror in them; her cheeks and mouth livid as those of one that died awhile ago in mortal pain. As I looked at her, her lips moved a little, and an awful hoarse voice, not like hers in the least, said, "Oh! my God, I have seen it!" and then she fell down suddenly, like a log, with a heavy noise. Hearing the noise audible all through the thin walls and floors of a London house, Benson came running in, and between us we managed to lift her on to the bed, and tried to bring her to herself by rubbing her feet and hands, and holding strong salts to her nostrils. And all the while we kept glancing over our shoulders, in a vague cold terror of seeing some awful, shapeless apparition. Two long hours she lay in a state of utter unconsciousness. Meanwhile Harry, who had been down to his club, returned. At the end of two hours we succeeded in bringing her back to sensation and life, but only to make the awful discovery that she was raving mad. She became so violent that it required all the combined strength of Harry and

Phillips (our butler) to hold her down in the bed. Of course, we sent instantly for a doctor, who, as she grew a little calmer towards evening, removed her in a cab to his own house. He has just been here to tell me that she is now pretty quiet, not from any return to sanity, but from sheer exhaustion. We are, of course, utterly in the dark as to *what* she saw, and her ravings are far too disconnected and unintelligible to afford us the slightest clue. I feel so completely shattered and upset by this awful occurrence, that you will excuse me, dear, I'm sure, if I write incoherently. One thing I need hardly tell you, and that is, that no earthly consideration would induce me to allow Adela to occupy that terrible room. I shudder and run by quickly as I pass the door.

"Yours, in great agitation,
"Cecilia."

MRS. DE WYNT TO MRS. MONTRESOR.

"The Lord Warden, Dover,
"May 28th.

"Dearest Cecilia

"Yours just come; how very dreadful! But I am still unconvinced as to the house being in fault. You know I feel a sort of godmother to it, and responsible for its good behaviour. Don't you think that what the girl had might have been a fit? Why not? I myself have a cousin who is subject to seizures of the kind, and immediately on being attacked his whole body becomes rigid, his eyes glassy and staring, his complexion livid, exactly as in the case you describe. Or, if not a fit, are you sure that she has not been subject to fits of madness? *Please* be sure and ascertain whether there is not insanity in her family. You know my utter disbelief in ghosts. I am convinced that most of them, if run to earth, would turn out about as genuine as the famed Cock Lane one. But even allowing the possibility, nay, the actual unquestioned existence of ghosts in the abstract, is it likely that there should be anything to be seen so horribly fear-inspiring, as to send a perfectly sane person *in one instant* raving mad, which you, after three weeks' residence in the house, have never caught a glimpse of? According to your hypothesis, your whole household ought, by this time, to be stark staring mad. Let me implore you not to give way to a panic which may, possibly, probably prove utterly

groundless. Oh, how I wish I were with you, to make you listen to
reason! Artie ought to be the best prop ever woman's old age was
furnished with, to indemnify me for all he and his hooping-cough have
made me suffer. Write immediately, please, and tell me how the poor
patient progresses. Oh, had I the wings of a dove! I shall be on wires till
I hear again.

"Yours,
"BESSY."

MRS. MONTRESOR TO MRS. DE WYNT.

"No 5, BOLTON STREET, PICCADILLY,
"June 12th.

"DEAREST BESSY,

"You will see that we have left that terrible house. How I wish we
had escaped from it sooner! Oh, my dear Bessy, I shall never be the
same again. Let me try to be coherent, and to tell you what has happened. And first, as to the housemaid, she has been removed to a lunatic
asylum, where she remains in much the same state. She has had several
lucid intervals, and during them has been closely, pressingly questioned
as to what it was she saw; but she has maintained an absolute, hopeless
silence, and only shudders, moans, and hides her face in her hands when
the subject is broached. Three days ago I went to see her, and on my return was sitting resting in the drawing-room, before going to dress for
dinner, talking to Adela about my visit, when Ralph Gordon walked in.
He has always been walking in the last ten days, and Adela has always
flushed up and looked happy whenever he made his appearance. He
looked very handsome, dear fellow, just come in from the park; seemed
in tremendous spirits, and was as sceptical as even you could be, as to
the ghostly origin of Sarah's seizure. 'Let me come here to-night and
sleep in that room; do, Mrs. Montresor,' he said, looking very eager and
excited. 'With the gas lit and a poker, I'll engage to exorcise every
demon that shows his ugly nose.'

" 'You don't mean really?' I asked, incredulously. 'Don't I? that's all,'
he answered emphatically. 'I should like nothing better. Well, is it a
bargain?' Adela turned quite pale. 'Oh, don't,' she said, hurriedly,
'please, don't! why should you run such a risk? How do you know that
you might not be sent mad too?' He laughed very heartily, and coloured

a little with pleasure at seeing the interest she took in his safety. 'Never fear,' he said, 'it would take more than a whole squadron of ghosts with the devil at their head, to send me crazy.' He was so eager, so persistent, so thoroughly in earnest, that I yielded at last, though with a certain strong reluctance, to his entreaties. Adela's blue eyes filled with tears, and she walked away hastily to the conservatory. Nevertheless, Ralph got his own way; it was so difficult to refuse him anything. We gave up all our engagements for the evening, and he did the same. At about ten o'clock he arrived, accompanied by a friend and brother officer, Captain Burton, who was anxious to see the result of the experiment. 'Let me go up at once,' he said, looking very happy and animated. 'I don't know when I have felt in such good tune; a new sensation is a luxury not to be had every day of one's life; turn the gas up as high as it will go; provide a good stout poker, and leave the issue to Providence and me.' We did as he bid. 'It's all ready now,' Henry said, coming downstairs after having obeyed his orders; 'the room is nearly as light as day. Well, good luck to you, old fellow!' 'Good-bye, Miss Bruce,' Ralph said, going over to Adela, and taking her hand with a look, half laughing, half sentimental

> " ' "Fare thee well, and if for ever,
> Then for ever, fare thee well."

that is my last dying speech and confession. Now mind,' he went on, standing by the table, and addressing us all; 'if I ring once, *don't* come. I may be flurried, and lay hold of the bell without thinking; if I ring twice, *come*.' Then he went, jumping up the stairs three steps at a time, and humming a tune. As for us, we sat in different attitudes of expectation and listening about the drawing-room. At first we tried to talk a little, but it would not do; our whole souls seemed to have passed into our ears. The clock's ticking sounded as loud as a church bell. Addy lay on the sofa, with her white face hidden in the cushions. So we sat for exactly an hour; but it seemed like two years, and just as the clock began to strike eleven, a sharp *ting, ting, ting,* rang clear and shrill through the house. 'Let us go,' said Addy, starting up and running to the door. 'Let us go,' I cried too, following her. But Captain Burton stood in the way, and intercepted our progress. 'No,' he said, decisively, 'you must not go; remember Gordon told us distinctly, if he rang once *not* to come. I know the sort of fellow he is, and that nothing would annoy him more than having his directions disregarded.'

"'Oh, nonsense!' Addy cried, passionately, 'he would never have rung if he had not seen something dreadful; let us go!' she ended, clasping her hands. But she was overruled, and we all went back to our seats. Ten minutes more of suspense, unendurable; I felt a lump in my throat, a gasping for breath;—ten minutes on the clock, but a thousand centuries on our hearts. Then again, loud, sudden, violent, the bell rang! We made a simultaneous rush to the door. I don't think we were one second flying upstairs. Addy was first. Almost simultaneously she and I burst into the room. There he was, standing in the middle of the floor, rigid, petrified, with that same look—that look that is burnt into my heart—of awful, unspeakable fear on his brave young face. For one instant he stood thus; then stretching out his arms stiffly before him, he groaned in a terrible husky voice, 'Oh, my God! I have seen it!' and fell down *dead*. Not in a swoon or in a fit, but *dead*. Vainly we tried to bring back the life to that strong young heart; it will never come back again till that day when the earth and the sea give up the dead that are therein. I cannot see the page for the tears that are blinding me; he was such a dear fellow! I can't write any more today.

"Your broken-hearted
"CECILIA."

THE LOST GHOST

BY MARY WILKINS FREEMAN

THE AMERICAN writer Mary E. Wilkins Freeman was innovative. She turned her back upon the overwrought and over-
worked Gothic influences of Europe, and wrote directly and simply
about the region she knew best, New England. It was a New England whose village life was declining, socially, economically, and
culturally as the young departed for the city with its advantages.

To Mary Freeman that village life contained stories, tales filled
with the "local color" that was becoming fashionable in the latter
part of the nineteenth century. She found publication easy in such
magazines as *Harper's New Monthly,* and was soon being praised by
such worthies as William Dean Howells.

Mary Wilkins Freeman introduced the modern ghost story to
America. She abandoned the idea of the long ghostly novel—the
ghost of the early nineteenth century stalked leisurely through three-
decker novels—and settled for the modern ghost short story. Readers
and ghosts became more impatient; the short story was about to
reach a golden age. And Mrs. Freeman knew there had to be a new
solidity to the fragile ghost story, and new emotions too, the poign-
ancy, for example, that is so magnificently expressed in "The Lost
Ghost." ટે

MRS. JOHN EMERSON, sitting with her needlework beside the window, looked out and saw Mrs. Rhoda Meserve coming down the street,
and knew at once by the trend of her steps and the cant of her head

that she meditated turning in at her gate. She also knew by a certain something about her general carriage—a thrusting forward of the neck, a bustling hitch of the shoulders—that she had important news. Rhoda Meserve always had the news as soon as the news was in being, and generally Mrs. John Emerson was the first to whom she imparted it. The two women had been friends ever since Mrs. Meserve had married Simon Meserve and come to the village to live.

Mrs. Meserve was a pretty woman, moving with graceful flirts of ruffling skirts; her clear-cut, nervous face, as delicately tinted as a shell, looked brightly from the plumy brim of a black hat at Mrs. Emerson in the window. Mrs. Emerson was glad to see her coming. She returned the greeting with enthusiasm, then rose hurriedly, ran into the cold parlour and brought out one of the best rocking-chairs. She was just in time, after drawing it up beside the opposite window, to greet her friend at the door.

"Good-afternoon," said she. "I declare, I'm real glad to see you. I've been alone all day. John went to the city this morning. I thought of coming over to your house this afternoon, but I couldn't bring my sewing very well. I am putting the ruffles on my new black dress skirt."

"Well, I didn't have a thing on hand except my crochet work," responded Mrs. Meserve, "and I thought I'd just run over a few minutes."

"I'm real glad you did," repeated Mrs. Emerson. "Take your things right off. Here, I'll put them on my bed in the bedroom. Take the rocking-chair."

Mrs. Meserve settled herself in the parlour rocking-chair, while Mrs. Emerson carried her shawl and hat into the little adjoining bedroom. When she returned Mrs. Meserve was rocking peacefully and was already at work hooking blue wool in and out.

"That's real pretty," said Mrs. Emerson.

"Yes, I think it's pretty," replied Mrs. Meserve.

"I suppose it's for the church fair?"

"Yes. I don't suppose it'll bring enough to pay for the worsted, let alone the work, but I suppose I've got to make something."

"How much did that one you made for the fair last year bring?"

"Twenty-five cents."

"It's wicked, ain't it?"

"I rather guess it is. It takes me a week every minute I can get to make one. I wish those that bought such things for twenty-five cents had to make them. Guess they'd sing another song. Well, I suppose I oughtn't to complain as long as it is for the Lord, but sometimes it does seem as if the Lord didn't get much out of it."

"Well, it's pretty work," said Mrs. Emerson, sitting down at the opposite window and taking up her dress skirt.

"Yes, it is real pretty work. I just *love* to crochet."

The two women rocked and sewed and crocheted in silence for two or three minutes. They were both waiting. Mrs. Meserve waited for the other's curiosity to develop in order that her news might have, as it were, a befitting stage entrance. Mrs. Emerson waited for the news. Finally she could wait no longer.

"Well, what's the news?" said she.

"Well, I don't know as there's anything very particular," hedged the other woman, prolonging the situation.

"Yes, there is; you can't cheat me," replied Mrs. Emerson.

"Now, how do you know?"

"By the way you look."

Mrs. Meserve laughed consciously and rather vainly.

"Well, Simon says my face is so expressive I can't hide anything more than five minutes no matter how hard I try," said she. "Well, there is some news. Simon came home with it this noon. He heard it in South Dayton. He had some business over there this morning. The old Sargent place is let."

Mrs. Emerson dropped her sewing and stared.

"You don't say so!"

"Yes, it is."

"Who to?"

"Why, some folks from Boston that moved to South Dayton last year. They haven't been satisfied with the house they had there—it wasn't large enough. The man has got considerable property and can afford to live pretty well. He's got a wife and his unmarried sister in the family. The sister's got money, too. He does business in Boston and it's just as easy to get to Boston from here as from South Dayton, and so they're coming here. You know the old Sargent house is a splendid place."

"Yes, it's the handsomest house in town, but——"

"Oh, Simon said they told him about that and he just laughed. Said he wasn't afraid and neither was his wife and sister. Said he'd risk ghosts rather than little tucked-up sleeping-rooms without any sun, like they've had in the Dayton house. Said he'd rather risk *seeing* ghosts, than risk being ghosts themselves. Simon said they said he was a great hand to joke."

"Oh, well," said Mrs. Emerson, "it is a beautiful house, and maybe there isn't anything in those stories. It never seemed to me they came very straight anyway. I never took much stock in them. All I thought was—if his wife was nervous."

"Nothing in creation would hire me to go into a house that I'd ever heard a word against of that kind," declared Mrs. Meserve with emphasis. "I wouldn't go into that house if they would give me the rent. I've seen enough of haunted houses to last me as long as I live."

Mrs. Emerson's face acquired the expression of a hunting hound.

"Have you?" she asked in an intense whisper.

"Yes, I have. I don't want any more of it."

"Before you came here?"

"Yes; before I was married—when I was quite a girl."

Mrs. Meserve had not married young. Mrs. Emerson had mental calculations when she heard that.

"Did you really live in a house that was——" she whispered fearfully.

Mrs. Meserve nodded solemnly.

"Did you really ever—see—anything——"

Mrs. Meserve nodded.

"You didn't see anything that did you any harm?"

"No, I didn't see anything that did me harm looking at it in one way, but it don't do anybody in this world any good to see things that haven't any business to be seen in it. You never get over it."

There was a moment's silence. Mrs. Emerson's features seemed to sharpen.

"Well, of course I don't want to urge you," said she, "if you don't feel like talking about it; but maybe it might do you good to tell it out, if it's on your mind, worrying you."

"I try to put it out of my mind," said Mrs. Meserve.

"Well, it's just as you feel."

"I never told anybody but Simon," said Mrs. Meserve. "I never felt as if it was wise perhaps. I didn't know what folks might think. So many don't believe in anything they can't understand, that they might think my mind wasn't right. Simon advised me not to talk about it. He said he didn't believe it was anything supernatural, but he had to own up that he couldn't give any explanation for it to save his life. He had to own up that he didn't believe anybody could. Then he said he wouldn't talk about it. He said lots of folks would sooner tell folks my head wasn't right than to own up they couldn't see through it."

"I'm sure I wouldn't say so," returned Mrs. Emerson reproachfully. "You know better than that, I hope."

"Yes, I do," replied Mrs. Meserve. "I know you wouldn't say so."

"And I wouldn't tell it to a soul if you didn't want me to."

"Well, I'd rather you wouldn't."

"I won't speak of it even to Mr. Emerson."

"I'd rather you wouldn't even to him."

"I won't."

Mrs. Emerson took up her dress skirt again; Mrs. Meserve hooked up another loop of blue wool. Then she began:

"Of course," said she, "I ain't going to say positively that I believe or disbelieve in ghosts, but all I tell you is what I saw. I can't explain it. I don't pretend I can, for I can't. If you can, well and good; I shall be glad, for it will stop tormenting me as it has done and always will otherwise. There hasn't been a day nor a night since it happened that I haven't thought of it, and always I have felt the shivers go down my back when I did."

"That's an awful feeling," Mrs. Emerson said.

"Ain't it? Well, it happened before I was married, when I was a girl and lived in East Wilmington. It was the first year I lived there. You know my family all died five years before that. I told you."

Mrs. Emerson nodded.

"Well, I went there to teach school, and I went to board with a Mrs. Amelia Dennison and her sister, Mrs. Bird. Abby, her name was—Abby Bird. She was a widow; she had never had any children. She had a little money—Mrs. Dennison didn't have any—and she had come to East Wilmington and bought the house they lived in. It was a real pretty house, though it was very old and run down. It had cost Mrs. Bird a good deal to put it in order. I guess that was the reason they took me to board. I guess they thought it would help along a little. I guess what I paid for my board about kept us all in victuals. Mrs. Bird had enough to live on if they were careful, but she had spent so much fixing up the old house that they must have been a little pinched for awhile.

"Anyhow, they took me to board, and I thought I was pretty lucky to get in there. I had a nice room, big and sunny and furnished pretty, the paper and paint all new, and everything as neat as wax. Mrs. Dennison was one of the best cooks I ever saw, and I had a little stove in my room, and there was always a nice fire there when I got home from school. I thought I hadn't been in such a nice place since I lost my own home, until I had been there about three weeks.

"I had been there about three weeks before I found it out, though I guess it had been going on ever since they had been in the house, and that was most four months. They hadn't said anything about it, and I didn't wonder, for there they had just bought the house and been to so much expense and trouble fixing it up.

"Well, I went there in September. I begun my school the first Monday. I remember it was a real cold fall, there was a frost the middle of September, and I had to put on my winter coat. I remember when I came home that night (let me see, I began school on a Monday, and that was two weeks from the next Thursday), I took off my coat downstairs and laid it on the table in the front entry. It was a real nice coat—heavy black broadcloth trimmed with fur; I had had it the winter before. Mrs. Bird called after me as I went upstairs that I ought not to leave it in the front entry for fear somebody might come in and take it, but I only laughed and called back to her that I wasn't afraid. I never was much afraid of burglars.

"Well, though it was hardly the middle of September, it was a real cold night. I remember my room faced west, and the sun was getting low, and the sky was a pale yellow and purple, just as you see it sometimes in the winter when there is going to be a cold snap. I rather think that was the night the frost came the first time. I know Mrs. Dennison covered up some flowers she had in the front yard, anyhow. I remember looking out and seeing an old green plaid shawl of hers over the verbena bed. There was a fire in my little wood-stove. Mrs. Bird made it, I know. She was a real motherly sort of woman; she always seemed to be the happiest when she was doing something to make other folks happy and comfortable. Mrs. Dennison told me she had always been so. She said she had coddled her husband within an inch of his life. 'It's lucky Abby never had any children,' she said, 'for she would have spoilt them.'

"Well, that night I sat down beside my nice little fire and ate an apple. There was a plate of nice apples on my table. Mrs. Bird put them there. I was always very fond of apples. Well, I sat down and ate an apple, and was having a beautiful time, and thinking how lucky I was to have got board in such a place with such nice folks, when I heard a queer little sound at my door. It was such a little hesitating sort of sound that it sounded more like a fumble than a knock, as if some one very timid, with very little hands, was feeling along the door, not quite daring to knock. For a minute I thought it was a mouse. But I waited and it came again, and then I made up my mind it was a knock, but a very little scared one, so I said, 'Come in.'

"But nobody came in, and then presently I heard the knock again. Then I got up and opened the door, thinking it was very queer, and I had a frightened feeling without knowing why.

"Well, I opened the door, and the first thing I noticed was a draught of cold air, as if the front door downstairs was open, but there was a strange close smell about the cold draught. It smelled more like a cellar that had been shut up for years, than out-of-doors. Then I saw something. I saw my coat first. The thing that held it was so small that I couldn't see much of anything else. Then I saw a little white face with eyes so scared and wishful that they seemed as if they might eat a hole in anybody's heart. It was a dreadful little face, with something about it which made it different from any other face on earth, but it was so pitiful that somehow it did away a good deal with the dreadfulness. And there were two little hands spotted purple with the cold, holding up my winter coat, and a strange little far-away voice said: 'I can't find my mother.'

"'For Heaven's sake,' I said, 'who are you?'

"Then the little voice said again: 'I can't find my mother.'

"All the time I could smell the cold and I saw that it was about the child; that cold was clinging to her as if she had come out of some deadly cold place. Well, I took my coat, I did not know what else to do, and the cold was clinging to that. It was as cold as if it had come off ice. When I had the coat I could see the child more plainly. She was dressed in one little white garment made very simply. It was a nightgown, only very long, quite covering her feet, and I could see dimly through it her little thin body mottled purple with the cold. Her face did not look so cold; that was a clear waxen white. Her hair was dark, but it looked as if it might be dark only because it was so damp, almost wet, and might really be light hair. It clung very close to her forehead, which was round and white. She would have been very beautiful if she had not been so dreadful.

" 'Who are you?' says I again, looking at her.

"She looked at me with her terrible pleading eyes and did not say anything.

" 'What are you?' says I. Then she went away. She did not seem to run or walk like other children. She flitted, like one of those little filmy white butterflies, that don't seem like real ones they are so light, and move as if they had no weight. But she looked back from the head of the stairs. 'I can't find my mother,' said she, and I never heard such a voice.

" 'Who is your mother?' says I, but she was gone.

"Well, I thought for a moment I should faint away. The room got dark and I heard a singing in my ears. Then I flung my coat onto the bed. My hands were as cold as ice from holding it, and I stood in my door, and called first Mrs. Bird and then Mrs. Dennison. I didn't dare go down over the stairs where that had gone. It seemed to me I should go mad if I didn't see somebody or something like other folks on the face of the earth. I thought I should never make anybody hear, but I could hear them stepping about downstairs, and I could smell biscuits baking for supper. Somehow the smell of those biscuits seemed the only natural thing left to keep me in my right mind. I didn't dare go over those stairs. I just stood there and called, and finally I heard the entry door open and Mrs. Bird called back:

" 'What is it? Did you call, Miss Arms?'

" 'Come up here; come up here as quick as you can, both of you,' I screamed out; 'quick, quick, quick!'

"I heard Mrs. Bird tell Mrs. Dennison: 'Come quick, Amelia, some-thing is the matter in Miss Arms' room.' It struck me even then that she expressed herself rather queerly, and it struck me as very queer, indeed, when they both got upstairs and I saw that they knew what had hap-pened, or that they knew of what nature the happening was.

" 'What is it, dear?' asked Mrs. Bird, and her pretty, loving voice had a strained sound. I saw her look at Mrs. Dennison and I saw Mrs. Den-nison look back at her.

" 'For God's sake,' says I, and I never spoke so before—'for God's sake, what was it brought my coat upstairs?'

" 'What was it like?' asked Mrs. Dennison in a sort of failing voice, and she looked at her sister again and her sister looked back at her.

" 'It was a child I have never seen here before. It looked like a child,' says I, 'but I never saw a child so dreadful, and it had on a nightgown, and said she couldn't find her mother. Who was it? What was it?'

"I thought for a minute Mrs. Dennison was going to faint, but Mrs. Bird hung onto her and rubbed her hands, and whispered in her ear (she had the cooingest kind of voice), and I ran and got her a glass of cold water. I tell you it took considerable courage to go downstairs alone, but they had set a lamp on the entry table so I could see. I don't believe I could have spunked up enough to have gone downstairs in the dark, thinking every second that child might be close to me. The lamp and the smell of the biscuits baking seemed to sort of keep my courage up, but I tell you I didn't waste much time going down those stairs and out into the kitchen for a glass of water. I pumped as if the house was afire, and I grabbed the first thing I came across in the shape of a tumbler: it was a painted one that Mrs. Dennison's Sunday school class gave her, and it was meant for a flower vase.

"Well, I filled it and then ran upstairs. I felt every minute as if something would catch my feet, and I held the glass to Mrs. Dennison's lips, while Mrs. Bird held her head up, and she took a good long swallow, then she looked hard at the tumbler.

" 'Yes,' says I, 'I know I got this one, but I took the first I came across, and it isn't hurt a mite.'

"Don't get the painted flowers wet,' says Mrs. Dennison very feebly, 'they'll wash off if you do.'

" 'I'll be real careful,' says I. I knew she set a sight by that painted tumbler.

"The water seemed to do Mrs. Dennison good, for presently she pushed Mrs. Bird away and sat up. She had been laying down on my bed.

" 'I'm all over it now,' says she, but she was terribly white, and her eyes looked as if they saw something outside things. Mrs. Bird wasn't much better, but she always had a sort of settled sweet, good look that nothing could disturb to any great extent. I knew I looked dreadful, for I caught a glimpse of myself in the glass, and I would hardly have known who it was.

"Mrs. Dennison, she slid off the bed and walked sort of tottery to a chair. 'I was silly to give way so,' says she.

"'No, you wasn't silly, sister,' says Mrs. Bird. 'I don't know what this means any more than you do, but whatever it is, no one ought to be called silly for being overcome by anything so different from other things which we have known all our lives.'

"Mrs. Dennison looked at her sister, then she looked at me, then back at her sister again, and Mrs. Bird spoke as if she had been asked a question.

"'Yes,' says she, 'I do think Miss Arms ought to be told—that is, I think she ought to be told all we know ourselves.'

"'That isn't much,' said Mrs. Dennison with a dying-away sort of sigh. She looked as if she might faint away again any minute. She was a real delicate-looking woman, but it turned out she was a good deal stronger than poor Mrs. Bird.

"'No, there isn't much we do know,' says Mrs. Bird, 'but what little there is she ought to know. I felt as if she ought to when she first came here.'

"'Well, I didn't feel quite right about it,' said Mrs. Dennison, 'but I kept hoping it might stop, and any way, that it might never trouble her, and you had put so much in the house, and we needed the money, and I didn't know but she might be nervous and think she couldn't come, and I didn't want to take a man boarder.'

"'And aside from the money, we were very anxious to have you come, my dear,' says Mrs. Bird.

"'Yes,' says Mrs. Dennison, 'we wanted the young company in the house; we were lonesome, and we both of us took a great liking to you the minute we set eyes on you.'

"And I guess they meant what they said, both of them. They were beautiful women, and nobody could be any kinder to me than they were, and I never blamed them for not telling me before, and, as they said, there wasn't really much to tell.

"They hadn't any sooner fairly bought the house, and moved into it, than they began to see and hear things. Mrs. Bird said they were sitting together in the sitting-room one evening when they heard it the first time. She said her sister was knitting lace (Mrs. Dennison made beautiful knitted lace) and she was reading the *Missionary Herald* (Mrs. Bird was very much interested in mission work), when all of a sudden they heard something. She heard it first and she laid down her *Missionary Herald* and listened, and then Mrs. Dennison she saw her listening and she drops her lace. 'What is it you are listening to, Abby?' says she. Then it came again and they both heard, and the cold shivers went down their backs to hear it, though they didn't know why. 'It's the cat, isn't it?' says Mrs. Bird.

"'It isn't any cat,' says Mrs. Dennison.

"'Oh, I guess it *must* be the cat; maybe she's got a mouse,' says Mrs. Bird, real cheerful, to calm down Mrs. Dennison, for she saw she was 'most scared to death, and she was always afraid of her fainting away. Then she opens the door and calls, 'Kitty, kitty, kitty!' They had brought their cat with them in a basket when they came to East Wilmington to live. It was a real handsome tiger cat, a tommy, and he knew a lot.

"Well, she called 'Kitty, kitty, kitty!' and sure enough the kitty came, and when he came in the door he gave a big yawl that didn't sound unlike what they had heard.

"'There, sister, here he is; you see it was the cat,' says Mrs. Bird. 'Poor kitty!'

"But Mrs. Dennison she eyed the cat, and she give a great screech.

"'What's that? What's that?' says she.

"'What's what?' says Mrs. Bird, pretending to herself that she didn't see what her sister meant.

"'Somethin's got hold of that cat's tail,' says Mrs. Dennison. 'Somethin's got hold of his tail. It's pulled straight out, an' he can't get away. Just hear him yawl!'

"'It isn't anything,' says Mrs. Bird, but even as she said that she could see a little hand holding fast to that cat's tail, and then the child seemed to sort of clear out of the dimness behind the hand, and the child was sort of laughing then, instead of looking sad, and she said that was a great deal worse. She said that laugh was the most awful and the saddest thing she ever heard.

"Well, she was so dumfounded that she didn't know what to do, and she couldn't sense at first that it was anything supernatural. She thought it must be one of the neighbour's children who had run away and was making free of their house, and was teasing their cat, and that they must be just nervous to feel so upset by it. So she speaks up sort of sharp.

"'Don't you know that you mustn't pull the kitty's tail?' says she.

'Don't you know you hurt the poor kitty, and she'll scratch you if you don't take care. Poor kitty, you mustn't hurt her.'

"And with that she said the child stopped pulling that cat's tail and went to stroking her just as soft and pitiful, and the cat put his back up and rubbed and purred as if he liked it. The cat never seemed a mite afraid, and that seemed queer, for I had always heard that animals were dreadfully afraid of ghosts; but then, that was a pretty harmless little sort of ghost.

"Well, Mrs. Bird said the child stroked that cat, while she and Mrs. Dennison stood watching it, and holding onto each other, for, no matter how hard they tried to think it was all right, it didn't look right. Finally Mrs. Dennison she spoke.

" 'What's your name, little girl?' says she.

"Then the child looks up and stops stroking the cat, and says she can't find her mother, just the way she said it to me. Then Mrs. Dennison she gave such a gasp that Mrs. Bird thought she was going to faint away, but she didn't. 'Well, who is your mother?' says she. But the child just says again 'I can't find my mother—I can't find my mother.'

" 'Where do you live, dear?' says Mrs. Bird.

" 'I can't find my mother,' says the child.

"Well, that was the way it was. Nothing happened. Those two women stood there hanging onto each other, and the child stood in front of them, and they asked her questions, and everything she would say was; 'I can't find my mother.'

"Then Mrs. Bird tried to catch hold of the child, for she thought in spite of what she saw that perhaps she was nervous and it was a real child, only perhaps not quite right in its head, that had run away in her little nightgown after she had been put to bed.

"She tried to catch the child. She had an idea of putting a shawl around it and going out—she was such a little thing she could have carried her easy enough—and trying to find out to which of the neighbours she belonged. But the minute she moved toward the child there wasn't any child there; there was only that little voice seeming to come from nothing, saying 'I can't find my mother,' and presently that died away.

"Well, that same thing kept happening, or something very much the same. Once in awhile Mrs. Bird would be washing dishes, and all at once the child would be standing beside her with the dish-towel, wiping them. Of course, that was terrible. Mrs. Bird would wash the dishes all over. Sometimes she didn't tell Mrs. Dennison, it made her so nervous. Sometimes when they were making cake they would find the raisins all picked over, and sometimes little sticks of kindling wood would be found laying beside the kitchen stove. They never knew when they would come across that child, and always she kept saying over and over that she couldn't find her mother. They never tried talking to her, except once in awhile Mrs. Bird would get desperate and ask her something, but the child never seemed to hear it; she always kept right on saying that she couldn't find her mother.

"After they had told me all they had to tell about their experience with the child, they told me about the house and the people that had lived there before they did. It seemed something dreadful had happened in that house. And the land agent had never let on to them. I don't think they would have bought it if he had, no matter how cheap it was, for even if folks aren't really afraid of anything, they don't want to live in houses where such dreadful things have happened that you keep thinking about them. I know after they told me I should never have stayed there another night, if I hadn't thought so much of them, no matter how comfortable I was made; and I never was nervous, either. But I stayed. Of course, it didn't happen in my room. If it had I could not have stayed."

"What was it?" asked Mrs. Emerson in an awed voice.

"It was an awful thing. That child had lived in the house with her father and mother two years before. They had come—or the father had—from a real good family. He had a good situation: he was a drummer for a big leather house in the city, and they lived real pretty, with plenty to do with. But the mother was a real wicked woman. She was as handsome as a picture, and they said she came from good sort of people enough in Boston, but she was bad clean through, though she was real pretty spoken and most everybody liked her. She used to dress out and make a great show, and she never seemed to take much interest in the child, and folks began to say she wasn't treated right.

"The woman had a hard time keeping a girl. For some reason one wouldn't stay. They would leave and then talk about her awfully, telling all kinds of things. People didn't believe it at first; then they began to. They said that the woman made that little thing, though she wasn't much over five years old, and small and babyish for her age, do most of the work, what there was done; they said the house used to look like a pigsty when she didn't have help. They said the little thing used to stand on a chair and wash dishes, and they'd seen her carrying in sticks of wood most as big as she was many a time, and they'd heard her mother scolding her. The woman was a fine singer, and had a voice like a screech-owl when she scolded.

"The father was away most of the time, and when that happened he had been away out West for some weeks. There had been a married man hanging about the mother for some time, and folks had talked some; but they weren't sure there was anything wrong, and he was a man very high up, with money, so they kept pretty still for fear he would hear of it and make trouble for them, and of course nobody was sure, though folks did say afterward that the father of the child had ought to have been told.

"But that was very easy to say; it wouldn't have been so easy to find anybody who would have been willing to tell him such a thing as that, especially when they weren't any too sure. He set his eyes by his wife, too. They said all he seemed to think of was to earn money to buy things to deck her out in. And he about worshiped the child, too. They said he was a real nice man. The men that are treated so bad mostly are real nice men. I've always noticed that.

"Well, one morning that man that there had been whispers about was missing. He had been gone quite a while, though, before they really knew that he was missing, because he had gone away and told his wife that he had to go to New York on business and might be gone a week, and not to worry if he didn't get home, and not to worry if he didn't write, because he should be thinking from day to day that he might take the next train home and there would be no use in writing. So the wife waited, and she tried not to worry until it was two days over the week, then she run into a neighbour's and fainted dead away on the floor; and then they made inquiries and found out that he had skipped—with some money that didn't belong to him, too.

"Then folks began to ask where was that woman, and they found out by comparing notes that nobody had seen her since the man went away; but three or four women remembered that she had told them that she thought of taking the child and going to Boston to visit her folks, so when they hadn't seen her around, and the house shut, they jumped to the conclusion that was where she was. They were the neighbours that lived right around her, but they didn't have much to do with her, and she'd gone out of her way to tell them about her Boston plan, and they didn't make much reply when she did.

"Well, there was this house shut up, and the man and woman missing and the child. Then all of a sudden one of the women that lived the nearest remembered something. She remembered that she had waked up three nights running, thinking she heard a child crying somewhere, and once she waked up her husband, but he said it must be the Bisbees' little girl, and she thought it must be. The child wasn't well and was always crying. It used to have colic spells, especially at night. So she didn't think any more about it until this came up, then all of a sudden she did think of it. She told what she had heard, and finally folks began to think they had better enter that house and see if there was anything wrong.

"Well, they did enter it, and they found that child dead, locked in one of the rooms. (Mrs. Dennison and Mrs. Bird never used that room; it was a back bedroom on the second floor.)

"Yes, they found that poor child there, starved to death, and frozen, though they weren't sure she had frozen to death, for she was in bed with clothes enough to keep her pretty warm when she was alive. But she had been there a week, and she was nothing but skin and bone. It looked as if the mother had locked her into the house when she went away, and told her not to make any noise for fear the neighbours would hear her and find out that she herself had gone.

"Mrs. Dennison said she couldn't really believe that the woman had meant to have her own child starved to death. Probably she thought the little thing would raise somebody, or folks would try to get in the house and find her. Well, whatever she thought, there the child was, dead.

"But that wasn't all. The father came home, right in the midst of it; the child was just buried, and he was beside himself. And—he went on the track of his wife, and he found her, and he shot her dead; it was in all the papers at the time; then he disappeared. Nothing had been seen of him since. Mrs. Dennison said that she thought he had either made way with himself or got out of the country, nobody knew, but they did know there was something wrong with the house.

" 'I knew folks acted queer when they asked me how I liked it when we first came here,' says Mrs. Dennison, 'but I never dreamed why till we saw the child that night.' "

"I never heard anything like it in my life," said Mrs. Emerson, staring at the other woman with awestruck eyes.

"I thought you'd say so," said Mrs. Meserve. "You don't wonder that I ain't disposed to speak light when I hear there is anything queer about a house, do you?"

"No, I don't, after that," Mrs. Emerson said.

"But that ain't all," said Mrs. Meserve.

"Did you see it again?" Mrs. Emerson asked.

"Yes, I saw it a number of times before the last time. It was lucky I wasn't nervous, or I never could have stayed there, much as I liked the place and much as I thought of those two women; they were beautiful women, and no mistake. I loved those women. I hope Mrs. Dennison will come and see me sometime.

"Well, I stayed, and I never knew when I'd see that child. I got so I was very careful to bring everything of mine upstairs, and not leave any little thing in my room that needed doing, for fear she would come lugging up my coat or hat or gloves or I'd find things done when there'd been no live being in the room to do them. I can't tell you how I dreaded seeing her; and worse than the seeing her was the hearing her say, 'I can't find my mother.' It was enough to make your blood run cold. I never heard a living child cry for its mother that was anything so pitiful as that dead one. It was enough to break your heart.

"She used to come and say that to Mrs. Bird oftener than to any one else. Once I heard Mrs. Bird say she wondered if it was possible that the poor little thing couldn't really find her mother in the other world, she had been such a wicked woman.

"But Mrs. Dennison told her she didn't think she ought to speak so nor even think so, and Mrs. Bird said she shouldn't wonder if she was right. Mrs. Bird was always very easy to put in the wrong. She was a good woman, and one that couldn't do things enough for other folks. It seemed as if that was what she lived on. I don't think she was ever so scared by that poor little ghost, as much as she pitied it, and she was 'most heartbroken because she couldn't do anything for it, as she could have done for a live child.

" 'It seems to me sometimes as if I should die if I can't get that awful little white robe off that child and get her in some clothes and feed her and stop her looking for her mother,' I heard her say once, and she was in earnest. She cried when she said it. That wasn't long before she died.

"Now I am coming to the strangest part of it all. Mrs. Bird died very sudden. One morning—it was Saturday, and there wasn't any school—I went downstairs to breakfast, and Mrs. Bird wasn't there; there was nobody but Mrs. Dennison. She was pouring out the coffee when I came in. 'Why, where's Mrs. Bird?' says I.

" 'Abby ain't feeling very well this morning,' says she; 'there isn't much the matter, I guess, but she didn't sleep very well, and her head aches, and she's sort of chilly, and I told her I thought she'd better stay in bed till the house gets warm.' It was a very cold morning.

" 'Maybe she's got cold,' says I.

" 'Yes, I guess she has,' says Mrs. Dennison. 'I guess she's got cold. She'll be up before long. Abby ain't one to stay in bed a minute longer than she can help.'

"Well, we went on eating our breakfast, and all at once a shadow flickered across one wall of the room and over the ceiling the way a shadow will sometimes when somebody passes the window outside. Mrs. Dennison and I both looked up, then out of the window; then Mrs. Dennison she gives a scream.

" 'Why, Abby's crazy!' says she. 'There she is out this bitter cold morning, and—and——' She didn't finish, but she meant the child. For we were both looking out, and we saw, as plain as we ever saw anything in our lives, Mrs. Abby Bird walking off over the white snow-path with that child holding fast to her hand, nestling close to her as if she had found her own mother.

" 'She's dead,' says Mrs. Dennison, clutching hold of me hard. 'She's dead; my sister is dead!'

"She was. We hurried upstairs as fast as we could go, and she was dead in her bed, and smiling as if she was dreaming, and one arm and hand was stretched out as if something had hold of it; and it couldn't be straightened even at the last—it lay out over her casket at the funeral."

"Was the child ever seen again?" asked Mrs. Emerson in a shaking voice.

"No," replied Mrs. Meserve; "that child was never seen again after she went out of the yard with Mrs. Bird."

EERIE EDWARDIANS

(SPECTERS IN THE GASLIT AGE)

THE LOOKING-GLASS

BY WALTER DE LA MARE

WALTER DE LA MARE, the brilliant British poet, novelist, and anthologist, published his first book, *Henry Brocken*, in 1904, a book in which he refashioned famous personages of European literature into fantasy figures. For De la Mare fantasy was to be of major importance throughout his creative life; and it was inevitable that he should be the early twentieth-century creator of the "poetic" ghost story.

Reality could intervene in De La Mare's stories, but a superreality had to be more important. "In a ghost story," he said, "the isthmus —the brig o'dread—from any preternatural to a natural explanation should be of the very narrowest. The evidence on the one side and on the other is softly falling like imperceptible dust into the scale pans. But, finally, surely, that on the preternatural side should waver gently downwards."

That delicately macabre touch is reflected in *The Looking-Glass*. De la Mare was fascinated with mirrors. His first book of poetry for children, *Song of Childhood*, was published under the pseudonym Ramal, mirror writing for De la Mare, and he used the device of a looking-glass in his work in many ways: often to cast an oblique shadow on the world of the supernatural. ❧

FOR AN hour or two in the afternoon, Miss Lennox had always made it a rule to retire to her own room for a little rest, so that for this brief interval, at any rate, Alice was at liberty to do just what she pleased with herself. That "just what she pleased," no doubt, was a little limited in range; and "with herself" was at best no very vast oasis amid its sands.

She might, for example, like Miss Lennox, rest, too, if she pleased. Miss Lennox prided herself on her justice.

But then, Alice could seldom sleep in the afternoon because of her troublesome cough. She might at a pinch write letters, but they would need to be nearly all of them addressed to imaginary correspondents. And not even the most romantic of young human beings can write on indefinitely to one who vouchsafes *no* kind of an answer. The choice in fact merely amounted to that between being "in" or "out" (in *any* sense), and now that the severity of the winter had abated, Alice much preferred the solitude of the garden to the vacancy of the house.

With rain came an extraordinary beauty to the narrow garden—its trees drenched, refreshed, and glittering at break of evening, its early flowers stooping pale above the darkened earth, the birds that haunted there singing as if out of a cool and happy cloister—the stormcock wildly jubilant. There was one particular thrush on one particular tree which you might say all but yelled messages at Alice, messages which sometimes made her laugh, and sometimes almost ready to cry, with delight.

And yet ever the same vague influence seemed to haunt her young mind. Scarcely so much as a mood; nothing in the nature of a thought; merely an influence—like that of some impressive stranger met—in a dream, say,—long ago, and now half-forgotten.

This may have been in part because the low and foundering wall between the empty meadows and her own recess of greenery had always seemed to her like the boundary between two worlds. On the one side freedom, the wild; on this, Miss Lennox, and a sort of captivity. There Reality; here (her "duties" almost forgotten) the confines of a kind of waking dream. For this reason, if for no other, she at the same time longed for and yet in a way dreaded the afternoon's regular reprieve.

It had proved, too, both a comfort and a vexation that the old servant belonging to the new family next door had speedily discovered this little habit, and would as often as not lie in wait for her between a bush of lilac and a bright green chestnut that stood up like a dense umbrella midway along the wall that divided Miss Lennox's from its one neighbouring garden. And since apparently it was Alice's destiny in life to be always precariously balanced between extremes, Sarah had also turned out to be a creature of rather peculiar oscillations of temperament.

Their clandestine talks were, therefore, though frequent, seldom particularly enlightening. None the less, merely to see this slovenly ponderous woman enter the garden, self-centered, with a kind of dull arrogance, her louring face as vacant as contempt of the Universe could make it, was an event ever eagerly, though at times vexatiously, looked for, and seldom missed.

Until but a few steps separated them, it was one of Sarah's queer habits to make believe, so to speak, that Alice was not there at all. Then, as regularly, from her place of vantage on the other side of the wall, she would slowly and heavily lift her eyes to her face, with a sudden energy which at first considerably alarmed the young girl, and afterwards amused her. For certainly you *are* amused in a sort of fashion when any stranger you might suppose to be a little queer in the head proves perfectly harmless. Alice did not exactly like Sarah. But she could no more resist her advances, than the garden could resist the coming on of night.

Miss Lennox, too, it must be confessed, was a rather tedious and fretful companion for wits (like Alice's) always wool-gathering—wool, moreover, of the shimmering kind that decked the Golden Fleece. Her own conception of the present was of a niche in Time from which she was accustomed to look back on the dim, though once apparently garish, panorama of the past; while with Alice, Time had kept promises enough only for a surety of its immense resources—resources illimitable, even though up till now they had been pretty tightly withheld.

Or, if you so preferred, as Alice would say to herself, you could put it that Miss Lennox had all her eggs in a real basket, and that Alice had all hers in a basket that was *not* exactly real—only problematical. All the more reason, then, for Alice to think it a little queer that it had been Miss Lennox herself and not Sarah who had first given shape and substance to her vaguely bizarre intuitions concerning the garden—a walled-in space in which one might suppose intuition alone could discover anything in the least remarkable.

"When my cousin, Mary Wilson (the Wilsons of Aberdeen, as I may have told you), when my cousin lived in this house," she had informed her young companion one evening over her own milk and oatmeal biscuits, "there was a silly talk with the maids that it was haunted."

"The house?" Alice had enquired, with a sudden crooked look on a face that Nature, it seemed, had definitely intended to be frequently startled; "The house?"

"I didn't say the *house*," Miss Lennox testily replied—it always annoyed her to see anything resembling a flush on her young companion's cheek, "and even if I did, I certainly *meant* the garden. If I had meant the house, I should have used the word house. I meant the garden. It was quite unnecessary to correct or contradict me; and whether or not, it's all the purest rubbish—just a tale, though not the only one of the kind in the world, I fancy."

"Do you remember any of the other tales?" Alice had enquired, after a rather prolonged pause.

"No, none," was the flat reply.

And so it came about that to Sarah (though she could hardly be described as the Serpent of the situation) to Sarah fell the opportunity of enjoying to the full an opening for her fantastic "lore." By insinuation, by silences, now with contemptuous scepticism, now with enormous warmth, she cast her spell, weaving an eager imagination through and through with rather gaudy threads of superstition.

"Lor', no, *Crimes*, maybe not, though blood is in the roots for all *I* can say." She had looked up almost candidly in the warm, rainy wind, her deadish-looking hair blown back from her forehead.

"Some'll tell you only the old people have eyes to see the mystery; and some, old or young, if so be they're ripe. Nothing to me either way; I'm gone past such things. And *what* it is, 'orror and darkness, or golden like a saint in heaven, or pictures in dreams, or just like dying fireworks in the air, the Lord alone knows, Miss, for I don't. But this I *will* say," and she edged up her body a little closer to the wall, the raindrops the while dropping softly on bough and grass, "Mayday's the day, and midnight's the hour, for such as be wakeful and brazen and stoopid enough to watch it out. And what you've got to look for in a manner of speaking is what comes up out of the darkness from behind them trees there!"

She drew back cunningly.

The conversation was just like clockwork. It recurred regularly—except that there was no need to wind anything up. It wound itself up over-night, and with such accuracy that Alice soon knew the complete series of question and answer by heart or by rote—as if she had learned them out of the Child's Guide to Knowledge, or the Catechism. Still there were interesting points in it even now.

"*And what you've got to look for*"—the *you* was so absurdly imper-

sonal when muttered in that thick coarse privy voice. And Alice invariably smiled at this little juncture; and Sarah as invariably looked at her
and swallowed.

"But have *you* looked for—for what you say, you know?" Alice would
then enquire, still with face a little averted towards the black low-
boughed group of broad-leafed chestnuts, positive candelabra in their
own season of wax-like speckled blossom.

"Me? *Me?* I was old before my time, they used to say. Why, besides
my poor sister up in Yorkshire there, there's not a mouth utters my
name." Her large flushed face smiled in triumphant irony. "Besides my
bed-rid mistress there, and my old what they call feeble-minded sister,
Jane Mary, in Yorkshire, I'm as good as in my grave. I may be dull and
hot in the head at times, but I stand *alone*—eat alone, sit alone, sleep
alone, think alone. There's never been such a lonely person before.
Now, what should such a lonely person as me, Miss, I ask you, or what
should you, either, for that matter, be meddling with your Maydays and
your haunted gardens for?" She broke off and stared with angry confusion around her, and, lifting up her open hand a little, she added hotly,
"Them birds!—My God, I drats 'em for their squealin'!"

"But, why?" said Alice, frowning slightly.

"The Lord only knows, Miss; I hate the sight of 'em! If I had what
they call a blunderbuss in me hand I'd blow 'em to ribbings."

And Alice never could quite understand why it was that the normal
pronunciation of the word would have suggested a less complete dis-
memberment of the victims.

It was on a bleak day in March that Alice first heard really explicitly
the conditions of the quest.

"Your hows and whys! What I say is, I'm sick of it all. Not so much
of you, Miss, which is all greens to me, but of the rest of it all! Anyhow,
fast you must, like the Catholics, and you with a frightful hacking
cough and all. Come like a new-begotten bride you must in a white
gown, and a wreath of lilies or rorringe-blossom in your hair, same
pretty much as I made for my mother's coffin this twenty years ago, and
which I wouldn't do now not for respectability even. And me and my
mother, let me tell you, were as close as hens in a roost. . . . But I'm
off me subject. There you sits, even if the snow itself comes sailing in on
your face, and alone you must be, neither book nor candle, and the
house behind you shut up black abed and asleep. But, there; you so wan

and sickly a young lady. What ghost would come to you, I'd like to know. You want some fine dark loveyer for a ghost—that's your ghost. Oo-ay! There's not a want in the world but's dust and ashes. That's my bit of schooling."

She gazed on impenetrably at Alice's slender fingers. And without raising her eyes she leaned her large hands on the wall. "Meself, Miss, meself's *my* ghost, as they say. Why, bless me! it's all thro' the place now, like smoke."

What was all through the place now like smoke Alice perceived to be the peculiar clarity of the air-discernible in the garden at times. The clearness as it were of glass, of a looking-glass, which conceals all behind and beyond it, returning only the looker's wonder, or simply her vanity, or even her gaiety. Why, for the matter of that, thought Alice smiling, there are people who look into looking-glasses, actually see themselves there, and yet never turn a hair. There *wasn't* any glass of course. This—this mirage sprang only out of the desire of her eyes, a kind of restless hunger of the mind—just to possess her soul in patience till the first favourable May evening came along and then once and for all to set everything at rest. It was a thought which fascinated her so completely, that it influenced her habits, her words, her actions. She even began to long for the afternoon solely to be alone with it; and in the midst of the reverie it charmed into her mind, she would glance up as startled as a Dryad to see the "cook-general's" dark face fixing its still cold gaze on her from over the moss-greened wall. As for Miss Lennox, she became testier and more "rational" than ever as she narrowly watched the day approaching when her need for a new companion would become extreme.

Who, however, the lover might be, and where the trysting-place, was unknown even to Alice, though, maybe, not absolutely unsurmised by her, and with a kind of cunning perspicacity perceived only by Sarah.

"I see my old tales have tickled you up, Miss," she said one day, lifting her eyes from the clothes-line she was carrying, to the girl's alert and mobile face. "What they call old wives' tales I fancy, too."

"Oh, I don't think so," Alice answered. "I can hardly tell, Sarah. I am only at peace *here*, I know that. I get out of bed at night to look down from the window and wish myself here. When I'm reading, just as if it were a painted illustration—in the book, you know—the scene of it all floats in between me and the print. Besides, I can do just what I like with it. In my mind, I mean. I just imagine; and there it all is. So you see I could not bear *now* to go away."

"There's no cause to worry your head about that," said the woman darkly, "and as for picking and choosing I never saw much of it for them that's under of a thumb. Why, when *I* was young, I couldn't have borne to live as I do now with just meself wandering to and fro. Muttering I catch meself, too. And, to be sure, surrounded in the air by shapes, and shadows, and noises, and winds, so as sometimes I can neither see nor hear. It's true, God's gospel, Miss—the body's like a clump of wood, it's that dull. And you can't get t'other side, so to speak."

So lucid a portrayal of her own exact sensations astonished the girl. "Well, but what is it, what is it, Sarah?"

Sarah strapped the air with the loose end of the clothesline. "Part, Miss, the hauntin' of the garden. Part as them black-jacketed clergymen would say, because we's we. And part 'cos it's all death the other side—all death."

She drew her head slowly in, her puffy cheeks glowed, her small black eyes gazed as fixedly and deadly as if they were anemones on a rock.

The very fulness of her figure seemed to exaggerate her vehemence. She gloated—a heavy somnolent owl puffing its feathers. Alice drew back, swiftly glancing as she did so over her shoulder. The sunlight was liquid wan gold in the meadow, between the black tree-trunks. They lifted their cumbrous branches far above the brick human house, stooping their leafy twigs. A starling's dark iridescence took her glance as he minced pertly in the coarse grass.

"I can't quite see why *you* should think of death," Alice ventured to suggest.

"Me? Not me! Where I'm put, I stay. I'm like a stone in the grass, I am. Not that if I were that old mealy-smilin' bag of bones flat on her back on her bed up there with her bits of beadwork and slops through a spout, I wouldn't make sure over-night of not being waked next mornin'. There's something in me that won't let me rest, what they call a volcano, though no more to eat in that beetle cupboard of a kitchen than would keep a Tom Cat from the mange."

"But, Sarah," said Alice, casting a glance up at the curtained windows of the other house, "she looks such a quiet, *patient* old thing. I don't think I *could* stand having not even enough to eat. Why do you stay?"

Sarah laughed for a full half-minute in silence, staring at Alice meanwhile. " 'Patient'!" she replied at last, "Oo-ay. Not to my knowledge did I ever breathe the contrary. As for staying; you'd stay all right if that loveyer of yours come along. You'd stand anything—them pale narrow-chested kind; though me, I'm neether to bend nor break. And if the old man was to look down out of the blue up there this very minute, ay, and shake his fist at me, I'd say it to his face. I loathe your whining psalm-singers. A trap's a trap. You wait and see!"

"But how do you mean?" Alice said slowly, her face stooping.

There came no answer. And, on turning, she was surprised to see the bunchy alpaca-clad woman already disappearing round the corner of the house.

The talk softly subsided in her mind like the dust in an empty room. Alice wandered on in the garden, extremely loth to go in. And gradually a curious happiness at last descended upon her heart, like a cloud of morning dew in a dell of wild-flowers. It seemed in moments like these, as if she had been given the power to think—or rather to be conscious, as it were, of thoughts not her own—thoughts like vivid pictures, follow-ing one upon another with extraordinary rapidity and brightness through her mind. As if, indeed, thoughts could be like fragments of glass, reflecting light at their every edge and angle. She stood tiptoe at the meadow wall and gazed greedily into the green fields, and across to the pollard aspens by the waterside. Turning, her eyes recognised clear in the shadow and the blue grey air of the garden her solitude—its soli-tude. And at once all thinking ceased.

"The Spirit is *me*: I haunt this place!" she said aloud, with sudden as-surance, and almost in Sarah's own words. "And I don't mind—not the least bit. It can be only my thankful, thankful self that is here. And that can never be lost."

She returned to the house, and seemed as she moved to see—almost as if she were looking down out of the sky on herself—her own dwarf figure walking beneath the trees. Yet there was at the same time a curious in-dividuality in the common things, living and inanimate, that were peep-ing at her out of their secrecy. The silence hung above them as apparent as their own clear reflected colours above the brief spring flowers. But when she stood tidying herself for the usual hour of reading to Miss Lennox, she was conscious of an almost unendurable weariness.

That night Alice set to work with her needle upon a piece of sprigged muslin to make her "watch-gown" as Sarah called it. She was excited.

She hadn't much time, she fancied. It was like hiding in a story. She worked with extreme pains, and quickly. And not till the whole flimsy thing was finished did she try on or admire any part of it. But, at last, in the early evening of one of the middle days of April, she drew her bedroom blind up close to the ceiling, to view herself in her yellow grained looking-glass.

The gown, white as milk in the low sunlight, and sprinkled with even whiter embroidered nosegays of daisies, seemed to accentuate a girlish figure, already very slender. She had arranged her abundant hair with unusual care, and her own clear, inexplicable eyes looked back upon her beauty, bright it seemed with tidings they could not speak.

She regarded closely that narrow, flushed, intense face in an unforeseen storm of compassion and regret, as if with the conviction that she herself was to blame for the inevitable leavetaking. It seemed to gaze like an animal its mute farewell in the dim discoloured glass.

And when she had folded and laid away the gown in her wardrobe, and put on her everyday clothes again, she felt an extreme aversion for the garden. So, instead of venturing out that afternoon, she slipped off its faded blue ribbon from an old bundle of letters which she had hoarded all these years from a school-friend long since lost sight of, and spent the evening reading them over, till headache and an empty despondency sent her to bed.

Lagging Time brought at length the thirtieth of April. Life was as usual. Miss Lennox had even begun to knit her eighth pair of woollen mittens for the annual Church bazaar. To Alice the day passed rather quickly; a cloudy, humid day with a furtive continual and enigmatical stir in the air. Her lips were parched; it seemed at any moment her skull might crack with the pain as she sat reading her chapter of Macaulay to Miss Lennox's sparking and clicking needles. Her mind was a veritable rookery of forebodings, flying and returning. She scarcely ate at all, and kept to the house, never even approaching a window. She wrote a long and rather unintelligible letter, which she destroyed when she had read it over. Then suddenly every vestige of pain left her.

And when at last she went to bed—so breathless that she thought her heart at any moment would jump out of her body, and so saturated with expectancy she thought she would die—her candle was left burning calmly, unnodding, in its socket upon the chest of drawers; the blind of her window was up, towards the houseless byroad; her pen stood in the inkpot.

She slept on into the morning of Mayday, in a sheet of eastern sunshine, till Miss Lennox, with a peevishness that almost amounted to resolution, decided to wake her. But then, Alice, though unbeknown in any really conscious sense to herself, perhaps, had long since decided not to be awakened.

Not until the evening of that day did the sun in his diurnal course for a while illumine the garden, and then very briefly: to gild, to lull, and to be gone. The stars wheeled on in the thick-sown waste of space, and even when Miss Lennox's small share of the earth's wild living creatures had stirred and sunk again to rest in the ebb of night, there came no watcher—not even the very ghost of a watcher—to the garden, in a watch-gown. So that what peculiar secrets found reflex in its dark mirror no human witness was there to tell.

As for Sarah, she had long since done with looking-glasses once and for all. A place was a place. There was still the washing to be done on Mondays. Fools and weaklings would continue to come and go. But give her *her* way, she'd have blown them and their looking-glasses all to ribbons—with the birds.

THE REAL RIGHT THING

BY HENRY JAMES

THE HOUSE of fiction," said the American expatriate writer Henry James, "has not one window, but a million." At each window, he felt, stands a figure with a pair of eyes. Each viewer sees differently; "one seeing more, the other seeing less, one seeing black where the other sees white . . ." And sometimes, one seeing, feeling something that the other does not see at all. A ghost.

James was born into an extraordinary family; his father Henry James, Senior, was a Boston Brahmin, a close friend of the literary world that ranged from Emerson to Margaret Fuller; his brother, William, was America's first important psychologist. All of the family was fascinated by what they called the invisible reality. In Henry James's case, fiction was such an expression for this reality, and the ghost story, a compelling, salable outlet.

James's masterpiece *The Turn of the Screw* is the greatest example of a macabre novella in the literature of the United States, but he also wrote a series of remarkable shorter stories.

"The Real Right Thing" was based on a comment from one of his contemporaries who was writing the life of an author, just deceased, and felt "he might come in." At the same time James was invited to write the biography of America's sculptor William Westmore Story, but biography at the time did not interest him. Instead, he felt himself drawn by an almost ghostly hand to write "The Real Right Thing." ॐ

I

WHEN, AFTER the death of Ashton Doyne—but three months after—
George Withermore was approached, as the phrase is, on the subject of
a "volume," the communication came straight from his publishers, who
had been, and indeed much more, Doyne's own; but he was not surprised to learn, on the occurrence of the interview they next suggested,
that a certain pressure as to the early issue of a Life had been applied
them by their late client's widow. Doyne's relations with his wife had
been to Withermore's knowledge a special chapter—which would present itself, by the way, as a delicate one for the biographer; but a sense
of what she had lost, and even of what she had lacked, had betrayed itself, on the poor woman's part, from the first days of her bereavement,
sufficiently to prepare an observer at all initiated for some attitude of
reparation, some espousal even exaggerated of the interests of a distinguished name. George Withermore was, as he felt, initiated; yet what
he had not expected was to hear that she had mentioned him as the person in whose hands she would most promptly place the materials for a
book.

These materials—diaries, letters, memoranda, notes, documents of
many sorts—were her property and wholly in her control, no conditions
at all attaching to any portion of her heritage; so that she was free at
present to do as she liked—free in particular to do nothing. What
Doyne would have arranged had he had time to arrange could be but
supposition and guess. Death had taken him too soon and too suddenly,
and there was all the pity that the only wishes he was known to have expressed were wishes leaving it positively out. He had broken short
off—that was the way of it; and the end was ragged and needed trim-
ming. Withermore was conscious, abundantly, of how close he had
stood to him, but also was not less aware of his comparative obscurity.
He was young, a journalist, a critic, a hand-to-mouth character, with little, as yet, of any striking sort, to show. His writings were few and small,
his relations scant and vague. Doyne, on the other hand, had lived long
enough—above all had had talent enough—to become great, and among
his many friends gilded also with greatness were several to whom his
wife would have affected those who knew her as much more likely to ap-
peal.

The preference she had at all events uttered—and uttered in a roundabout considerate way that left him a measure of freedom—made our young man feel that he must at least see her and that there would be in any case a good deal to talk about. He immediately wrote to her, she as promptly named an hour, and they had it out. But he came away with his particular idea immensely strengthened. She was a strange woman, and he had never thought her an agreeable, yet there was something that touched him now in her bustling blundering zeal. She wanted the book to make up, and the individual whom, of her husband's set, she probably believed she might most manipulate was in every way to help it to do so. She hadn't taken Doyne seriously enough in life, but the biography should be a full reply to every imputation on herself. She had scantly known how such books were constructed, but she had been looking and had learned something. It alarmed Withermore a little from the first to see that she'd wish to go in for quantity. She talked of "volumes," but he had his notion of that.

"My thought went straight to *you,* as his own would have done," she had said almost as soon as she rose before him there in her large array of mourning—with her big black eyes, her big black wig, her big black fan and gloves, her general gaunt ugly tragic, but striking and, as might have been thought from a certain point of view, "elegant" presence. "You're the one he liked most; oh *much!"*—and it had quite sufficed to turn Withermore's head. It little mattered that he could afterwards wonder if she had known Doyne enough, when it came to that, to be sure. He would have said for himself indeed that her testimony on such a point could scarcely count. Still, there was no smoke without fire; she knew at least what she meant, and he wasn't a person she could have an interest in flattering. They went up together without delay to the great man's vacant study at the back of the house and looking over the large green garden—a beautiful and inspiring scene to poor Withermore's view—common to the expensive row.

"You can perfectly work here, you know," said Mrs. Doyne: "you shall have the place quite to yourself—I'll give it all up to you; so that in the evenings in particular, don't you see? it will be perfection for quiet and privacy."

Perfection indeed, the young man felt as he looked about—having explained that, as his actual occupation was an evening paper and his earlier hours, for a long time yet, regularly taken up, he should have to come always at night. The place was full of their lost friend; everything in it had belonged to him; everything they touched had been part of his life. It was all at once too much for Withermore—too great an honour and even too great a care; memories still recent came back to him, so that, while his heart beat faster and his eyes filled with tears, the pressure of his loyalty seemed almost more than he could carry. At the sight of his tears Mrs. Doyne's own rose to her lids, and the two for a minute only looked at each other. He half-expected her to break out "Oh help me to feel as I know you know I want to feel!" And after a little one of them said, with the other's deep assent—it didn't matter which: "It's here that we're *with* him." But it was definitely the young man who put it, before they left the room, that it was there he was with themselves.

The young man began to come as soon as he could arrange it, and then it was, on the spot, in the charmed stillness, between the lamp and the fire and with the curtains drawn, that a certain intenser consciousness set in for him. He escaped from the black London November; he passed through the large hushed house and up the red-carpeted staircase where he only found in his path the whisk of a soundless trained maid or the reach, out of an open room, of Mrs. Doyne's queenly weeds and approving tragic face; and then, by a mere touch of the well-made door that gave so sharp and pleasant a click, shut himself in for three or four warm hours with the spirit—as he had always distinctly declared it—of his master. He was not a little frightened when, even the first night, it came over him that he had really been most affected, in the whole matter, by the prospect, the privilege and the luxury, of this sensation. He hadn't, he could now reflect, definitely considered the question of the book—as to which there was here even already much to consider: he had simply let his affection and admiration—to say nothing of his gratified pride—meet to the full the temptation Mrs. Doyne had offered them.

How did he know without more thought, he might begin to ask himself, that the book was on the whole to be desired? What warrant had he ever received from Ashton Doyne himself for so direct and, as it were, so familiar an approach? Great was the art of biography, but there were lives and lives, there were subjects and subjects. He confusedly recalled, so far as that went, old words dropped by Doyne over contemporary compilations, suggestions of how he himself discriminated as to other heroes and other panoramas. He even remembered how his friend would at moments have shown himself as holding that the "literary" career might—save in the case of a Johnson and a Scott, with a Boswell and a Lockhart to help—best content itself to be represented. The artist was what he *did*—he was nothing else. Yet how on the other hand wasn't *he*, George Withermore, poor devil, to have jumped at the chance of spending his winter in an intimacy so rich? It had been simply dazzling—that was the fact. It hadn't been the "terms," from the publishers—though these were, as they said at the office, all right; it had been Doyne himself, his company and contact and presence, it had been just what it was turning out, the possibility of an intercourse closer than that of life. Strange that death, of the two things, should have the fewer mysteries and secrets! The first night our young man was alone in the room it struck him his master and he were really for the first time together.

II

Mrs. Doyne had for the most part let him expressively alone, but she had on two or three occasions looked in to see if his needs had been met, and he had had the opportunity of thanking her on the spot for the judgement and zeal with which she had smoothed his way. She had to some extent herself been looking things over and had been able already to muster several groups of letters; all the keys of drawers and cabinets she had moreover from the first placed in his hands, with helpful information as to the apparent whereabouts of different matters. She had put him, to be brief, in the fullest possible possession, and whether or no her husband had trusted her she at least, it was clear, trusted her husband's friend. There grew upon Withermore nevertheless the impression that in spite of all these offices she wasn't yet at peace and that a certain unassuageable anxiety continued even to keep step with her confidence. Though so full of consideration she was at the same time perceptibly *there*: he felt her, through a supersubtle sixth sense that the whole connexion had already brought into play, hover, in the still hours, at the top of landings and on the other side of doors; he gathered from the soundless brush of her skirts the hint of her watchings and waitings. One evening when, at his friend's table, he had lost himself in the depths of correspondence, he was made to start and turn by the suggestion that some one was behind him. Mrs. Doyne had come in without his hearing the door, and she gave a strained smile, as he sprang to his feet. "I hope," she said, "I haven't frightened you."

"Just a little—I was so absorbed. It was as if, for the instant," the young man explained, "it had been himself."

The oddity of her face increased in her wonder. "Ashton?"

"He does seem so near," said Withermore.

"To you too?"

This naturally struck him. "He does then to you?"

She waited, not moving from the spot where she had first stood, but looking round the room as if to penetrate its duskier angles. She had a way of raising to the level of her nose the big black fan which she apparently never laid aside and with which she thus covered the lower half of her face, her rather hard eyes, above it, becoming the more ambiguous. "Sometimes."

"Here," Withermore went on, "it's as if he might at any moment come in. That's why I jumped just now. The time's so short since he really used to—it only *was* yesterday. I sit in his chair, I turn his books, I use his pens, I stir his fire—all exactly as if, learning he would presently be back from a walk, I had come up here contentedly to wait. It's delightful—but it's strange."

Mrs. Doyne, her fan still up, listened with interest. "Does it worry you?"

"No—I like it."

Again she faltered. "Do you ever feel as if he were—a—quite—a—personally in the room?"

"Well, as I said just now," her companion laughed, "on hearing you behind me I seemed to take it so. What do we want, after all," he asked, "but that he shall be with us?"

"Yes, as you said he'd be—that first time." She gazed in full assent. "He *is* with us."

She was rather portentous, but Withermore took it smiling. "Then we must keep him. We must do only what he'd like."

"Oh only that of course—only. But if he *is* here—?" And her sombre eyes seemed to throw it out in vague distress over her fan.

"It proves he's pleased and wants only to help? Yes, surely; it must prove that."

She gave a light gasp and looked again round the room. "Well," she said as she took leave of him, "remember that I too want only to help." On which, when she had gone, he felt sufficiently that she had come in simply to see he was all right.

He was all right more and more, it struck him after this, for as he began to get into his work he moved, as it appeared to him, but the closer to the idea of Doyne's personal presence. When once this fancy had begun to hang about him he welcomed it, persuaded it, encouraged it, quite cherished it, looking forward all day to feeling it renew itself in the evening, and waiting for the growth of dusk very much as one of a pair of lovers might wait for the hour of their appointment. The smallest accidents humoured and confirmed it, and by the end of three or four weeks he had come fully to regard it as the consecration of his enterprise. Didn't it just settle the question of what Doyne would have thought of what they were doing? What they were doing was what he wanted done, and they could go on from step to step without scruple or doubt. Withermore rejoiced indeed at moments to feel this certitude: there were times of dipping deep into some of Doyne's secrets when it was particularly pleasant to be able to hold that Doyne desired him, as it were, to know them. He was learning many things he hadn't suspected—drawing many curtains, forcing many doors, reading many riddles, going, in general, as they said, behind almost everything. It was at an occasional sharp turn of some of the duskier of these wanderings "behind" that he really, of a sudden, most felt himself, in the intimate sensible way, face to face with his friend; so that he could scarce have told, for the instant, if their meeting occurred in the narrow passage and tight squeeze of the past or at the hour and in the place that actually held him. Was it a matter of '67?—or but of the other side of the table?

Happily, at any rate, even in the vulgarest light publicity could ever shed, there would be the great fact of the way Doyne was "coming out." He was coming out too beautifully—better yet than such a partisan as Withermore could have supposed. All the while as well, nevertheless, how would this partisan have represented to any one else the special state of his own consciousness? It wasn't a thing to talk about—it was only a thing to feel. There were moments for instance when, while he bent over his papers, the light breath of his dead host was as distinctly in his hair as his own elbows were on the table before him. There were moments when, had he been able to look up, the other side of the table would have shown him this companion as vividly as the shaded lamp-light showed him his page. That he couldn't at such a juncture look up was his own affair, for the situation was ruled—that was but natural—by deep delicacies and fine timidities, the dread of too sudden or too rude an advance. What was intensely in the air was that if Doyne *was* there it wasn't nearly so much for himself as for the young priest of his altar. He hovered and lingered, he came and went, he might almost have been, among the books and the papers, a hushed discreet librarian, doing the particular things, rendering the quiet aid, liked by men of letters.

Withermore himself meanwhile came and went, changed his place, wandered on quests either definite or vague; and more than once when, taking a book down from a shelf and finding in it marks of Doyne's pencil, he got drawn on and lost he had heard documents on the table behind him gently shifted and stirred, had literally, on his return, found some letter mislaid pushed again into view, some thicket cleared by the opening of an old journal at the very date he wanted. How should he have gone so, on occasion, to the special box or drawer, out of fifty receptacles, that would help him, had not his mystic assistant happened, in fine prevision, to tilt its lid or pull it half-open, just in the way that would catch his eye?—in spite, after all, of the fact of lapses and intervals in which, *could* one have really looked, one would have seen somebody standing before the fire a trifle detached and over-erect—somebody fixing one the least bit harder than in life.

III

That this auspicious relation had in fact existed, had continued, for two or three weeks, was sufficiently shown by the dawn of the distress with which our young man found himself aware of having, for some reason, from the close of a certain day, begun to miss it. The sign of that was an abrupt surprised sense—on the occasion of his mislaying a marvellous unpublished page which, hunt where he would, remained stupidly irrecoverably lost—that his protected state was, with all said, exposed to some confusion and even to some depression. If, for the joy of the business, Doyne and he had, from the start, been together, the situation had within a few days of his first suspicion of it suffered the odd change of their ceasing to be so. That was what was the matter, he mused, from the moment an impression of mere mass and quantity struck him as taking, in his happy outlook at his material, the place of the pleasant assumption of a clear course and a quick pace. For five nights he struggled; then, never at his table, wandering about the room, taking up his references only to lay them down, looking out of the window, poking the fire, thinking strange thoughts and listening for signs and sounds not as he suspected or imagined, but as he vainly desired and invoked them, he yielded to the view that he was for the time at least forsaken.

The extraordinary thing thus became that it made him not only sad but in a high degree uneasy not to feel Doyne's presence. It was somehow stranger he shouldn't be there than it had ever been he *was*—so strange indeed at last that Withermore's nerves found themselves quite illogically touched. They had taken kindly enough to what was of an order impossible to explain, perversely reserving their sharpest state for the return to the normal, the supersession of the false. They were remarkably beyond control when finally, one night after his resisting them an hour or two, he simply edged out of the room. It had now but for the first time become impossible to him to stay. Without design, but panting a little and positively as a man scared, he passed along his usual corridor and reached the top of the staircase. From this point he saw Mrs. Doyne look up at him from the bottom quite as if she had known he would come; and the most singular thing of all was that, though he had been conscious of no motion to resort to her, had only been prompted to relieve himself by escape, the sight of her position made him recognise it as just, quickly feel it as a part of some monstrous oppression that was closing over them both. It was wonderful how, in the mere modern London hall, between the Tottenham Court Road rugs and the electric light, it came up to him from the tall black lady, and went again from him down to her, that he knew what she meant by looking as if he would know. He descended straight, she turned into her own little lower room, and there, the next thing, with the door shut, they were, still in silence and with queer faces, confronted over confessions that had taken sudden life from these two or three movements. Withermore gasped as it came to him why he had lost his friend. "He has been with *you?*"

With this it was all out—out so far that neither had to explain and that, when "What do you suppose is the matter?" quickly passed between them, one appeared to have said it as much as the other. Withermore looked about at the small bright room in which, night after night, she had been living her life as he had been living his own upstairs. It was pretty, cosy, rosy; but she had by turns felt in it what he had felt and heard in it what he had heard. Her effect there—fantastic black, plumed and extravagant, upon deep pink—was that of some "decadent" coloured print, some poster of the newest school. "You understood he had left me?" he asked.

She markedly wished to make it clear. "This evening—yes. I've made things out."

"You knew—before—that he was with me?"

She hesitated again. "I felt he wasn't with *me*. But on the stairs—"

"Yes?"

"Well—he passed; more than once. He was in the house. And at your door—"

"Well?" he went on as she once more faltered.

"If I stopped I could sometimes tell. And from your face," she added, "to-night, at any rate, I knew your state."

"And that was why you came out?"

"I thought you'd come to me."

He put out to her, on this, his hand, and they thus for a minute of silence held each other clasped. There was no peculiar presence for either now—nothing more peculiar than that of each for the other. But the place had suddenly become as if consecrated, and Withermore played over it again his anxiety. "What *is* then the matter?"

"I only want to do the real right thing," she returned after her pause.

"And aren't we doing it?"

"I wonder. Aren't *you*?"

He wondered too. "To the best of my belief. But we must think."

"We must think," she echoed. And they did think—thought with intensity the rest of that evening together, and thought independently (Withermore at least could answer for himself) during many days that followed. He intermitted a little his visits and his work, trying, all critically, to catch himself in the act of some mistake that might have accounted for their disturbance. Had he taken, on some important point— or looked as if he might take—some wrong line or wrong view? had he somewhere benightedly falsified or inadequately insisted? He went back at last with the idea of having guessed two or three questions he might have been on the way to muddle; after which he had abovestairs, another period of agitation, presently followed by another interview below with Mrs. Doyne, who was still troubled and flushed.

"He's there?"

"He's there."

"I knew it!" she returned in an odd gloom of triumph. Then as to make it clear: "He hasn't been again with *me*."

"Nor with me again to help," said Withermore.

She considered. "Not to help?"

"I can't make it out—I'm at sea. Do what I will I feel I'm wrong."

She covered him a moment with her pompous pain. "How do you feel it?"

"Why by things that happen. The strangest things. I can't describe them—and you wouldn't believe them."

"Oh yes I should!" Mrs. Doyne cried.

"Well, he intervenes." Withermore tried to explain. "However I turn I find him."

She earnestly followed. " 'Find' him?"

"I meet him. He seems to rise there before me."

Staring, she waited a little. "Do you mean you see him?"

"I feel as if at any moment I may. I'm baffled. I'm checked." Then he added: "I'm afraid."

"Of *him*?" asked Mrs. Doyne.

He thought. "Well—of what I'm doing."

"Then what, that's so awful, *are* you doing?"

"What you proposed to me. Going into his life."

She showed, in her present gravity, a new alarm. "And don't you *like* that?"

"Doesn't *he*? That's the question. We lay him bare. We serve him up. What is it called? We give him to the world."

Poor Mrs. Doyne, as if on a menace to her hard atonement, glared at this for an instant in deeper gloom. "And why shouldn't we?"

"Because we don't know. There are natures, there are lives, that shrink. He mayn't wish it," said Withermore. "We never asked him."

"How *could* we?"

He was silent a little. "Well, we ask him now. That's after all what our start has so far represented. We've put it to him."

"Then—if he has been with us—we've had his answer."

Withermore spoke now as if he knew what to believe. "He hasn't been 'with' us—he has been against us."

"Then why did you think—"

"What I *did* think at first—that what he wishes to make us feel is his sympathy? Because I was in my original simplicity mistaken. I was—I don't know what to call it—so excited and charmed that I didn't understand. But I understand at last. He only wanted to communicate. He strains forward out of his darkness, he reaches toward us out of his mystery, he makes us dim signs out of his horror."

" 'Horror'?" Mrs. Doyne gasped with her fan up to her mouth.

"At what we're doing." He could by this time piece it all together. "I see now that at first—"

"Well, what?"

"One had simply to feel he was there and therefore not indifferent. And the beauty of that misled me. But he's there as a protest."

"Against *my* Life?" Mrs. Doyne wailed.

"Against *any* Life. He's there to *save* his Life. He's there to be let alone."

"So you give up?" she almost shrieked.

He could only meet her. "He's there as a warning."

For a moment, on this, they looked at each other deep. "You *are* afraid!" she at last brought out.

It affected him, but he insisted. "He's there as a curse!"

With that they parted, but only for two or three days; her last word to him continuing to sound so in his ears that, between his need really to satisfy her and another need presently to be noted, he felt he mightn't yet take up his stake. He finally went back at his usual hour and found her in her usual place. "Yes, I *am* afraid," he announced as if he had turned that well over and knew now all it meant. "But I gather you're not."

She faltered, reserving her word. "What is it you fear?"

"Well, that if I go on I *shall* see him."

"And then—?"

"Oh then," said George Withermore, "I *should* give up!"

She weighed it with her proud but earnest air. "I think, you know, we must have a clear sign."

"You wish me to try again?"

She debated. "You see what it means—for me—to give up."

"Ah but *you* needn't," Withermore said.

She seemed to wonder, but in a moment went on. "It would mean that he won't take from me—" But she dropped for despair.

"Well, what?"

"Anything," said poor Mrs. Doyne.

He faced her a moment more. "I've thought myself of the clear sign. I'll try again."

As he was leaving her however she remembered. "I'm only afraid that to-night there's nothing ready—no lamp and no fire."

"Never mind," he said from the foot of the stairs; "I'll find things."

To which she answered that the door of the room would probably at any rate be open; and retired again as to wait for him. She hadn't long to wait; though, with her own door wide and her attention fixed, she may not have taken the time quite as it appeared to her visitor. She heard him, after an interval, on the stair, and he presently stood at her entrance, where, if he hadn't been precipitate, but rather, for step and sound, backward and vague, he showed at least as livid and blank.

"I give up."

"Then you've seen him?"

"On the threshold—guarding it."

"Guarding it?" She glowed over her fan. "Distinct?"

"Immense. But dim. Dark. Dreadful," said poor George Withermore.

She continued to wonder. "You didn't go in?"

The young man turned away. "He forbids!"

"You say I needn't," she went on after a moment. "Well then need I?"

"See him?" George Withermore asked.

She waited an instant. "Give up."

"You must decide." For himself he could at last but sink to the sofa with his bent face in his hands. He wasn't quite to know afterwards how long he had sat so; it was enough that what he did next know was that he was alone among her favourite objects. Just as he gained his feet however, with this sense and that of the door standing open to the hall, he found himself afresh confronted, in the light, the warmth, the rosy space, with her big black perfumed presence. He saw at a glance, as she offered him a huger bleaker stare over the mask of her fan, that she had been above; and so it was that they for the last time faced together their strange question. "You've seen him?" Withermore asked.

He was to infer later on from the extraordinary way she closed her eyes and, as if to steady herself, held them tight and long, in silence, that beside the unutterable vision of Ashton Doyne's wife his own might rank as an escape. He knew before she spoke that all was over. "I give up."

THE FURNISHED ROOM

BY O. HENRY

I F FICTION, as Henry James said, had a million windows—then, to O. Henry it seemed New York City had a million stories. It often appeared, as he wrote one weekly, that he had to tell each one himself.

O. Henry was born William Sydney Porter, in Greensboro, North Carolina, but by the time he arrived in Manhattan in 1902, he had had a varied career as a ranch hand, journalist, reporter, bankteller, and finally jailbird—having been convicted and jailed for embezzlement. New York, that thriving city of four million, allowed him to adopt a new name (which he adapted from an old cowboy song) and a new identity. He became the most popular chronicler of Bagdad-on-the-Subway, as he called it, the teeming city. One of his earliest biographers said, that from O. Henry's work, if all other records were lost, one could "rebuild a grotesque and alluring city that would somehow be the city of that decade from 1900 to 1910, echoing its voice, expressing the moods of its four million."

Despite his success, O. Henry was always penniless. He knew the poverty of living in furnished rooms, the anxiety of the anonymity of New York life. He loved that anonymity, but he knew it was tragic for those who did not; every room, yes, every room had a story, and some had a ghost as well. ɜଓ

Restless, shifting, fugacious as time itself is a certain vast bulk of the population of the red brick district of the lower West Side. Homeless, they have a hundred homes. They flit from furnished room to furnished room, transients forever—transients in abode, transients in heart and mind. They sing "Home, Sweet Home" in ragtime; they carry their *lares et penates* in a bandbox; their vine is entwined about a picture hat; a rubber plant is their fig tree.

Hence the houses of this district, having had a thousand dwellers, should have a thousand tales to tell, mostly dull ones, no doubt, but it would be strange if there could not be found a ghost or two in the wake of all these vagrant guests.

One evening after dark a young man prowled among these crumbling red mansions, ringing their bells. At the twelfth he rested his lean hand-luggage upon the step and wiped the dust from his hat-band and forehead. The bell sounded faint and far away in some remote, hollow depths.

To the door of this, the twelfth house whose bell he had rung, came a housekeeper who made him think of an unwholesome, surfeited worm that had eaten its nut to a hollow shell and now sought to fill the vacancy with edible lodgers.

He asked if there was a room to let.

"Come in," said the housekeeper. Her voice came from her throat; her throat seemed lined with fur. "I have the third floor back, vacant since a week back. Should you wish to look at it?"

The young man followed her up the stairs. A faint light from no particular source mitigated the shadows of the halls. They trod noiselessly upon a stair carpet that its own loom would have forsworn. It seemed to have become vegetable; to have degenerated in that rank, sunless air to lush lichen or spreading moss that grew in patches to the staircase and was viscid under the foot like organic matter. At each turn of the stairs were vacant niches in the wall. Perhaps plants had once been set within them. If so they had died in that foul and tainted air. It may be that statues of the saints had stood there, but it was not difficult to conceive that imps and devils had dragged them forth in the darkness and down to the unholy depths of some furnished pit below.

"This is the room," said the housekeeper, from her furry throat. "It's a nice room. It ain't often vacant. I had some most elegant people in it last summer—no trouble at all, and paid in advance to the minute. The water's at the end of the hall. Sprowls and Mooney kept it three months. They done a vaudeville sketch. Miss B'retta Sprowls—you may have heard of her—Oh, that was just the stage names—right there over the dresser is where the marriage certificate hung, framed. The gas is here, and you see there is plenty of closet room. It's a room everybody likes. It never stays idle long."

"Do you have many theatrical people rooming here?" asked the young man.

"They comes and goes. A good proportion of my lodgers is connected with theatres. Yes, sir, this is the theatrical district. Actor people never stays long anywhere. I get my share. Yes, they comes and they goes."

He engaged the room, paying for a week in advance. He was tired, he said, and would take possession at once. He counted out the money. The room had been made ready, she said, even to towels and water. As the housekeeper moved away he put, for the thousandth time, the question that he carried at the end of his tongue.

"A young girl—Miss Vashner—Miss Eloise Vashner—do you remember such a one among your lodgers? She would be singing on the stage, most likely. A fair girl, of medium height, and slender, with reddish, gold hair and a dark mole near her left eyebrow."

"No, I don't remember the name. Them stage people has names they change as often as their rooms. They comes and they goes. No, I don't call that one to mind."

No. Always no. Five months of ceaseless interrogation and the inevitable negative. So much time spent by day in questioning managers, agents, schools and choruses; by night among the audiences of theatres from all-star casts down to music halls so low that he dreaded to find what he most hoped for. He who had loved her best had tried to find her. He was sure that since her disappearance from home this great, water-girt city held her somewhere, but it was like a monstrous quicksand, shifting its particles constantly, with no foundation, its upper granules of today buried tomorrow in ooze and slime.

The furnished room received its latest guest with a first glow of pseudo-hospitality, a hectic, haggard, perfunctory welcome like the specious smile of a demirep. The sophistical comfort came in reflected gleams from the decayed furniture, the ragged brocade upholstery of a couch and two chairs, a foot-wide cheap pier glass between the two windows, from one or two gilt picture frames and a brass bedstead in a corner.

The guest reclined, inert, upon a chair, while the room, confused in speech as though it were an apartment in Babel, tried to discourse to him of its divers tenantry.

A polychromatic rug like some brilliant-flowered rectangular, tropical islet lay surrounded by a billowy sea of soiled matting. Upon the gay-papered wall were those pictures that pursue the homeless one from house to house—The Huguenot Lovers, The First Quarrel, The Wedding Breakfast, Psyche at the Fountain. The mantel's chastely severe outline was ingloriously veiled behind some pert drapery drawn rakishly askew like the sashes of the Amazonian ballet. Upon it was some desolate flotsam cast aside by the room's marooned when a lucky sail had borne them to a fresh port—a trifling vase or two, pictures of actresses, a medicine bottle, some stray cards out of a deck.

One by one, as the characters of a cryptograph become explicit, the little signs left by the furnished room's procession of guests developed a significance. The threadbare space in the rug in front of the dresser told that lovely women had marched in the throng. Tiny fingerprints on the wall spoke of little prisoners trying to feel their way to sun and air. A splattered stain, raying like a shadow of a bursting bomb, witnessed where a hurled glass or bottle had splintered with its contents against the wall. Across the pier glass had been scrawled with a diamond in staggering letters the name "Marie." It seemed that the succession of dwellers in the furnished room had turned in fury—perhaps tempted beyond forbearance by its garish coldness—and wreaked upon it their passions. The furniture was chipped and bruised, the couch, distorted by bursting springs, seemed a horrible monster that had been slain during the stress of some grotesque convulsion. Some more potent upheaval had cloven a great slice from the marble mantel. Each plank in the floor owned its particular cant and shriek as from a separate and individual agony. It seemed incredible that all this malice and injury had been wrought upon the room by those who had called it for a time their home; and yet it may have been the cheated home instinct surviving blindly, the resentful rage at false household gods that had kindled their wrath. A hut that is our own we can sweep and adorn and cherish.

The young tenant in the chair allowed these thoughts to file, soft-shod, through his mind, while there drifted into the room furnished sounds and furnished scents. He heard in one room a tittering and incontinent, slack laughter; in others the monologue of a scold, the rattling of dice, a lullaby, and one crying dully; above him a banjo tinkled with spirit. Doors banged somewhere, the elevated trains roared intermittently; a cat yowled miserably upon a back fence. And he breathed the breath of the house—a dank savour rather than a smell—a cold, musty effluvium as from underground vaults mingled with the reeking exhalations of linoleum and mildewed and rotten woodwork.

Then, suddenly, as he rested there, the room was filled with the strong, sweet odour of mignonette. It came as upon a single buffet of wind with such sureness and fragrance and emphasis that it almost seemed a living visitant. And the man cried aloud: "What, dear?" as if he had been called, and sprang up and faced about. The rich odour clung to him and wrapped him around. He reached out his arms for it, all his senses for the time confused and commingled. How could one be peremptorily called by an odour? Surely it must have been a sound. But, was it not the sound that had touched, that had caressed him?

"She has been in this room," he cried, and he sprang to wrest from it a token, for he knew he would recognise the smallest thing that had belonged to her or that she had touched. This enveloping scent of mignonette, the odour that she had loved and made her own—whence came it?

The room had been but carelessly set in order. Scattered upon the flimsy dresser scarf were half a dozen hairpins—those discreet, indistinguishable friends of womankind, feminine of gender, infinite of mood and uncommunicative of tense. These he ignored, conscious of their triumphant lack of identity. Ransacking the drawers of the dresser he came upon a discarded, tiny, ragged handkerchief. He pressed it to his face. It was racy and insolent with heliotrope; he hurled it to the floor. In another drawer he found odd buttons, a theatre programme, a pawnbroker's card, two lost marshmallows, a book on the divination of dreams. In the last was a woman's black satin hair-bow, which halted him, poised between ice and fire. But the black satin hairbow also is femininity's demure, impersonal, common ornament, and tells no tales.

And then he traversed the room like a hound on the scent, skimming the walls, considering the corners of the bulging matting on his hands and knees, rummaging mantel and tables, the curtains and hangings, the drunken cabinet in the corner, for a visible sign, unable to perceive that she was there beside, around, against, within, above him, clinging to him, wooing him, calling him so poignantly through the finer senses that even his grosser ones became cognisant of the call. Once again he answered loudly: "Yes, dear!" and turned wild-eyed, to gaze on vacancy, for he could not yet discern form and colour and love and outstretched arms in the odour of mignonette. Oh, God! whence that odour, and since when have odours had a voice to call? Thus he groped.

He burrowed in crevices and corners, and found corks and cigarettes. These he passed in passive contempt. But once he found in a fold of the matting a half-smoked cigar, and this he ground beneath his heel with a green and trenchant oath. He sifted the room from end to end. He found dreary and ignoble small records of many a peripatetic tenant; but of her whom he sought, and who may have lodged there, and whose spirit seemed to hover there, he found no trace.

And then he thought of the housekeeper.

He ran from the haunted room downstairs and to a door that showed a crack of light. She came out to his knock. He smothered his excitement as best he could.

"Will you tell me, madam," he besought her, "who occupied the room I have before I came?"

"Yes, sir. I can tell you again. 'Twas Sprowls and Mooney, as I said. Miss B'retta Sprowls it was in the theatres, but Missis Mooney she was. My house is well known for respectability. The marriage certificate hung, framed, on a nail over——"

"What kind of a lady was Miss Sprowls—in looks, I mean?"

"Why, black-haired, sir, short, and stout, with a comical face. They left a week ago Tuesday."

"And before they occupied it?"

"Why, there was a single gentleman connected with the draying business. He left owing me a week. Before him was Missis Crowder and her two children, they stayed four months; and back of them was old Mr. Doyle, whose sons paid for him. He kept the room six months. That goes back a year, sir, and further I do not remember."

He thanked her and crept back to his room. The room was dead. The essence that had vivified it was gone. The perfume of mignonette had departed. In its place was the old, stale odour of mouldy house furniture, of atmosphere in storage.

The ebbing of his hope drained his faith. He sat staring at the yellow, singing gaslight. Soon he walked to the bed and began to tear the sheets into strips. With the blade of his knife he drove them tightly into every crevice around windows and door. When all was snug and taut he turned out the light, turned the gas full on again and laid himself gratefully upon the bed.

It was Mrs. McCool's night to go with the can for beer. So she fetched it and sat with Mrs. Purdy in one of those subterranean retreats where house-keepers forgather and the worm dieth seldom.

"I rented out my third floor, back, this evening," said Mrs. Purdy, across a fine circle of foam. "A young man took it. He went up to bed two hours ago."

"Now, did ye, Missis Purdy, ma'am?" said Mrs. McCool, with intense admiration. "You do be a wonder for rentin' rooms of that kind. And did ye tell him, then?" she concluded in a husky whisper, laden with misery.

"Rooms," said Mrs. Purdy, in her furriest tones, "are furnished for to rent. I did not tell him, Mrs. McCool."

"'Tis right ye are, ma'am, 'tis by renting rooms we kape alive. Ye have the rale sense for business, ma'am. There be many people will rayjict the rentin' of a room if they be tould a suicide has been after dyin' in the bed of it."

"As you say, we has our living to be making," remarked Mrs. Purdy.

"Yis, ma'am, 'tis true. 'Tis just one wake ago this day I helped ye lay out the third floor, back. A pretty slip of a colleen she was to be killin' herself wid the gas—a swate little face she had, Mrs. Purdy, ma'am."

"She'd a-been called handsome, as you say," said Mrs. Purdy, assenting but critical, "but for that mole she had a-growin' by her left eyebrow. Do fill up your glass again, Missis McCool."

THE GHOSTS

BY LORD DUNSANY

I NEVER write of the things I have seen—which hundreds of others can do as well," said Lord Dunsany, "but only of the things I have imagined." His imagination and his literary output were prodigious; he once declared he could write a story about anything, the mud of the Thames River, for example, and promptly did so.

Edward John Moreton Drax Plunkett, eighteenth Baron Dunsany, held one of the oldest titles in the British peerage. Castle Dunsany, not far from Dublin in Ireland, had been in the family for generations. By the time Lord Dunsany was born, the world of the robber barons, in which the Dunsany family had once participated, had long disappeared into fantasy. Dunsany created his own world, a world of great primal gods and forces of nature.

He also created a handful of great ghost stories. "Read him—read him," H. P. Lovecraft said, "he is the preeminent fanta-siste." ह

THE ARGUMENT that I had with my brother in his great lonely house will scarcely interest my readers. Not those, at least, whom I hope may be attracted by the experiment that I undertook, and by the strange things that befell me in that hazardous region into which so lightly and so ignorantly I allowed my fancy to enter. It was at Oneleigh that I had visited him.

Now Oneleigh stands in a wide isolation, in the midst of a dark gathering of old whispering cedars. They nod their heads together when the North Wind comes, and nod again and agree, and furtively grow still again, and say no more awhile. The North Wind is to them like a nice problem among wise old men; they nod their heads over it, and mutter it all together. They know much, those cedars, they have been there so long. Their grandsires knew Lebanon, and the grandsires of these were the servants of the King of Tyre and came to Solomon's court. And amidst these black-haired children of grey-headed Time stood the old house of Oneleigh. I know not how many centuries had lashed against it their evanescent foam of years; but it was still unshattered, and all about it were the things of long ago, as cling strange growths to some sea-defying rock. Here, like the shells of long-dead limpets, was armour that men encased themselves in long ago; here, too, were tapestries of many colours, beautiful as seaweed; no modern flotsam ever drifted hither, no early Victorian furniture, no electric light. The great trade routes that littered the years with empty meat tins and cheap novels were far from here. Well, well, the centuries will shatter it and drive its fragments on to distant shores. Meanwhile, while it yet stood, I went on a visit there to my brother, and we argued about ghosts. My brother's intelligence on this subject seemed to me to be in need of correction. He mistook things imagined for things having an actual existence; he argued that second-hand evidence of persons having seen ghosts proved ghosts to exist. I said that even if they had seen ghosts, this was no proof at all; nobody believes that there are red rats, though there is plenty of first-hand evidence of men having seen them in delirium. Finally, I said I would see ghosts myself, and continue to argue against their actual existence. So I collected a handful of cigars and drank several cups of very strong tea, and went without my dinner, and retired into a room where there was dark oak and all the chairs were covered with tapestry, and my brother went to bed bored with our argument and trying hard to dissuade me from making myself uncomfortable. All the way up the old stairs as I stood at the bottom of them, and as his candle went winding up and up, I heard him still trying to persuade me to have supper and go to bed.

It was a windy winter, and outside the cedars were muttering I know not what about; but I think they were Tories of a school long dead, and were troubled about something new. Within, a great damp log upon the fireplace began to squeak and sing, and struck up a whining tune, and a tall flame stood up over it and beat time, and all the shadows crowded round and began to dance. In distant corners old masses of darkness sat still like chaperones and never moved. Over there, in the darkest part of the room, stood a door that was always locked. It led into the hall, but no one ever used it; near that door something had happened once of which the family are not proud. We do not speak of it. There in the firelight stood the venerable forms of the old chairs; the hands that had made their tapestries lay far beneath the soil, the needles with which they wrought were many separate flakes of rust. No one wove now in that old room—no one but the assiduous ancient spiders who, watching by the deathbed of the things of yore, worked shrouds to hold their dust. In shrouds about the cornices already lay the heart of the oak wainscot that the worm had eaten out.

Surely at such an hour, in such a room, a fancy already excited by hunger and strong tea might see the ghosts of former occupants. I expected nothing less. The fire flickered and the shadows danced, memories of strange historic things rose vividly in my mind; but midnight chimed solemnly from a seven-foot clock, and nothing happened. My imagination would not be hurried, and the chill that is with the small hours had come upon me, and I had nearly abandoned myself to sleep, when in the hall adjoining there arose the rustling of silk dresses that I had waited for and expected. Then there entered two by two the high-born ladies and their gallants of Jacobean times. They were little more than shadows—very dignified shadows, and almost indistinct; but you have all read ghost stories before, you have all seen in museums the dresses of those times—there is little need to describe them; they entered, several of them, and sat down on the old chairs, perhaps a little carelessly considering the value of the tapestries. Then the rustling of their dresses ceased.

Well—I had seen ghosts, and was neither frightened nor convinced that ghosts existed. I was about to get up out of my chair and go to bed, when there came a sound of pattering in the hall, a sound of bare feet coming over the polished floor, and every now and then a foot would slip and I heard claws scratching along the wood as some four-footed thing lost and regained its balance. I was not frightened, but uneasy. The pattering came straight towards the room that I was in, then I heard the sniffing of expectant nostrils; perhaps "uneasy" was not the most suitable word to describe my feelings then. Suddenly a herd of

black creatures larger than bloodhounds came galloping in; they had
large pendulous ears, their noses were to the ground sniffing, they went
up to the lords and ladies of long ago and fawned about them disgust-
ingly. Their eyes were horribly bright, and ran down to great depths.
When I looked into them I knew suddenly what these creatures were,
and I was afraid. They were the sins, the filthy, immortal sins of those
courtly men and women.

How demure she was, the lady that sat near me on an old-world chair
—how demure she was, and how fair, to have beside her with its jowl
upon her lap a sin with such cavernous red eyes, a clear case of murder.
And you, yonder lady with the golden hair, surely not you—and yet that
fearful beast with the yellow eyes slinks from you to yonder courtier
there, and whenever one drives it away it slinks back to the other. Over
there a lady tries to smile as she strokes the loathsome furry head of another's sin, but one of her own is jealous and intrudes itself under her
hand. Here sits an old nobleman with his grandson on his knee, and one
of the great black sins of the grandfather is licking the child's face and
has made the child its own. Sometimes a ghost would move and seek another chair, but always his pack of sins would move behind him. Poor
ghosts, poor ghosts! how many flights they must have attempted for two
hundred years from their hated sins, how many excuses they must have
given for their presence, and the sins were with them still—and still
unexplained. Suddenly one of them seemed to scent my living blood,
and bayed horribly, and all the others left their ghosts at once and
dashed up to the sin that had given tongue. The brute had picked up
my scent near the door by which I had entered, and they moved slowly
nearer to me sniffing along the floor, and uttering every now and then
their fearful cry. I saw that the whole thing had gone too far. But now
they had seen me, now they were all about me, they sprang up trying to
reach my throat; and whenever their claws touched me, horrible
thoughts came into my mind and unutterable desires dominated my
heart. I planned bestial things as these creatures leaped around me, and
planned them with a masterly cunning. A great red-eyed murder was
among the foremost of those furry things from whom I feebly strove to
defend my throat. Suddenly it seemed to me good that I should kill my
brother. It seemed important to me that I should not risk being
punished. I knew where a revolver was kept; after I shot him, I would
dress the body up and put flour on the face like a man that had been

acting as a ghost. It would be very simple. I would say that he had frightened me—and the servants had heard us talking about ghosts. There were one or two trivialities that would have to be arranged, but nothing escaped my mind. Yes, it seemed to me very good that I should kill my brother as I looked into the red depths of this creature's eyes. But one last effort as they dragged me down—"If two straight lines cut one another," I said, "the opposite angles are equal. Let AB, CD, cut one another at E, then the angles CEA, CEB equal two right angles (prop. xiii). Also CEA, AED equal two right angles."

I moved toward the door to get the revolver; a hideous exultation arose among the beasts. "But the angle CEA is common, therefore AED equals CEB. In the same way CEA equals DEB. Q.E.D." It was proved. Logic and reason re-established themselves in my mind, there were no dark hounds of sin, the tapestried chairs were empty. It seemed to me an inconceivable thought that a man should murder his brother.

RATS

BY M. R. JAMES

THE CONNOISSEUR of the ghost story turns to M. R. James as a master practitioner. Many writers have dashed off a ghost story, so compelling that they had to relate it, but they were never to write another; others have written many tales, but only a few might be truly successful. Only each James story is perfect.

Montague Rhodes James had a precocious childhood; before he was ten he had written the lives of nineteen saints. He followed this flurry of scholarship by an astounding career as a scholar at Eton, a consistent prizewinner at Cambridge. His interests in archeology took him to excavations in Cyprus. He catalogued medieval manuscripts and was a director of the Fitzwilliam Museum. A famous educator, he served as Provost at Cambridge and at Eton. It was there, in that famous boys' school, that he enthralled the students with his stories of the unknown, the unseen, the dank, and the dark.

M. R. James discoursed, too, on the writing of the ghost story: "As a rule, the setting should be fairly familiar and the majority of the characters and their talk such as you may meet or hear any day." The impression any such story should have was simple.

"If I'm not very careful, something of this kind may happen to me!" ॐ

"And if you was to walk through the bedrooms now, you'd see the ragged, mouldy bedclothes a-heaving and a-heaving like seas." "And a-heaving and a-heaving with what?" he says. "Why, with the rats under 'em."

B UT W AS it with the rats? I ask because in another case it was not. I cannot put a date to the story, but I was young when I heard it, and the teller was old. It is an ill-proportioned tale, but that is my fault, not his.

It happened in Suffolk, near the coast. In a place where the road makes a sudden dip and then a sudden rise, as you go northward, at the top of that rise, stands a house on the left of the road. It is a tall red-brick house, narrow for its height; perhaps it was built about 1770. The top of the front is a low triangular pediment with a round window in the centre. Behind it are stables and offices, and such garden as it has is behind them. Scraggy Scotch firs are near it: an expanse of gorse-covered land stretches away from it. It commands a view of the distant sea from the upper windows of the front. A sign on a post stands before the door, or did so stand, for though it was an inn of repute once, I believe it is so no longer.

To this inn came my acquaintance, Mr. Thomson, when he was a young man, on a fine spring day, coming from the University of Cambridge, and desirous of solitude in tolerable quarters, and time for reading. These he found, for the landlord and his wife had been in service and could make a visitor comfortable, and there was no one else staying in the inn. He had a large room on the first floor commanding the road and the view, and if it faced east, why, that could not be helped; the house was well built and warm.

He spent very tranquil and uneventful days: work all the morning, an afternoon perambulation of the country round, a little conversation with country company or the people of the inn in the evening over the then fashionable drink of brandy-and-water, a little more reading and writing, and bed; and he would have been content that this should continue for the full month he had at disposal, so well was his work progressing, and so fine was the April of that year—which I have reason to believe was that which Orlando Whistlecraft chronicles in his weather record as the "charming year."

One of his walks took him along the northern road, which stands high and traverses a wide common, called a heath. On the bright afternoon when he first chose this direction his eye caught a white object some hundreds of yards to the left of the road, and he felt it necessary to make sure what this might be. It was not long before he was standing by it, and found himself looking at a square block of white stone fashioned somewhat like the base of a pillar, with a square hole in the upper surface. Just such another you may see at this day on Thetford Heath. After taking stock of it, he contemplated for a few minutes the view, which offered a church tower or two, some red roofs of cottages, and windows winking in the sun, and the expanse of sea—also with an occasional wink and gleam upon it—and so pursued his way.

In the desultory evening talk in the bar, he asked why the white stone was there on the common.

"A' old-fashioned thing, that is," said the landlord (Mr. Betts); "we was none of us alive when that was put there." "That's right," said another. "It stands pretty high," said Mr. Thomson, "I dare say a sea-mark was on it some time back." "Ah, yes," Mr. Betts agreed, "I 'ave 'eard they could see it from the boats; but whatever there was, it's fell to bits this long time." "Good job, too," said a third; "'twarn't a lucky mark, by what the old men used to say; not lucky for the fishin', I mean to say." "Why ever not?" said Thomson. "Well, I never see it myself," was the answer, "but they 'ad some funny ideas, what I mean, peculiar, them old chaps, and I shouldn't wonder but what they made away with it theirselves."

It was impossible to get anything clearer than this: the company, never very voluble, fell silent, and when next someone spoke it was of village affairs and crops. Mr. Betts was the speaker.

Not every day did Thomson consult his health by taking a country walk. One very fine afternoon found him busily writing at three o'clock. Then he stretched himself and rose, and walked out of his room into the passage. Facing him was another room, then the stair-head, then two more rooms, one looking out to the back, the other to the south. At the south end of the passage was a window, to which he went, considering with himself that it was rather a shame to waste such a fine afternoon. However, work was paramount just at the moment; he thought he would just take five minutes off and go back to it, and those five minutes he would employ—the Bettses could not possibly object—to looking at the other rooms in the passage, which he had never seen. Nobody at all, it seemed, was indoors; probably, as it was market day, they were all gone to the town, except perhaps a maid in the bar. Very still the house was, and the sun shone really hot; early flies buzzed in the window-panes. So he explored.

The room facing his own was undistinguished except for an old print of Bury St. Edmunds; the two next him on his side of the passage were gay and clean, with one window apiece, whereas his had two. Remained the south-west room, opposite to the last which he had entered. This was locked; but Thomson was in a mood of quite indefensible curiosity, and, feeling confident that there could be no damaging secrets in a place so easily got at, he proceeded to fetch the key of his own room, and, when that did not answer, to collect the keys of the other three. One of them fitted, and he opened the door. The room had two windows looking south and west, so it was as bright and the sun as hot upon it as could be. Here there was no carpet, but bare boards; no pictures, no washing-stand, only a bed in the farther corner: an iron bed, with mattress and bolster, covered with a bluish check counterpane.

As featureless a room as you can well imagine, and yet there was something that made Thomson close the door very quickly and quietly behind him and lean against the windowsill in the passage, actually quivering all over. It was this: that under the counterpane someone lay, and not only lay, but stirred. That it was some*one* and not some*thing* was certain, because the shape of a head was unmistakable on the bolster; and yet it was all covered, and no one lies with covered head but a dead person; and this was not dead, not truly dead, for it heaved and shivered. If he had seen these things in dusk or by the light of a flickering candle, Thomson could have comforted himself and talked of fancy. On this bright day that was impossible.

What was to be done? First, lock the door at all costs. Very gingerly he approached it and, bending down, listened, holding his breath; perhaps there might be a sound of heavy breathing and a prosaic explanation. There was absolute silence. But as, with a rather tremulous hand, he put the key into its hole and turned it, it rattled, and on the instant a stumbling padding tread was heard coming towards the door. Thomson fled like a rabbit to his room and locked himself in: futile enough, he knew it was; would doors and locks be any obstacle to what he suspected? But it was all he could think of at the moment, and in fact nothing happened; only there was a time of acute suspense—followed by a misery of doubt as to what to do. The impulse, of course, was to slip away as soon as possible from a house which contained such an inmate.

But only the day before he had said he should be staying for at least a week more, and how, if he changed plans, could he avoid the suspicion of having pried into places where he certainly had no business? Moreover, either the Bettses knew all about the inmate, and yet did not leave the house; or knew nothing, which equally meant that there was nothing to be afraid of; or knew just enough to make them shut up the room, but not enough to weigh on their spirits: in any of these cases it seemed that not much was to be feared, and certainly so far he had had no sort of ugly experience. On the whole, the line of least resistance was to stay.

Well, he stayed out his week. Nothing took him past that door, and, often as he would pause in a quiet hour of day or night in the passage, and listen and listen, no sound whatever issued from that direction. You might have thought that he would have made some attempt at ferreting out stories connected with the inn—hardly perhaps from Betts, but from the parson of the parish, or old people in the village; but no, the reticence which commonly falls on people who have had strange experiences, and believe in them, was upon him. Nevertheless, as the end of his stay drew near, his yearning after some kind of explanation grew more and more acute. On his solitary walks he persisted in planning out some way, the least obtrusive, of getting another daylight glimpse into that room, and eventually arrived at this scheme. He would leave by an afternoon train—about four o'clock. When his fly was waiting, and his luggage on it, he would make one last expedition upstairs to look round his own room and see if anything was left unpacked, and then, with that key, which he had contrived to oil (as if that made any difference!) the door should once more be opened for a moment, and shut.

So it worked out. The bill was paid, the consequent small talk gone through while the fly was loaded: "Pleasant part of the country—been very comfortable, thanks to you and Mrs. Betts—hope to come back some time," on one side; on the other: "Very glad you've found satisfaction, sir, done our best—always glad to 'ave your good word—very much favoured we've been with the weather, to be sure." Then, "I'll just take a look upstairs in case I've left a book or something out—no, don't trouble, I'll be back in a minute." And as noiselessly as possible he stole to the door and opened it. The shattering of the illusion! He almost laughed aloud. Propped, or you might say sitting, on the edge of the bed was—nothing in the round world but a scarecrow! A scarecrow out of the garden, of course, dumped into the deserted room. . . . Yes; but here amusement ceased. Have scarecrows bare, bony feet? Do their heads loll on to their shoulders? Have they iron collars and links of chain about their necks? Can they get up and move, if ever so stiffly, across a floor, with wagging head and arms close at their sides? And shiver?

The slam of the door, the dash to the stair-head, the leap downstairs were followed by a faint. Awaking, Thomson saw Betts standing over him with the brandy-bottle and a very reproachful face. "You shouldn't 'a' done so, sir, really you shouldn't. It ain't a kind way to act by persons as done the best they could for you." Thomson heard words of this kind, but what he said in reply he did not know. Mr. Betts, and perhaps even more Mrs. Betts, found it hard to accept his apologies and his assurances that he would say no word that could damage the good name of the house. However, they *were* accepted. Since the train could not now be caught, it was arranged that Thomson should be driven to the town to sleep there.

Before he went the Bettses told him what little they knew. "They says he was landlord 'ere a long time back, and was in with the 'ighwaymen that 'ad their beat about the 'eath. That's how he come by his end: 'ung in chains, they say, up where you see that stone what the gallus stood in. Yes, the fishermen made away with that, I believe, because they see it out at sea and it kep' the fish off, according to their idea. Yes, we 'ad the account from the people that 'ad the 'ouse before we come. 'You keep that room shut up,' they says, 'but don't move the bed out, and you'll find there won't be no trouble.' And no more there 'as been; not once he haven't come out into the 'ouse, though what he may do now there ain't no sayin'. Anyway, you're the first I know on that's seen him since we've been 'ere; I never set eyes on him myself, nor don't want. And ever since we've made the servants' rooms in the stablin', we ain't 'ad no difficulty that way. Only I do 'ope, sir, as you'll keep a close tongue, considerin' 'ow an 'ouse do get talked about"; with more to this effect.

The promise of silence was kept for many years. The occasion of my hearing the story at last was this: that when Mr. Thomson came to stay with my father it fell to me to show him to his room, and instead of letting me open the door for him, he stepped forward and threw it open himself, and then for some moments stood in the doorway holding up his candle and looking narrowly into the interior. Then he seemed to recollect himself and said: "I beg your pardon. Very absurd, but I can't help doing that, for a particular reason." What that reason was I heard some few days afterwards and you have heard now.

Twentieth-Century Touch of Terror
(THE CONTEMPORARY APPARITION)

THE THING IN THE MOONLIGHT

BY H. P. LOVECRAFT

OWARD PHILLIPS LOVECRAFT, one of the great twentieth-century masters of the world of shades and shadows, began to publish regularly in the 1920s. He chose to write at night, or at least in a darkened room, appropriate settings for a man whose stories were peopled by creatures of darkness.

Lovecraft published in such collector's magazines as *Astounding Stories, Amazing Stories, Tales of Magic and Mystery*, and the extraordinary *Weird Tales*. In order to supplement his meager earnings, he was also a "ghost writer" in another sense, rewriting material for others, among whom was The Great Houdini, whose magic hardly extended to words.

The impression of a childhood steeped in Gothic horrors, real and imagined, were never to desert H. P. Lovecraft. Guilt-haunted, witch-haunted, horror-haunted, he easily identified with the perils of living in old New England. He insisted he felt more "at home" then. Contemporary persons were nothing but ironic shadows or phantoms; his writing (even though it often discouraged and depressed him) was a reality stronger than any stranger jostling him on the streets of twentieth-century America.

Lovecraft was a great nocturnal walker; he roamed the once Colonial streets of his native Providence, preferring to see it in moonlight. It was not surprising that he should see . . . "The Thing."

MORGAN IS not a literary man; in fact he cannot speak English with any degree of coherency. That is what makes me wonder about the words he wrote, though others have laughed.

He was alone the evening it happened. Suddenly an unconquerable urge to write came over him, and taking pen in hand he wrote the following:

My name is Howard Phillips. I live at 66 College Street, in Providence, Rhode Island. On November 24, 1927—for I know not even what the year may be now—, I fell asleep and dreamed, since when I have been unable to awaken.

My dream began in a dank, reed-choked marsh that lay under a gray autumn sky, with a rugged cliff of lichen-crusted stone rising to the north. Impelled by some obscure quest, I ascended a rift or cleft in this beetling precipice, noting as I did so the black mouths of many fearsome burrows extending from both walls into the depths of the stony plateau.

At several points the passage was roofed over by the choking of the upper parts of the narrow fissure; these places being exceeding dark, and forbidding the perception of such burrows as may have existed there. In one such dark space I felt conscious of a singular accession of fright, as if some subtle and bodiless emanation from the abyss were engulfing my spirit; but the blackness was too great for me to perceive the source of my alarm.

At length I emerged upon a tableland of moss-grown rock and scanty soil, lit by a faint moonlight which had replaced the expiring orb of day. Casting my eyes about, I beheld no living object; but was sensible of a very peculiar stirring far below me, amongst the whispering rushes of the pestilential swamp I had lately quitted.

After walking for some distance, I encountered the rusty tracks of a street railway, and the worm-eaten poles which still held the limp and sagging trolley wire. Following this line, I soon came upon a yellow, vestibuled car numbered 1852—of a plain, double-trucked type common from 1900 to 1910. It was untenanted, but evidently ready to start; the trolley being on the wire and the air-brake now and then throbbing beneath the floor. I boarded it and looked vainly about for the light switch —noting as I did so the absence of the controller handle, which thus implied the brief absence of the motorman. Then I sat down in one of the cross seats of the vehicle. Presently I heard a swishing in the sparse grass toward the left, and saw the dark forms of two men looming up in the moonlight. They had the regulation caps of a railway company, and I could not doubt but that they were conductor and motorman. Then one of them *sniffed* with singular sharpness, and raised his face to howl to the moon. The other dropped on all fours to run toward the car.

I leaped up at once and raced madly out of that car and across endless leagues of plateau till exhaustion forced me to stop—doing this not because the conductor had dropped on all fours, but because the face of the motorman was a mere white cone tapering to one blood-red-tentacle. . . .

I was aware that I only dreamed, but the very awareness was not pleasant.

Since that fearful night, I have prayed only for awakening—it has not come!

Instead I have found myself an *inhabitant* of this terrible dreamworld! That first night gave way to dawn, and I wandered aimlessly over the lonely swamp-lands. When night came, I still wandered, hoping for awakening. But suddenly I parted the weeds and saw before me the ancient railway car—and to one side a cone-faced thing lifted its head and in the streaming moonlight howled strangely!

It has been the same each day. Night takes me always to that place of horror. I have tried not moving, with the coming of nightfall, but I must walk in my slumber, for always I awaken with the thing of dread howling before me in the pale moonlight, and I turn and flee madly.

God! when will I awaken?

That is what Morgan wrote. I would go to 66 College Street in Providence, but I fear for what I might find there.

ESCORT

BY DAPHNE DU MAURIER

D APHNE DU MAURIER, winner of the National Book
Award for her novel *Rebecca*, and narrator of that unforget-
table story "The Birds," started early in her long and productive
literary career. She was influenced, she said, in particular by Kath-
erine Mansfield and Guy de Maupassant, but her father Gerald du
Maurier, the actor and novelist, certainly contributed to her sure
sense of drama.

Miss du Maurier has also been gifted with an almost uncanny
sense of place, a prerequisite for any writer in the supernatural field.
One of the places that has haunted her over the years is her beloved
Cornwall in the west of Great Britain, a coastal area permeated with
legends of sunken cities, mermaids, haunted ships and haunted sea-
men.

The twentieth-century ghost story has changed in the telling, but
not always in its subject matter. Some themes are almost traditional,
and cry out to be repeated in every generation. Probably the most
fascinating sea phantom is *The Flying Dutchman*, the ship that sails
forever without being able to return to its home port. Miss de Maurier escorts a twentieth-century tramp steamer into another
world. ੬ॐ

THERE IS nothing remarkable about the *Ravenswing*, I can promise
you that. She is between six and seven thousand tons, was built in 1926,
and belongs to the Condor Line, Port of Register, Hull. You can look

her up in Lloyd's, if you have a mind. There is little to distinguish her from hundreds of other tramp steamers of her particular tonnage. She had sailed that same route and travelled those same waters for the three years I had served in her, and she was on the job some time before that. No doubt she will continue to do so for many years more and will eventually end her days peacefully on the mud like her predecessor, the old *Gullswing*, did before her; unless the U-boats get her first.

She has escaped them once, but next time we may not have our escort. Perhaps I had better make it clear, too, that I myself am not a fanciful man. My name is William Blunt, and I have the reputation of living up to it. I never have stood for nonsense of any sort, and have no time for superstition. My father was a Nonconformist minister, and maybe that had something to do with it. I tell you this to prove my reliability, but, for that matter, you can ask anyone in Hull. And now, having introduced myself and the ship, I can get on with my story.

We were homeward bound from a Scandinavian port in the early part of the autumn. I won't give you the name of the port—the censor might stop me—but we had already made the trip there and back three times since the outbreak of war. The convoy system had not started in those first days, and the strain on the captain and myself was severe. I don't want you to infer that we were windy, or the crew either, but the North Sea in wartime is not a bed of roses, and I'll leave it at that.

When we left port that October afternoon, I could not help thinking it seemed a hell of a long way home, and it did not put me in what you would call a rollicking humour when our little Scandinavian pilot told us with a grin that a Grimsby ship, six hours ahead of us, had been sunk without warning. The Nazi government had been giving out on the wireless, he said, that the North Sea could be called the German Ocean, and the British Fleet could not do anything about it. It was all right for the pilot: he was not coming with us. He waved a cheerful farewell as he climbed over the side, and soon his boat was a black speck bobbing astern of us at the harbour entrance, and we were heading for the open sea, our course laid for home.

It was about three o'clock in the afternoon, the sea was very still and grey, and I remember thinking to myself that a periscope would not be easy to miss; at least we would have fair warning, unless the glass fell and it began to blow. However, it did the nerves no good to envisage something that was not going to happen, and I was pretty short with the first engineer when he started talking about the submarine danger, and why the hell did not the Admiralty do something about it?

"Your job is to keep the old *Ravenswing* full steam ahead for home and beauty, isn't it?" I said. "If Winston Churchill wants your advice, no doubt he'll send for you." He had no answer to that, and I lit my pipe and went on to the bridge to take over from the captain.

I suppose I'm not out-of-the-way observant about my fellow men, and I certainly did not notice then that there was anything wrong with the captain. He was never much of a talker at any time. The fact that he went to his cabin at once meant little or nothing. I knew he was close at hand if anything unusual should happen.

It turned very cold, after nightfall, and later a thin rain began to fall. The ship rolled slightly as she met the longer seas. The sky was overcast with the rain, and there were no stars. The autumn nights are always black, of course, in northern waters, but this night the darkness seemed intensified. There would be small chance of sighting a periscope, I thought, under these conditions, and it might well be that we should receive no other intimation than the shock of the explosion. Someone said the other day that the U-boats carried a new type of torpedo, supercharged, and that explained why the ships attacked sank so swiftly.

The *Ravenswing* would founder in three or four minutes if she was hit right amidships and it might be that we should never even sight the craft that sank us. The submarine would vanish in the darkness; they would not bother to pick up survivors. They could not see them if they wanted to, not in this darkness. I glanced at the chap at the wheel, he was a little Welshman from Cardiff, and he had a trick of sucking his false teeth and clicking them back again every few minutes. We stood a pretty equal chance, he and I, standing side by side together on the bridge. It was then I turned suddenly and saw the captain standing in the entrance to his cabin. He was holding on for support, his face was very flushed, and he was breathing heavily.

"Is anything wrong, sir?" I said.

"This damn pain in my side," he gasped; "started it yesterday, and thought I'd strained myself. Now I'm doubled up with the bloody thing. Got any aspirin?"

Aspirin my foot, I thought. If he has not got acute appendicitis, I'll eat my hat. I'd seen a man attacked like that before; he'd been rushed to a hospital and operated on in less than two hours. They'd taken an appendix out of him swollen as big as a fist.

"Have you a thermometer there?" I asked the captain.

"Yes," he said. "What the hell's the use of that? I haven't got a temperature. I've strained myself, I tell you. I want some aspirin."

I took his temperature. It was a hundred and four. The sweat was pouring down his forehead. I put my hand on his stomach, and it was rigid, like a brick wall. I helped him to his berth and covered him up with blankets. Then I made him drink half a glass of brandy neat. It may be the worst thing you can do for appendicitis, but when you are hundreds of miles from a surgeon and in the middle of the North Sea in wartime you are apt to take chances.

The brandy helped to dull the pain a little, and that was the only thing that mattered. Whatever the result to the captain, it had but one result for me. I was in command of the *Ravenswing* from now on, and mine was the responsibility of bringing her home through those submarine-infested waters. I, William Blunt, had got to see this through.

It was bitter cold. All feeling had long since left my hands and feet. I was conscious of a dull pain in those parts of my body where my hands and feet should have been. But the effect was curiously impersonal. The pain might have belonged to someone else, the sick captain himself even, back there in his cabin, lying moaning and helpless as I had left him last, some forty-eight hours before. He was not my charge; I could do nothing for him. The steward nursed him with brandy and aspirin, and I remember feeling surprised, in a detached sort of way, that he did not die.

"You ought to get some sleep. You can't carry on like this. Why don't you get some sleep?"

Sleep. That was the trouble. What was I doing at that moment but rocking on my two feet on the borderline of oblivion, with the ship in my charge, and this voice in my left ear the sound that brought me to my senses. It was Carter, the second mate. His face looked pinched and anxious.

"Supposing you get knocked up?" he was saying. "What am I going to do? Why don't you think of me?"

I told him to go to hell, and stamped down the bridge to bring the life back to my numbed feet, and to disguise the fact from Carter that sleep had nearly been victorious.

"What else do you think has kept me on the bridge for forty-eight hours but the thought of you," I said, "and the neat way you let the stern hawser drop adrift, with the second tug alongside, last time we were in Hull? Get me a cup of tea and a sandwich and shut your bloody mouth," I said.

My words must have relieved him, for he grinned back at me and shot down the ladder like a Jack-in-the-box. I held on to the bridge and stared ahead, sweeping the horizon for what seemed like the hundred thousandth time, and seeing always the same blank face of the sea, slate grey and still. There were low-banked clouds to the westward, whether mist or rain I could not tell, but they gathered slowly without wind and the glass held steady, while there was a certain smell about the air, warning of fog. I swallowed my cup of tea and made short work of a sandwich, and I was feeling in my pocket for my pipe and a box of matches when the thing happened for which, I suppose, I had consciously been training myself since the captain went sick some forty-eight hours before.

"Object to port. Three-quarters of a mile distant. Looks like a periscope."

The words came from the lookout on the fo'c'sle head, and so flashed back to the watch on deck. As I snatched my glasses I caught a glimpse of the faces of the men lining the ship's side, curiously uniform they were, half eager, half defiant.

Yes. There she was. No doubt now. A thin grey line, like a needle away there on our port bow, leaving a narrow wake behind her like a jagged ripple. Once again I was aware of Carter beside me, tense, expectant, and I noticed that his hands trembled slightly as he lifted the glasses in his turn. I gave the necessary alteration of our course, and telegraphed the corresponding change of speed down to the first engineer, and then took up my glasses once more. The change of course had brought the periscope right ahead, and for a few minutes or so the thin line continued on its way as though indifferent to our manœuvre, and then, as I had feared and foreseen, the submarine altered course, even as we had done, and the periscope bore down upon us, this time to starboard.

"She's seen us," said Carter.

"Yes," I said. He looked up at me, his brown eyes troubled like a spaniel puppy's. We altered course again and increased our speed, this time bringing our stern to the thin grey needle, so that for a moment it seemed as though the gap between us would be widened and she would pass away behind us, but, swift and relentless, she bore up again on our quarter, and little Carter began to swear, fluently and passionately, the futility of words a sop to his own fear. I sympathised, seeing in a flash, as the proverbial drowning man is said to do, an episode in my own childhood when my father lectured me for lying, and even as I remembered this picture of a long-forgotten past I spoke down the mouth tube to the engine-room once more and ordered yet another alteration in our speed.

The watch below had now all hurriedly joined the watch on deck. They lined the side of the ship, as though hypnotised by the unwavering grey line that crept closer, ever closer.

"She's breaking surface," said Carter. "Watch that line of foam."

The periscope had come abeam of us and had drawn ahead. It was now a little over a mile distant, on our port bow. Carter was right. She was breaking surface, even as he said. We could see the still water become troubled and disturbed and then slowly, inevitably, the squat conning tower appeared and the long, lean form rose from the depths like a black slug, the water streaming from its decks.

"The bastards," whispered Carter to himself: "the filthy, stinking bastards."

The men clustered together below me on the deck watched the submarine with a strange indifference, like spectators at some show with which they had no concern. I saw one fellow point out some technical detail of the submarine to the man by his side; and then light a cigarette. His companion laughed, and spat over the side of the ship into the water. I wondered how many of them could swim.

I gave the final order through to the engine-room, and then ordered all hands on deck, to boat stations. My next order would depend on the commander of the submarine.

"They'll shell the boats," said Carter, "they won't let us get away, they'll shell the boats."

"Oh, for God's sake," I began, the pallor of his face begetting in me a furious senseless anger, when suddenly I caught sight of the wall of fog that was rolling down upon us from astern. I swung Carter round by the shoulders to meet it. "Look there," I said, "look there," and his jaw dropped, and he grinned stupidly. Already the visibility around us was

no more than a cable's length on either side, and the first drifting
vapour stung us with its cold, sour smell. Above us the air was thick and
clammy. In a moment our after shrouds were lost to sight. I heard one
fellow strike up the opening chorus of a comic song in a high falsetto
voice, and he was immediately cursed to silence by his companions.
Ahead of us lay the submarine, dark and immobile, the water still running from its sides, the decks as yet unmanned, and her long snout
caught unexpectedly in a sudden shaft of light. Then the white fog that
enveloped us crept forward and beyond, the sky descended, and our
world was blotted out.

It wanted two minutes to midnight, I crouched low under cover of
the bridge and flashed a torch on to my watch. No bell had been
sounded since the submarine had first been sighted, some eight hours
earlier. We waited. Darkness had travelled with the fog, and night fell
early. There was silence everywhere, but for the creaking of the ship as
she rolled in the swell and the thud of water slapping her sides as she lay
over, first on one side, then on the other. Still we waited. The cold was
no longer so intense as it had been. There was a moist, clammy feeling
in the air. The men talked in hushed whispers beneath the bridge. We
went on waiting. Once I entered the cabin where the captain lay sick,
and flashed my torch on to him. His face was flushed and puffy. His
breathing was heavy and slow. He was sleeping fitfully, moaning now
and again, and once he opened his eyes, but he did not recognise me. I
went back to the bridge. The fog had lifted slightly, and I could see our
forward shrouds and the fo'c'sle head. I went down on to the deck and
leant over the ship's side. The tide was running strongly to the south. It
had turned three hours before, and for the fourth time that evening I
began to calculate our drift. I was turning to the ladder to climb to the
bridge once more, when I heard footsteps running along the deck, and a
man cannonaded into me.

"Fog's lifting astern," he said breathlessly, "and there's something
coming up on our starboard quarter."

I ran back along the deck with him. A group of men were clustered at
the ship's side, talking eagerly. "It's a ship all right, sir," said one.
"Looks like a Finnish barque. I can see her canvas."

I peered into the darkness with them. Yes, there she was, about a
hundred yards distant, and bearing down upon us. A great three-masted
vessel, with a cloud of canvas aloft. It was too late in the year for the

grain ships. What the hell was she doing in these waters in wartime? Unless she was carrying timber. Had she seen us, though? That was the point. Here we were, without lights, skulking in the trough of the sea because of that damned submarine, and now risking almost certain collision with some old timber ship.

If only I could be certain that the tide and the fog had put up a number of miles between us and the enemy. She was coming up fast, the old-timer, God knows where she found her wind—there was none on my left cheek that would blow out a candle. If she passed us at this rate there would be fifty yards to spare, no more, and with that hell ship waiting yonder in the darkness somewhere, the Finn would go straight to kingdom come.

"All right," I said, "she's seen us; she's bearing away." I could only make out her outline in the darkness as she travelled past abeam. A great, high-sided vessel she was, in ballast probably, or there would never have been so much of her out of the water. I'd forgotten they had such bulky afterdecks. Her spars were not the clean things I remembered either; these were a mass of rigging, and the yards an extraordinary length, necessary, no doubt, for all that bunch of canvas.

"She's not going to pass us," said somebody, and I heard the blocks rattle and jump, and the rigging slat, as the great yards swung over. And was that faint high note, curious and immeasurably distant, the pipe of a boatswain's whistle? But the fog vapour was drifting down on us again, and the ship was hidden. We strained our eyes in the darkness, seeing nothing, and I was about to turn back to the bridge again when a thin call came to us across the water.

"Are you in distress?" came the hail. Whether her nationality was Finnish or not, at least her officer spoke good English, even if his phrasing was a little unusual. I was wary though, and I did not answer. There was a pause and then the voice travelled across to us once more. "What ship are you, and where are you bound?"

And then, before I could stop him, one of our fellows bellowed out: "There's an enemy submarine come to the surface about half a mile ahead of us." Someone smothered the idiot half a minute too late and, for better or worse, our flag had been admitted.

We waited. None of us moved a finger. All was silent. Presently we heard the splash of oars and the low murmur of voices. They were sending a boat across to us from the barque. There was something furtive and strange about the whole business. I was suspicious. I did not like it. I felt for the hard butt of my revolver, and was reassured. The sound of oars drew nearer. A long, low boat like a West Country gig drew out of the shadows, manned by half a dozen men. There was a fellow with a lantern in the bows. Someone, an officer I presumed, stood up in the stern. It was too dark for me to see his face. The boat pulled up beneath us, and the men rested on their oars.

"Captain's compliments, gentlemen, and do you desire an escort?" inquired the officer.

"What the hell!" began one of our men, but I cursed him to quiet. I leaned over the side, shading my eyes from the light of the boat's lantern.

"Who are you?" I said.

"Lieutenant Arthur Mildmay, at your service, sir," replied the voice.

There was nothing foreign in his intonation. I could swear to that, but again I was struck by his phraseology. No snottie in the Navy ever talked like this. The Admiralty might have bought up a Finnish barque, of course, and armed her, like Von Luckner did in the last week, but the idea seemed unlikely.

"Are you camouflaged?" I asked.

"I beg your pardon?" he replied in some surprise. Then his English was not so fluent as I thought. Once again I felt for my revolver. "You're not trying to make a fool of me by any chance, are you?" I said sarcastically.

"Not in the least," replied the voice. "I repeat the captain sends his compliments, and as you gave him to understand we are in the immediate vicinity of the enemy, he desires me to offer you his protection. Our orders are to escort any merchant ships we find to a port of safety."

"And who issued those orders?" I said.

"His Majesty King George, of course," replied the voice.

It was then, I think, that I felt for the first time a curious chill of fear. I remember swallowing hard. My throat felt dry, and I could not answer at once. I looked at the men around me, and they wore, one and all, a silly, dumb, unbelieving expression on their faces.

"He says the King sent him," said the fellow beside me, and then his voice trailed away uncertainly, and he fell silent.

I heard Carter tap me on the shoulder, "Send them away," he whispered. "There's something wrong; it's a trap."

The man kneeling in the bow of the gig flashed his lantern in my face, blinding me. The young lieutenant stepped across the thwarts and took the lantern from him. "Why not come aboard and speak to the captain yourself, if you are in doubt?" he said.

Still I could not see his face, but he wore some sort of cloak round his shoulders, and the hand that held the lantern was long and slim. The lantern that dazzled me brought a pain across my eyes so severe that for a few moments I could neither speak nor think, and then, to my own surprise, I heard myself answer: "Very well, make room for me, then, in your boat."

Carter laid his hand on my arm.

"You're crazy," he said. "You can't leave the ship."

I shook him off, obstinate for no reason, determined on my venture. "You're in charge, Carter," I said. "I shan't be long away. Let me go, you damn' fool."

I ordered the ladder over the side, and wondered, with a certain irritation, why the stupid fellows gaped at me as they obeyed. I had that funny reckless feeling that comes upon you when you're half drunk, and I wondered if the reason for it was my own lack of sleep for over forty-eight hours.

I landed with a thud in the gig, and stumbled to the stern beside the officer. The men bent on their oars, and the boat began to creep across the water to the barque. It was bitter cold. The clammy mugginess was gone. I turned up the collar of my coat and tried to catch a closer glimpse of my companion, but it was black as pitch in the boat and his features were completely hidden from me.

I felt the seat under me, with my hand. It was like ice, freezing to the touch and I plunged my hands deep in my pockets. The cold seemed to penetrate my greatcoat, and find my flesh. My teeth chattered, and I could not stop them. The chap in front of me, bending to his oar, was a great burly brute, with shoulders like an ox. His sleeves were rolled up above his elbows, his arms were bare. He was whistling softly between his teeth.

"You don't feel the cold, then?" I asked.

He did not answer, and I leant forward and looked into his face. He stared at me, as though I did not exist, and went on whistling between his teeth. His eyes were deep set, sunken in his head. His cheekbones were very prominent and high. He wore a queer, stovepipe of a hat, shiny and black.

"Look here," I said, tapping him on his knee, "I'm not here to be fooled, I can tell you that."

And then the lieutenant, as he styled himself, stood up beside me in the stern. "Ship ahoy," he called, his two hands to his mouth, and looking up, I saw we were already beneath the barque, her great sides towering above us. A lantern appeared on the bulwark by the ladder, and again my eyes were dazzled by the sickly yellow light.

The lieutenant swung on to the ladder, and I followed him, hand over fist, breathing hard, for the bitter cold caught at me and seemed to strike right down into my throat. I paused when I reached the deck, with a stitch in my side like a kicking horse, and in that queer half-light that came from the flickering lanterns I saw that this was no Finnish barque with a load of timber, no grain ship in ballast, but a raider bristling with guns. Her decks were cleared for action, and the men were there ready at their stations. There was much activity and shouting, and a voice from for'ard calling out orders in a thin high voice.

There seemed to be a haze of smoke thick in the air, and a heavy sour stench, and with it all the cold dank chill I could not explain.

"What is it?" I called. "What's the game?" No one answered. Figures passed me and brushed me, shouting and laughing at one another. A lad of about thirteen ran by me, with a short blue jacket and long white trousers, while close beside me, crouching by his gun, was a great bearded fellow like my oarsman of the gig, with a striped stocking cap upon his head. Once again, above the hum and confusion, I heard the thin, shrill piping of the boatswain's whistle and, turning, I saw a crowd of jostling men running barefooted to the afterdeck, and I caught the gleam of steel in their hands.

"The captain will see you, if you come aft," said the lieutenant.

I followed him, angry and bewildered. Carter was right, I had been fooled; and yet as I stumbled in the wake of the lieutenant I heard English voices shouting on the deck, and funny unfamiliar English oaths.

We pushed through the door of the afterdeck, and the musty rank smell became more sour and more intense. It was darker still. Blinking, I found myself at the entrance of a large cabin, lit only by flickering lantern light, and in the centre of the cabin was a long table, and a man was sitting there in a funny high-backed chair. Three or four other men stood behind him, but the lantern light shone on his face alone. He was very thin, very pale, and his hair was ashen grey. I saw by the patch he wore that he had lost the sight of one eye, but the other eye looked through me in the cold abstracted way of someone who would get his business done, and has little time to spare.

"Your name, my man?" he said, tapping with his hand upon the table before him.

"William Blunt, sir," I said, and I found myself standing to attention, with my cap in my hands, my throat as dry as a bone, and that same funny chill of fear in my heart.

"You report there is an enemy vessel close at hand, I understand?"

"Yes, sir," I said. "A submarine came to the surface about a mile distant from us, some hours ago. She had been following us for half an hour before she broke surface. Luckily the fog came down and hid us. That was at about half-past four in the afternoon. Since then we have not attempted to steam, but have drifted without lights."

He listened to me in silence. The figures behind him did not move. There was something sinister in their immobility and his, as though my words meant nothing to them, as though they did not believe me or did not understand.

"I shall be glad to offer you my assistance, Mr. Blunt," he said at last. I stood awkwardly, still turning my cap in my hands. He did not mean to make game of me, I realised that, but what use was his ship to me?

"I don't quite see," I began, but he held up his hand. "The enemy will not attack you while you are under my protection," he said; "if you care to accept my escort, I shall be very pleased to give you safe-conduct to England. The fog has lifted, and luckily the wind is with us."

I swallowed hard. I did not know what to say.

"We steam at eleven knots," I said awkwardly, and when he did not reply I stepped forward to his table, thinking he had not heard.

"Supposing the blighter is still there?" I said. "He'll get the pair of us. She'll blow up like matchwood, this ship of yours. You stand even less chance than us."

The man seated by the table leant back in his chair. I saw him smile. "I've never run from a Frenchman yet," he said.

Once again I heard the boatswain's whistle, and the patter of bare feet overhead upon the deck. The lanterns swayed, in a current of air from the swinging door. The cabin seemed very musty, very dark. I felt faint and queer, and something like a sob rose in my throat which I could not control.

"I'd like your escort," I stammered, and even as I spoke he rose in his chair and leant towards me. I saw the faded blue of his coat, and the ribbon across it. I saw his pale face very close, and the one blue eye. I saw him smile, and I felt the strength of the hand that held mine and saved me from falling.

They must have carried me to the boat and down the ladder, for when I opened my eyes again, with a queer dull ache at the back of my head, I was at the foot of my own gangway, and my own chaps were hauling me aboard. I could just hear the splash of oars as the gig pulled away back to the barque.

"Thank God you're back!" said Carter. "What the devil did they do to you. You're as white as chalk. Were they Finns or Boche?"

"Neither," I said curtly; "they're English, like ourselves. I saw the captain. I've accepted his escort home."

"Have you gone raving mad?" said Carter.

I did not answer, I went up to the bridge and gave orders for steaming. Yes, the fog was lifting, and above my head I could see the first pale glimmer of a star. I listened, well content, to the familiar noises of the ship as we got under way again. The throb of the screw, the thrash of the propeller. The relief was tremendous. No more silence, no more inactivity. The strain was broken, and the men were themselves again, cheerful, cracking jokes at one another. The cold had vanished, and the curious dead fatigue that had been part of my mind and body for so long. The warmth was coming back to my hands and my feet.

Slowly we began to draw ahead once more, ploughing our way in the swell, while to starboard of us, some hundred yards distant, came our escort, the white foam hissing from her bows, her cloud of canvas billowing to a wind that none of us could feel. I saw the helmsman beside me glance at her out of the tail of his eye, and when he thought I was not looking he wet his finger and held it in the air. Then his eye met mine, and fell again, and he whistled a song to show he did not care. I wondered if he thought me as mad as Carter did. Once I went in to see the captain. The steward was with him, and when I entered he switched on the lamp above the captain's berth.

"His fever's down," he said. "He's sleeping naturally at last. I don't think we're going to lose him, after all."

"No, I guess he'll be all right," I said.

I went back to the bridge, whistling the song I had heard from the sailor in the gig. It was a jaunty, lilting tune, familiar in a rum sort of way, but I could not put a name to it. The fog had cleared entirely, and the sky was ablaze with stars. We were steaming now at our full rate of knots, but still our escort kept abeam, and sometimes, if anything, she drew just a fraction ahead.

Whether the submarine was on the surface still, or whether she had dived, I neither knew nor cared, for I was full of that confidence that I had lacked before and which, after a while, seemed to possess the helmsman in his turn, so that he grinned at me, jerking his head at our escort, and said, "There don't seem to be no flies on Nancy, do there?" and fell, as I did, to whistling that nameless jaunty tune. Only Carter remained sullen and aloof. His fear had given way to sulky silence, and at last, sick of the sight of his moody face staring through the chartroom window, I ordered him below, and was aware of a new sense of freedom and relief when he had gone.

So the night wore on, and we, plunging and rolling in the wake of our escort, saw never a sight of periscope or lean grey hull again. At last the sky lightened to the eastward, and low down on the horizon appeared the streaky pallid dawn. Five bells struck, and away ahead of us, faint as a whisper, came the answering pipe of a boatswain's whistle. I think I was the one that heard it. Then I heard the weak, tired voice of the captain calling me from his cabin. I went to him at once. He was propped up against his pillows, and I could tell from his face he was as weak as a rat, but his temperature was normal, even as the steward had said.

"Where are we, Blunt?" he said. "What's happened?"

"We'll be safely berthed before the people ashore have rung for breakfast," I said. "The coast's ahead of us now."

"What's the date, man?" he asked. I told him.

"We've made good time," he said. I agreed.

"I shan't forget what you've done, Blunt," he said. "I'll speak to the owners about you. You'll be getting promotion for this."

"Promotion my backside," I said. "It's not me that needs thanking, but our escort away on the starboard bow."

"Escort?" he said, staring at me. "What escort? Are we travelling with a bloody convoy?"

Then I told him the story, starting with the submarine, and the fog, and so on to the coming of the barque herself, and my own visit aboard her, and not missing out an account of my own nerves and jumpiness, either. He listened to me, dazed and bewildered on his pillow.

"What's the name of your barque?" he said slowly, when I had finished.

I smote my hand on my knee. "It may be Old Harry for all I know; I never asked them," I said, and I began whistling the tune that the fellow had sung as he bent to his oars in the gig.

"I can't make it out," said the captain; "you know as well as I do there aren't any sailing ships left on the British register."

I shrugged my shoulders. Why the hell couldn't he accept the escort as naturally as I and the men had done?

"Get me a drink, and stop whistling that confounded jig," said the captain. I laughed, and gave him his glass.

"What's wrong with it?" I said.

"It's 'Lilliburlero,' centuries old. What makes you whistle that?" he said. I stared back at him, and I was not laughing any longer.

"I don't know," I said, "I don't know."

He drank thirstily, watching me over the rim of his glass. "Where's your precious escort now?" he said.

"On the starboard bow," I repeated, and I went forward to the bridge again and gazed seaward, where I knew her to be.

The sun, like a great red globe, was topping the horizon, and the night clouds were scudding to the west. Far ahead lay the coast of England. But our escort had gone.

I turned to the fellow steering. "When did she go?" I asked.

"Beg pardon, sir?" he said.

"The sailing ship. What's happened to her?" I repeated.

The man looked puzzled, and cocked his eye at me curiously.

"I've seen no sailing ship," he said. "There's a destroyer been abeam of us some time. She must have come up with us under cover of darkness. I've only noticed her since the sun rose."

I snatched up my glasses and looked to the west. The fellow was not dreaming. There was a destroyer with us, as he said. She plunged into the long seas, churning up the water and chucking it from her like a great white wall of foam. I watched her for a few minutes in silence, and then I lowered my glasses. The fellow steering gazed straight in front of him. Now daylight had come he seemed changed in a queer, indefinable way. He no longer whistled jauntily. He was his usual stolid seaman self.

"We shall be docked by nine-thirty. We've made good time," I said.

"Yes, sir," he said.

Already I could see a black dot far ahead, and a wisp of smoke. The tugs were lying off for us. Carter was in my old place on the fo'c'sle head. The men were at their stations. I, on the captain's bridge, would bring his ship to port. He called me to him, five minutes before the tugs took us in tow, when the first gulls were wheeling overhead.

"Blunt," he said, "I've been thinking. That captain fellow you spoke to in the night, on board that sailing craft. You say he wore a black patch over one eye. Did he by any chance have an empty sleeve pinned to his breast as well?"

I did not answer. We looked at one another in silence. Then a shrill whistle warned me that the pilot's boat was alongside. Somewhere, faint and far, the echo sounded like a boatswain's pipe.

THE LAKE

BY RAY BRADBURY

R AY BRADBURY, whose imagination visited the space world
of the moon and planets long before the astronauts and contemporary scientific equipment, was, he said, once greeted by laughter. "Now nobody laughs." Nobody laughs at his supernatural stories
either. Shiver certainly, but no one laughs.

The particular terror and immediacy that Ray Bradbury has
brought to the contemporary supernatural story can be explained by
his own comments on his writing process. He writes every day and
lets the character that emerges on his pages take the lead: "The author uses the character as his Ouija board, I'd guess you'd say, trust-
ing in him to write the story. There is no paradox here. One simply
trusts one's secret self, subconscious, whatever you want to call it.
The character is always the medium in a séance held between
author and secret self."

Winner of innumerable awards, one of the best-selling authors of
our time, Ray Bradbury has gone a long way since he founded and
mimeographed a science fiction quarterly in high school.

Attuned to outer space and the supernatural world, he finds some
contemporary adjustments difficult; he dislikes flying and has never
driven a car. 🦢

THEY CUT the sky down to my size and threw it over the Michigan
Lake, put some kids yelling on yellow sand with bouncing balls, a gull
or two, a criticizing parent, and me breaking out of a wet wave and
finding this world bleary and moist.

I ran up on the beach.

Mama swabbed me with a furry towel. "Stand there and dry," she said.

I stood there and watched the sun take away the water beads on my arms. I replaced them with goose-pimples.

"My, there's a wind," said Mama. "Put on your sweater."

"Wait'll I watch my goose-bumps," I said.

"Harold," said Mama.

I inserted me into my sweater and watched the waves come up and fall down on the beach. But not clumsily. On purpose, with a green sort of elegance. Even a drunken man could not collapse with such elegance as those waves.

It was September. In the last days when things are getting sad for no reason. The beach was so long and lonely with only about six people on it. The kids quit bouncing the ball because somehow the wind made them sad, too, whistling the way it did, and they sat down and felt autumn come along the long beach.

All the hot dog places were boarded up with strips of golden planking, sealing in all the mustard, onion, meat odors of the long, joyful summer. It was like nailing summer into a series of coffins. One by one the places slammed their covers down, padlocked their doors, and the wind came and touched the sand, blowing away all of the million footprints of July and August. It got so that now, in September, there was nothing but the mark of my rubber tennis shoes and Donald and Delaus Schabold's feet, and their father down by the water curve.

Sand blew up in curtains on the sidewalks, and the merry-go-round was hidden with canvas, all the horses frozen in mid-air on their brass poles, showing teeth, galloping on. With only the wind for music, slipping through canvas.

I stood there. Everyone else was in school. I was not. Tomorrow I would be on my way westward across the United States on a train. Mom and I had come to the beach for one last brief moment.

There was something about the loneliness that made me want to get away by myself. "Mama, I want to run up the beach aways," I said.

"All right, but hurry back, and don't go near the water."

I ran. Sand spun under me and the wind lifted me. You know how it is, running, arms out so you feel veils from your fingers, caused by wind. Like wings.

Mama withdrew into the distance, sitting. Soon she was only a brown speck and I was all alone. Being alone is a newness to a twelve-year-old child. He is so used to people around. The only way he can be alone is in his mind. That's why children imagine such fantastic things. There are so many real people around, telling children what and how to do, that a boy has to run off down a beach, even if it's only in his mind, to get by himself in his own world with his own miniature values.

So now I was really alone.

I went down to the water and let it cool up to my stomach. Always before, with the crowd, I hadn't dared to look. But now— Sawing a man in half. A magician. Water is like that. It feels as if you were sawed in half and part of you, sugar, is dissolving away. Cool water, and once in a while a very elegantly stumbling wave that fell with a flourish of lace.

I called her name. A dozen times I called it.

"Tally! Tally! Oh, Tally!"

Funny, but you really expect answers to your calling when you are young. You feel that whatever you may think can be real. And sometimes maybe that is not so wrong.

I thought of Tally, swimming out into the water last May, with her pigtails trailing, blonde. She went laughing, and the sun was on her small twelve-year-old shoulders. I thought of the water settling quiet, of the life-guard leaping into it, of Tally's mother screaming, and how Tally never came out. . . .

The life-guard tried to persuade her to come out, but she did not. He came back with only bits of water weed in his big knuckled fingers, and Tally was gone. She would not sit across from me at school any longer, or chase indoor balls on the brick street on summer nights. She had gone too far out, and the lake would not let her come back in.

And now in the lonely autumn when the sky was huge and the water was huge and the beach was so very long, I had come down for the last time, alone.

I called her name over and over. Tally, oh, Tally!

The wind blew so very softly, over my ears, the way wind blows over the mouth of seashells and sets them whispering. The water rose and embraced my chest and then to my knees, and up and down, one way and another, sucking under my heels.

"Tally! Come back, oh, Tally!"

I was only twelve. But I know how much I loved her. It was that love that comes before all significance of body and morals. It was that love that is no more bad than wind and sea and sand lying side by side forever. It was made of all the warm long days together at the beach, and the humming quiet days of droning education at the school. All the long autumn days of the years passed when I had carried her books home from school.

Tally!

I called her name for the last time. I shivered. I felt water on my face and did not know how it got there. The waves had splashed me there. My own tide was coming in and I downed in it.

Turning, I retreated to the sand and stood there for half an hour, hoping for one glimpse, one side, one little bit of Tally to remember. Then, in a sort of symbol, I knelt and built a castle of sand, shaping it fine and building it up as Tally and I had often built them, so many of them. But this time I only built half of it. Then I got up.

"Tally, if you hear me, come in and build the rest."

I began to walk off toward that faraway speck that was Mama. The water came in and blended the sea castle circle by circle, mashing it down little by little, into the original smoothness.

I could not help but think that there are no castles in life that one builds that some wave does not spread down into the old, old formlessness.

Silently, I walked up the beach.

Far away, a merry-go-round jangled faintly, but it was only the wind.

I went away on the train the next day.

Across the cornlands of Illinois. A train has a poor memory. It soon puts all behind it. It forgets the rivers of childhood, the bridges, the lakes, the valleys, the cottages, the pains and joys. It spreads them out behind and they drop back of a horizon.

I lengthened my bones, put flesh on them, changed my young mind for an older one, threw away clothes as they no longer fitted, shifted from grammar to high-school, to college books, to law-books. And then there was a young woman in Sacramento, there was a preacher, and there were words and kisses.

I continued with my law study. By the time I was twenty-two, I had almost forgotten what the East was like.

Margaret suggested that our delayed honeymoon trip be taken back in that direction.

A train works both ways, like a memory. It brings rushing back all those things you left behind so many years before.

Lake Bluff, population 10,000, came up over the sky. Margaret looked so handsome in her fine new clothes. She kept watching me as I watched my old world gather me back into its living. Her strong white hands held onto mine as the train slid into Bluff station and our baggage was escorted out.

So many years, and the things they do to people's faces and bodies. When we walked through the town, arm in arm, I saw no one I recognized. There were faces with echoes in them. Echoes of hikes on ravine trails. Faces with small laughter in them from closed grammar schools and swinging on metal-linked swings and going up and down on teeter-totters. But I didn't speak. I just walked and looked and filled up inside with all those memories, like leaves stacked for burning in autumn.

Our days were happy there. Two weeks in all, revisiting all the places together. I thought I loved Margaret very well. At least I thought I did.

It was on one of the last days that we walked down by the shore. It was not quite as late in the year as that day so many years before, but the first evidences of desertion were coming upon the beach. The people were thinning out, several of the hot dog places had been shuttered and nailed, and the wind, as always, had been waiting there to sing for us.

I almost saw Mama sitting on the sand as she used to sit. I had that feeling again of wanting to be alone. But I could not force myself to say it to Margaret. I only held onto her and waited.

It got late in the day. Most of the children had gone home, and only a few men and women remained basking in the windy sun.

The life-guard boat pulled up on the shore. The life-guard stepped out of it, slowly, with something in his arms.

I froze there. I held my breath and I felt small, only twelve years old, very little, very infinitesimal and afraid. The wind howled. I could not see Margaret. I could see only the beach, the life-guard slowly emerging from his boat with a gray sack in his hands, not very heavy, and his face almost as gray and lined.

"Stay here, Margaret," I said. I don't know why I said it.

"But, why?"

"Just stay here, that's all—"

I walked slowly down the sand to where the life-guard stood. He looked at me.

"What is it?" I asked.

The life-guard kept looking at me for a long time and he couldn't speak. He put the gray sack down on the sand, the water whispered wet up around it and went back.

"What is it?" I insisted.

"She's dead," said the life-guard quietly.

I waited.

"Funny," he said softly, "funniest thing I ever saw. She's been dead— a long time."

I repeated his words. "A long time?"

"Ten years, I'd say. There haven't been any children drowned here *this* year. There were twelve children drowned here since 1933, but we recovered all their bodies before a few hours had passed. All except one, I remember. This body here, why it must be ten years in the water. It's not—pleasant."

"Open it," I said. I don't know why I said it. The wind was louder.

He fumbled with the sack. "The way I know it's a little girl, is because she's still wearing a locket. There's nothing much else to tell by—"

"Hurry, man *open it!*" I cried.

"I better not do that," he said. Then maybe he saw the way my face must have looked. "She was such a little girl—"

He opened it only part way. That was enough.

The beach was deserted. There was only the sky and the wind and the water and the autumn coming on lonely. I looked down at her there.

I said something, over and over. The life-guard looked at me. "Where did you find her?" I asked.

"Down the beach, in the shallow water. Down that way. It's a long, long time for her, ain't it?"

I shook my head.

"Yes, it is. Oh, God, yes it is."

I thought, people grow. I have grown. But she has not changed. She is still small. She is still young. Death does not permit growth or change. She still has golden hair. She will be forever young and I will love her forever, oh God, I will love her forever.

The life-guard tied up the sack again.

Down the beach, a few moments later, I walked by myself. I found something I didn't really expect. This is where the life-guard found her body, I said to myself.

There, at the water's edge, lay a sand-castle, only half built. Just like Tally and I used to make them. She—half. And I—half.

I looked at it. This is where they found Tally. I knelt beside the sand-castle and saw the little prints of feet coming in from the lake and going back out to the lake again—and not returning ever.

Then—I knew.

"I'll help you finish it," I said.

I did. I built the rest of it up very slowly, and then I arose and turned away and walked off, so as not to watch it crumble in the waves, as all things crumble.

I walked back up the beach to where a strange woman named Margaret waited for me, smiling. . . .

THE ROCK

BY SHIRLEY JACKSON

SHIRLEY JACKSON, the superb author of *The Lottery* and *The Haunting of Hill House*, was called by some of her friends, the Virginia Werewolf of séance fiction; others maintained she used a broomstick instead of a pen. In any case, ghosts and hauntings, phantoms and apparitions appeared frequently in her writing, which also had another outlet, humorous vignettes of the delights and turmoil of an extensive family life. "I write," she once said, "because it's the only chance I get to sit down."

When Miss Jackson sat down to create her world of the new American Gothic horror, she kept an open mind. When queried about whether she had ever seen a ghost, she answered that while she had been researching *The Haunting of Hill House*, "I had not the slightest desire to see a ghost. I was absolutely willing to go on the rest of my life without ever seeing even the slightest supernatural manifestation." But she found herself taking refuge in the pages of *Little Women* every night just to hold the spectral world at bay.

Her stories are not only brilliant but have a strange cryptic, haunted quality, particularly this little-known masterpiece that confronts the most final apparition of all. 𝕰𝕰

BEING ON the water was not precisely a unique, but rather an unusual, experience for Paula Ellison, and for the first few minutes that she sat on the small seat almost too close to the front of the boat, she was perfectly still, afraid not so much of upsetting the boat as of being unprepared when it surely did upset. She had gotten in first, and sat with her back to the island where they were going, watching the young man in the oilskin jacket as he helped first her sister-in-law Virginia, and then her brother Charles, into the more comfortable seats in the center of the boat. Charles, Paula thought, looked tired, and she thought further that she did not grudge him the better seat, or the reassurance of sitting next to Virginia, because Charles had certainly been so very ill, and was still not well, and looked tired after their journey.

"I'm so *excited*," Virginia said, and bounced in the boat almost like a child. Then she added, in the gentle voice both she and Paula were now using toward Charles, "How do you feel, darling?"

"Very well indeed," Charles said. "Very much better."

"It looks so *exciting*," Virginia said. "Look at it, all dark and rocky against the sky and that *perfect* sunset."

"What is that picture?" Charles asked. "*You* know the one."

"Like a pirate stronghold," Virginia continued ecstatically, "or a prison or some—"

Paula said with amusement, "Charles, do you think it entirely wise to bring Virginia to a place where she can indulge her romantic temperament so fully?"

Charles, without hearing her, said to Virginia, "Actually, I'm afraid it's only a rather ordinary summer resort." He smiled at his sister. "Do you think we might find one pirate for Virginia?"

Paula, without meaning to, looked over his head to the young man in the oilskin jacket who was running the boat, and found him at that moment looking at her, so that she turned quickly away and said, "It's cold."

"It *is* cold." Virginia pulled her coat closer around her.

"We're here so late in the year," Charles said.

Paula said immediately. "That's *much* better, you know; it means we'll be practically the only people and won't have to bother being sociable."

Virginia added, almost as quickly, "And I *always* think these early fall days are the best, after all. Relaxing," she added vaguely.

"Well, at least I didn't keep us from any vacation at all this year," Charles said.

"I never intended to take any vacation this year," Virginia said. "I *hate* going away in the summers, and the children are so much better off not going into public resorts."

"As you know," Paula said stiffly, "I rarely plan on a vacation at all. If it hadn't been for your insisting that you needed me—"

Charles laughed. "You worry too much," he said, turning from Virginia to Paula. "You don't have to fuss every time I mention being sick."

"You're not to think about it," Paula said.

"We all want to forget it," Virginia said.

"It's forgotten," Charles said. "How much longer will it take to reach the island?" From the inflection of his voice everyone immediately assumed that he was speaking to the young man in the oilskin jacket and did not know how otherwise to address him, whether as "driver" or "captain" or "ferryman" or perhaps "boy."

After a minute the young man said, "Nearly there."

"Does the island have a name?" Virginia asked.

"People round here call it mostly Rock Island," the young man said.

"Even *that* is exciting," Virginia said. She looked first at Charles and then at Paula. "Even that it should be named Rock Island. Like a stronghold, or a fort, or a—"

"Rock," Paula said.

"We land on the other side," the young man said, without being asked; it was as though every person whom he carried to the island asked the same series of questions, made the same comments, spoke of pirates and that picture, *you* know, and went on to ask how long now? and what was the name of the island, and as though the next question had to be "Where do we land?" or "Do we dock there?" or "How are you going to get the boat up onto those rocks?" and this time, for once, impatient and perhaps tired of ferrying, he answered the question before it could be asked. Paula, who thought that Virginia was again going to say "How exciting," said quickly, "Charles, are you tired?"

"No," he said, surprised. "Not tired at all; I'm feeling very well, really."

Although she had not intended to view this island, this site of her unexpected holiday, so soon, had meant ever since she stepped into the boat without being allowed a chance of turning around to keep her back steadfastly against the island and not turn, not turn, until she was close enough to touch it, Paula at last forgot her resolution and turned to look; she saw, looming impossibly large over her head and with the red sunset behind, a great black jagged rock, without signs of humanity or sympathy, with only dreadful reaching black rocks and sharp incredible outlines against the sunset and she said (thinking, I can always go back if it's *too* awful), "Charles, how do you feel?"

"I feel *fine*," he said sharply.

"It's just all *too* exciting," Virginia said.

As the boat came closer it appeared that the island was composed of a single rock instead of many; there were no pebbles or splinters of rock at the edges of the water in the little cove to which the young man guided the boat, and a series of steps leading up to the house above seemed to be carved out of the rock. The sun had gone by now and only a faint impression of the sunset lay in the sky; it had grown much colder and the coming darkness made the rock look blacker and the steps steep and wet.

"Can we get up there at all?" Paula said, leaning from the boat to look at the steps; realizing that she was expected to stand and move from the boat onto the steps she hesitated and then reflected that she could hardly stay on in the boat unless she chose to go back with the ferryman. I wish for once Virginia would move first, she thought, or Charles, and then rebuked herself with the recollection that after all Virginia could hardly climb over Paula in the end seat to get out, and Charles was ill. The young man stepped easily from the boat onto the rock and held out his hand to Paula, and she remembered that he had helped Virginia into the boat earlier, and took his hand and found herself with less grace than usual almost scrambling onto the rock steps. They were not wet, after all, or slippery, but seemed actually to press back against her feet as though holding firmly against her.

I like it here, she thought, surprising herself, and found the steps irresistible; before Virginia was even out of the boat Paula had turned and begun to climb. At first she only enjoyed the pressure of the steps under her feet, and then she raised her head and saw the house above her and she began to climb faster.

"Look at Paula, so far ahead," she heard Charles saying below her; he sounded cross, and she thought that perhaps he was annoyed with her for having spoken so much of his illness. Ahead of her the windows of the house showed light and then the door opened and someone came into the doorway, looking down and seeming to peer through the darkness.

"Who is it?" the woman in the doorway called.

Required to identify herself suddenly, Paula hesitated on the steps and then turned and looked behind her. Charles and Virginia were following her slowly, helping one another, and Paula felt first a small pang that she had not stayed with them, but had gone on so easily herself. Then, past the curve of the rock below her, she saw the boat going back, and was suddenly very frightened when she realized that the boat and the ferryman had never intended to stay with them; how will we ever get back? she wondered, and then smiled at herself, thinking that surely the ferryman must come back several times a day.

"Are you all right?" she called down to Charles and Virginia. "Shall I come back and help you?"

"We're all right," Virginia called up to her. "The steps are just a little steep for Charles."

Paula turned and climbed on up to the house while the woman in the doorway stood watching her. "So you've come," said the woman in the doorway when Paula was close enough for her to speak. "I'd almost given up expecting you."

Not a very gracious hostess, Paula thought. "We've been late for everything all day," she explained. "Trains, busses, meals, everything."

"You'll have to take what you can get here tonight," the woman said. "Dinner's been done with for an hour, and the dishes washed and put away."

"I'm sure we won't want much," Paula said. She was displeased, and as she came up onto the last, wider steps which led to the doorway she did not stop to look at the woman, but brushed past her and went inside. The room into which she came seemed to be made of the rock of the island, and for a minute she stood staring, forgetting the landlady behind her. A great fire burned on the far side of the huge room, and flickered against the walls in lines that might have been reflecting mica in rock, ran in light up and down the wide dark walls on which no pictures hung, and shattered itself oddly across and along the floor on which no rug lay. The furniture was huge and wooden, a great trestle table with benches on either side, and a long wooden bench with back and arms which brought the word "settle" to Paula's mind, and huge

square wooden chairs, worn and smooth with use. There were no orna-
ments of any kind and no light except from the great fire.

Paula heard the landlady, still behind her in the doorway, calling
down to Charles and Virginia that it was only a bit more to come, and
then the landlady added very quietly, "You'll want to put in curtains
and such, I daresay."

"Were you speaking to me?" Paula asked; there seemed no one else
around.

"And flowers, I suppose."

Paula advanced to the fire and stood warming her hands. "It's a most
unusual room," she said. She was trying to identify her own feelings;
over and above everything else was a great despair and impulsive dislike
of this house, this woman, this room; she tried to tell herself that it was
the usual reaction to finishing a long journey and finding less comfort
than she had been dreaming of since she left home. More than this,
however, she was discouraged; this did not seem at all the sort of place
in which to spend a belated vacation and she was anxious over how
Charles and Virginia would feel about it. It'll be better in the morning
when the sun is out, she told herself, and heard Charles and Virginia
greeting the landlady.

"Did our suitcases come?" Charles was asking immediately; he had
overseen their departure.

"This morning," said the landlady. "They're in your rooms."

"Splendid," said Charles. He came over to the fire and stood beside
Paula. "Chill in the air," he said.

"It gets cold nights, this time of year," the landlady said.

"This is an extraordinary room," Virginia said. "It looks as though it's
made out of rock."

"It *is* rock, as a matter of fact," said the landlady. "Most unusual.
The greater part of the house is made of rock; I have a small booklet
describing it for tourists, and I have put copies in your rooms. It is
regarded as a most unusual house."

"It is *most* unusual," said Charles. "You are Mrs. Carter, of course?"

"Mrs. Carter," said the landlady, nodding. "Mr. and Mrs. Ellison."

"And Miss Ellison," said Charles, indicating Paula.

"Of course," said the landlady. "I have your rooms ready."

"Splendid," Charles said; he had taken command again now that
there was no physical exertion required, and he looked patronizingly

over Paula to say to the landlady, "Any chance of our having something to eat?"

The landlady waved her head back and forth sadly. "You came so late, you know," she said. "I can give you cheese, and beer, and perhaps, if you wanted to wait for a broiled chicken . . ."

"Just some tea for me, thanks," said Virginia.

"I should like some tea," Paula said.

"Whatever you can find, then, in a minute or so," Charles said. "Nothing that means any trouble."

The landlady nodded politely and went out of the room, and Charles, looking around with an odd smile, said "Well."

"Isn't it wonderful?" said Virginia. "That marvelous old woman, and this house . . ." she gestured at the walls and then, remembering, laughed and turned to Paula. "You know what she said to me, that funny old woman?" she demanded. "When I was just coming in the door, she whispered to me, was the tall woman with our party?" She laughed again. "Meaning *you*," she said to Paula.

"She didn't seem to like me," Paula said.

"These women are unaccountable," Charles said. "Remember she lives practically alone on this island."

"In this *wonderful* house," Virginia said.

It was substantially better in the daylight. They had slept in rooms adjoining one another, Charles and Virginia in a huge fourposter bed with curtains, and Paula in a small room with windows overlooking the water almost directly, and in the morning, lying awake in her bed, Paula was for a minute surprised at the moving reflections on the ceiling of her room before she realized that it was only the reflection of the sun on the water, reflected again through her windows. She rose from the bed and went to look out on the water and was shocked to see the steep and immediate fall of the island below her; this was the side of the island away from the steps they had come up the night before, and all this part of the house almost hung over the water. Looking down, Paula thought how in many ways this might be extraordinarily good for Charles after his illness, and good for Virginia and Paula too, since the whole aspect of the island lacked that cloying servitude which they all three hated by now, Charles from receiving it for so long, and she and Virginia from giving it; there was here no sense of heavy luxury and overrich surroundings, but only a very clear and distinct effect of an island out of sight of the mainland, sharp and strong alone on the water, and nothing below but solid rock and nothing more to do, perhaps, than endure the constant and incessant triumphs of water over rock, rock over water.

"I could spend all day," she thought, almost speaking aloud, "just standing somewhere watching the horizon, or sitting on a high rock, or walking down to the water and up again."

She put on a pair of heavy shoes, since if she were going to climb rocks she must be protected against their animosity, and went down the wide wooden stairs of the house into the stone room, where already this morning a fire was burning and the heavy furniture looked burnished in the sunlight through the windows. A clean napkin lay on the long wooden table and on it a heavy cup like the one she had had her tea from the night before, and a wooden trencher. Paula went to the door which she had learned led to the kitchen, opened it slightly, and called "Good morning."

"Well, there," said the landlady from somewhere within. "With us already?"

She swung the kitchen door wide and came into the stone room with an earthenware jug which she set down on the table. "Coffee," she said. "You'll have eggs, perhaps? And bacon? Fresh-made rolls?"

"Thank you," Paula said. Even the landlady seemed more cheerful this morning, and Paula thought that perhaps this was because she herself was not so sullen. "I'll have anything I may," she said, smiling. "I never dreamed I could be so hungry."

"It's being near the water," the landlady said profoundly. "You'll always have good appetite here. I've known them eat a whole chicken at a sitting."

"Tell me," Paula said, coming closer to look at the earthenware jug of coffee, "your dishes are so unusual, and so lovely. Where did you ever find them?"

"They came with the house," the landlady said. "I keep them because people seem to think they belong."

"They do, indeed," Paula said.

"Hard to wash clean," said the landlady, disappearing again into the kitchen.

This morning the moving lines of the firelight on the stone walls were caught and pursued by reflections of sunlight, and the broad windows overlooking the sea and the rock glittered until Paula wondered if the island could be seen from the mainland as a bright light on the horizon. She poured herself a cup of coffee from the earthenware jug, admiring its weight and solidity, and stood with her cup by the window, looking out. When the kitchen door opened she said without turning, "What is the rock the island is made of? I'd really swear it was black."

"Jet?" said the landlady's voice, musing, "malachite? I don't remember, but it's in the little book."

Paula came to the table and sat down, and served herself with eggs and bacon onto the wooden trencher. The landlady stood by, silently, and when Paula began to eat she said, "You'll see my other guest this morning."

"Another guest?" said Paula.

"You'll be wanting to meet him as soon as possible," said the landlady.

"Who is he?" said Paula, but the landlady was going into the kitchen. She finished her breakfast and lighted a cigarette, and came back to the window with her cigarette and her coffee cup, and pulled one of the great wooden chairs around to sit in, so that she was almost hidden by the back of it and was surprised for a minute by the landlady's scolding voice until she realized it could not possibly be addressed to her.

"She's been and gone, of course," said the landlady. "You ought to have come an hour ago." There was the dull sound of the wooden trenchers being stacked together and the landlady's voice went on, "I can't after all keep coming to look for you when I want you; there are people here needing food and bedding and attention, and where you've gone I can never tell."

Since she was eavesdropping, Paula thought that the only thing to do was stand up immediately and go to the table for more coffee as though she had not been listening at all, which turned out to be more difficult than she thought, when she saw the landlady's surprised face.

"She's here again, then," the landlady said. "This will be the other guest, Miss."

I hope she doesn't fall to addressing all her guests so impertinently, Paula thought, and turned to smile at the other guest; she felt an immediate shock of recognition, as though this were someone she had known all her life, and then realized that she had never seen him before. "How do you do," she said, and then stopped because she did not know his name.

"How do you do, Miss Ellison," he said courteously but in such a low voice that she was not completely sure if he had called her by name. He seemed so frightened of her that she refrained from asking his name, but only smiled again and said, "I was admiring the view of the water from the window."

"That's why I like an island," he said. His tone and his manner were precisely those of someone excruciatingly shy, who cannot always stop to frame sensible remarks. He was very small, and held his hands in front of him in an attitude of cringing, and the only fact against his being so terribly shy was that he did not avoid looking at her, as a shy person would, but kept his eyes fixed upon her in a sort of hypnotized stare, and, staring back rudely, Paula thought that his eyes must be almost the color and texture of the rock itself.

"I was waiting for your sister-in-law, actually," he said.

"She'll be down in a while," said Paula, trying not to smile. Virginia was small and lovely, and shy little men like this always found her reassuring. "She was very tired after our trip yesterday, and I expect she'll sleep late."

"You'll *do*, of course," he said ineptly.

"Thank you," Paula said with gravity. "Have you been here long?"

"Quite a while," said the little man vaguely. "A very long time, in fact."

"I understand that this is quite a popular spot earlier in the year."

"Moderately so. Never more than a few people, that is." He looked at her earnestly. "Not many people feel at *home* on an island," he said.

"I suppose only a certain sort of person would find this stimulating," Paula said. She glanced out the window again and down to the sea below. "It's an excellent place for my brother to be, right now; he's been very ill, and needed precisely this kind of lonely, stimulating spot."

"It will probably do him a great deal of good," said the little man politely.

"I hope so," said Paula. She was thinking of how such a concrete, limited world as an island and the sea might be extraordinarily helpful to Charles, since he would be given no choice except rock or water, and could not waste his mind in a thousand distractions; he might come to see everything, as she sternly hoped, in terms of solidity and fluidity, and learn that the rock was, as a place to live, far preferable to the sea. Perhaps, even, confining Charles to an island for a while would result in his taking an island away with him and being thus enabled to preserve for himself this kind of firm rock to live on always . . . The little man disturbed her by saying, "You mustn't be *entirely* sure of the rock, you know."

"I beg your pardon?"

"Well, it's been here for a number of years, of course . . . and rock is a hard thing to get rid of . . ."

"I don't understand."

"It doesn't matter at all," he said nervously. "Your brother's illness— it's given you a good deal of worry?"

"Of course," she said; she had mentioned Charles's illness originally as a sort of warning; it would be wisest, she felt, to let the other guest know immediately that Charles had been very ill indeed and must not be disturbed, and must not, indeed, be allowed to disturb others with vagaries left over from his illness. She had not expected, however, that the conversation might allow this little man to feel that he had any right to ask more personal questions; a polite murmur of sympathy was the most she had felt was required of him.

"It's been very difficult for you," he said.

"Do you expect to be here long?" She hoped she did not sound too emphatic; these little men were sometimes hard to discourage and yet, on the other hand, they might be so easily affronted.

"Not much longer now." He smiled at her, and again she thought that his eyes in the timid face were much like the rock under her feet. "I intend to walk up to the high rock this morning," he said. "The highest point on the island. You can't miss it."

"It must be very interesting," she said flatly.

"I shall be there all morning," he said. "Just follow the path that be- gins under your windows. Good-by."

As she stood staring at the doorway out of which he had gone so sud- denly she heard footsteps on the stairs, and a moment later her sister-in- law came into the room.

"Charles is feeling very tired and plans to stay in bed," she said. "Good morning, Paula dear."

"Good morning, Virginia. I'm so sorry about Charles."

"Is this coffee?"

The landlady came in, bustling and fussing at Virginia; Virginia would have fresh-baked rolls and bacon, and perhaps a gently boiled egg? Would Virginia have peaches brought from the mainland this morning? And the poor sick gentleman; would he have a tray?

Paula stood at the window and watched Virginia breakfast; already the sharp air of the sea outside had made her impatient with being indoors, and she found herself unwilling to move into the room when Virginia invited her to sit at the table and take more coffee; the window was at present as close as she might reasonably go to the outdoors, and she must remain within sight of the sea.

"*Wonderful* coffee," said Virginia. "I'm so hungry."

The landlady came over to the window and leaned out, standing near Paula.

"He'll be up on the high rock," she said softly.

"I know, he—"

"Mrs. Carter," said Virginia, "might I possibly have another of your incredible muffins?"

The landlady hurried off and into the kitchen, and Virginia said, without turning around, "Isn't she unbelievable?"

"Would you like to go for a walk this morning?" Paula asked. "If Charles is resting, you and I could go exploring."

"*Love* to," said Virginia. "All over the island—I can't wait."

The kitchen door swung open and the landlady returned, saying as she came, "The tray has gone up to the poor gentleman, and I hope he feels the better for it."

"Mrs. Carter," said Paula deliberately, "will you tell me the name of your other guest?"

"You ladies will be wanting fresh coffee," said the landlady, peering into the coffee jug; "shame on me for letting you waste yourselves on this."

"What other guest?" said Virginia as the landlady hurried off again.

"An odd little man," Paula said.

"And the view," said the landlady, returning, "you'll be wanting to see the view."

"My sister and I thought we might walk over the island this morning," Paula said.

"Indeed you will," said the landlady, "and if the poor gentleman up-stairs calls, I'll be right here."

"Where would you suggest we start?" Paula asked.

"Well," said the landlady. She stopped, thinking, her hands on her broad hips, and frowning slightly. "Most people," she said, "prefer the steps down to the sea and then the path around the seashore. Or if you turn to the right as you leave the front door, you will find a path that takes you through our garden. If it were earlier in the year I might sug-gest bathing in the cove, but delicate young ladies do not care for bath-ing when the weather is chilled. Or perhaps—"

"What about the path that starts under my window?"

"That of course," said the landlady, "takes you just back down to the seashore again. Only if you go so far away and the poor gentleman up-stairs should happen to call . . ."

"We'd better stay near the house," Virginia said.

"You were asking about my kitchens," said the landlady to Virginia. "If the other lady chooses to go walking and yet you want to stay within hearing of the poor gentleman upstairs, I would account it a pleasure to show you my kitchens."

"I should love to see them," Virginia said. "Paula?"

"The other young lady is aching to be outside," the landlady said. "Some of us cannot resist the sea." She smiled politely at Paula and then turned again to Virginia. "If you are finished with your coffee," she said, "it might be as well to start before the day is much along." As Vir-ginia rose, the landlady said over her shoulder to Paula, "We'll see you back, then, by lunchtime. Mind the slippery rocks."

"Ah—Johnson," said the little man. "Yes, Johnson."

"I'm Paula Ellison, Mr. Johnson."

"Yes, of course. It was Virginia Ellison I was—yes, of course."

"Marvelous view up here."

"Isn't it? You'll be tired of the sound of your brother's voice, I ex-pect?"

"Why, I don't know that I am, particularly. Of course, he's been so very ill."

"Yes."

"It's been quite a strain on both of us."

"Both of us? Oh, yes, Virginia, I see."

"We've had to take *very* careful charge of him."

"Of course. It must have been most upsetting."

"Well—tiring."

"Your own brother. Yes, I quite understand. And his wife such a—may I say?—such a *dependent* person."

"She did as much as she was able."

"Of course. As much as she was able, yes."

"She is not strong. And she had the children."

"Let me confess—I *do* dislike children. You do too, I take it?"

"Well . . . not of course my own nieces."

"Of course not. Your own brother's children. But with the responsibility so much on you, and your sister-in-law so dependent, and the children too—it is not surprising you have been allowed to exhaust yourself."

"It has been very tiring, yes."

"And then of course in addition there would be the realization that there is actually no tie like that of flesh and blood. No love like that between brother and sister."

"We have always been very close, Mr. Johnson."

"Of course. Unusually so, I daresay."

"Perhaps we have. Too close, perhaps."

"Neither of you could do very well without the other, I suppose. And it is so hard when one is ill."

"Very hard."

"I suppose you have never been so ill?"

"Never."

"But I daresay if you *were*, your brother would care for you as attentively as you care for him."

"If he could, yes."

"He has so much more to worry about. His children, his wife."

"He would hardly have much time for *me*."

"His wife would need him. She is so dependent, she could hardly spare him to care for his sister. Only his sister, when his wife and children need him at home."

"I am sure she would be most concerned if anything happened to me."

"Most concerned, yes. She is really very fond of you, I suppose."

"We are very fond of each other. Quite companionable."

"Perhaps your mutual concern over your brother brought you even closer together. You share one dear object, after all."

"Charles is very dear to both of us."

"Of course. His wife is probably with him now."

"I ought to go back."

"Not at all. If she is there, you can hardly be needed."

"Now then," said the landlady heartily, "here you are, back again much before you're wanted. My little joke," she added, looking at Paula's frown. "I am indeed a great joker. And you didn't stay long. Nothing to worry about with your sister, neither. She's up with the poor gentleman has been so ill, and I daresay gives him better medicine than any of us could, with the smile on her sweet face. And so you met Mr. Arnold?"

"Arnold? He said his name was Johnson."

"And so it is, if he says so. I'll be calling you Arnold or Heathen or something, give me my head; I never could remember a name and that's the truth. So you met him, whatever he chooses to call himself?"

"I ran into him by accident."

"So you did, dear, so you did. And you'll be wanting to know now where you can meet him next?"

"Nothing of the sort," said Paula stiffly. "I was about to go up—"

"To the high rock again? He won't be *there* by now. Tomorrow maybe. Try late tonight in front of the great fire, after the rest of us are abed. *There* you will find him."

"Certainly not," said Paula.

"Well, then it'll take you a while," said the landlady. "And the things he can tell you and all. Solid rock," she continued smoothly as Virginia came into the room, "and standing here since no one knows when."

"How is Charles?" Paula asked Virginia.

"Feeling much better, thank you," Virginia said.

"I'll just go up for a minute."

"Please don't," said Virginia hastily. "I mean, he said he was going to try to sleep and it would be better not to disturb him."

"And then of course there's Virginia, so weak, and so safe."

"She's not entirely safe—"

"Not entirely. But for all you or I could do . . ."

"She's very fond of me."

"And very fond of Charles. But so dependent. So pretty, too, and so weak, and so fragile. Such a pretty girl."

"I have been very necessary to her."

"Of course now that Charles is better you will not be quite so necessary. They will have each other again."

"That is as it should be."

"As you say. That is as it should be. And you?"

"I shall go home again, I suppose."

"Home?"

"I have a small apartment. I left there of course while Charles was so very ill. It was necessary for me to stay with Virginia."

"But now you will go back?"

"I have not been asked to stay with Virginia."

"They have each other again. And the children, and their home. I suppose they will feel sorry for you?"

"Sorry for me?"

"That you have gone, I mean. Sorry to be without you."

"I suppose so."

"See how the fire shines on the walls. It is perfectly safe here in this room, of course. This room is solid rock. It is only in the rest of the house that fire might be a danger. The rest of the house is of wood."

"Virginia, will you come exploring with me *today?*" Paula stood by the window; it was her daily habit now to take her breakfast there, sitting in the great wooden chair, where she could keep sight of the sea. During the day she found the sound and the smell and the sight of the sea almost a necessity for her, and at night she either sat late in the rock room with the great fire roaring before her and the sound of the sea all outside, or lay straight and silent on her narrow bed with the windows open onto the cliffs below and the sea almost in her room. "We've been here almost a week, and I don't believe you've so much as stepped outdoors."

"It makes me nervous," said Virginia. She smiled across the coffee jug at Paula. "I think I'm beginning to feel caught in by the island. Almost homesick for land on all sides instead of sea."

"Charles likes it."

"Sometimes," said Virginia. "Sometimes he's as much afraid as I am."

"Afraid, Virginia?"

"*You* know," Virginia said, gesturing vaguely. "You get to feeling so sort of cut off from everything. No way of escape. No way to get home again."

"I thought I'd run up and see Charles after breakfast," Paula said. "Is he sleeping?"

"Resting, anyway. Why don't you put it off until after lunch?"

"I will probably not be back. I intended to take a lunch with me and spend all day on the rocks."

"What can you find to *do* out there?"

"I find it stimulating, nothing but the sea and the rocks and nothing between them but me."

"And do you run across the other guest?" Virginia asked innocently.

"I sometimes gather shells, but there are no very interesting ones."

"You spoke once of another guest," Virginia said insistently. "Didn't you once mention an odd little man?"

"Suppose I just run up and say good morning to Charles, and spend just a minute trying to cheer him up?"

"He's cheerful enough. Why don't you wait till tonight?"

"I'd like to see him now, if you're sure you don't mind."

Silently, Virginia followed Paula upstairs and into the room Virginia and Charles shared. Paula had been here daily since they came, but Charles had not yet come downstairs, protesting that he was convalescing well enough in his bed, with the smell of the sea in his room and its sound in his ears always, and the landlady's good food brought to him regularly. He looked better, Paula thought; he had more color in his face—surprising, since he had not been outdoors or even had fresh air in the room—and he was astonishingly vigorous for someone who had been so very ill for such a long time.

"Good morning, Charles dear," she said as she entered. "And how well you look today!"

"I feel splendidly well," Charles said from the bed. He hoisted himself up slightly and turned his cheek for his sister's morning kiss. "You look well, Paula."

"I love it here. I'm afraid Virginia is bored, though."

"Is she?" Charles smiled over Paula's head at Virginia. "I don't think so," he said.

"You must try to get outdoors, Charles, and get nearer the sea. I can't tell you how invigorating I find it."

"Perhaps *you* do," Charles said. "Virginia and I prefer it indoors. We like our sea through windows."

"And *here*'s the poor gentleman's breakfast," said the landlady, bustling in with her tray. "Did he think I had forgotten him? When I was only waiting for hot corncakes from the oven? And see that you eat all of it, my poor Mr. Ellison, and we will have you well in no time at all."

"Will you have your breakfast, darling?" Virginia asked. She came closer to the bed. "Excuse me, Paula; let me come in here and see that his tray is right. Darling, are you hungry? I had such a wonderful breakfast downstairs."

"Good morning, Miss Ellison," said Mr. Johnson from the doorway. Paula looked up, over the heads of Charles and Virginia and the landlady and saw him, somehow taller, standing leaning against the doorway. "And how are *you* this morning?"

"I had eggs, and homemade sausage, just as you have, only I didn't have these wonderful corncakes. Just try one, darling. I believe Mrs. Carter made them especially for you."

"And how is your poor sick brother? *Is* he any better? And your sister-in-law, how is she?"

"Good morning, Mr. Johnson," Paula said.

"I beg your pardon, dear?" said Virginia, looking back at Paula over her shoulder. "Did you ask Charles something?"

"I doubt if she will bother with *me*, Miss Ellison. I doubt very much if she would ever be interested in me now."

Paula turned and stared, first at Charles and Virginia, who was bending over him laughing and feeding him, and then at the landlady, who was watching Paula silently and with an expression which might have been humorous.

"Mrs. Carter—" Paula said.

Mrs. Carter shrugged.

Mr. Johnson went on smoothly, "It had to be one or the other of you, you see; I told you I was waiting for your sister-in-law, but you *would* come first. It was your decision, you know; I would have been satisfied with either."

"Just don't try to answer him, dear," Mrs. Carter whispered. "There's no answer he'll take." She put a protective arm around Paula. "Try to hide behind me," she said very softly.

"No use, Mrs. Carter," he said, and smiled sadly. "No use at all, you know." He nodded at Paula. "*She* knows," he said, and went swiftly and silently away.

ABOUT THE AUTHORS

CHARLES DICKENS, one of the world's great novelists, was born in England in 1812. The son of a navy clerk, he grew up in London. During one of his father's imprisonments for debt, the twelve-year-old Charles was apprenticed in a blacking warehouse and learned firsthand the horror of child labor. At seventeen he became a court shorthand reporter and subsequently a parliamentary reporter for the London *Morning Chronicle*. His sketches of London types (first signed "Boz" in 1834) began appearing in periodicals in 1833, and the collected *Sketches by Boz* (1836) enjoyed a great success. *The Posthumous Papers of the Pickwick Club* (1836–37) made Dickens and his characters Sam Weller and Mr. Pickwick famous. For his eager and ever more numerous readers Dickens worked vigorously, publishing first in monthly installments and then as books, *Oliver Twist* (1838), *Nicholas Nickleby* (1839), *The Old Curiosity Shop* (1841). He often worked on more than one novel at a time. After a visit to America in 1842, he wrote *America Notes* (1842) and *Martin Chuzzlewit* (1844), both sharply criticizing America's shortcomings. His many other novels, of which *David Copperfield* was his own favorite, were written while he was lecturing, managing his amateur theatrical company, and editing successively two magazines, *Household Words* and *All the Year Round*. Then in 1870, while finishing Chapter 23 of his crime and detective novel, *The Mystery of Edwin Drood*, Dickens became unconscious and died at the age of fifty-eight, leaving behind a work which still puzzles historians and writers of detective fiction—a mystery without a solution.

BRAM STOKER was born in Dublin, Ireland, in 1847, the son of a government official. In his childhood he was an invalid, but in after years he became one of the leading athletes of Dublin University, where he had a brilliant academic career. For ten years he worked in the Irish Civil Service, and in 1878 published *The Duties of Clerks of Petty Sessions in Ireland*. In the same year he became Henry Irving's acting manager at the Lyceum, and later (1906) he wrote *Personal Reminiscences of Henry Irving*. In 1893, Stoker spent several weeks in Scotland and subsequently used it for the locale of several of his short stories, including "The Secret of the

Growing Gold." In 1897 he published *Dracula*, which has been called the most blood-curdling horror story in English literature and which sold over a million copies. He died in 1912.

WILKIE COLLINS, English novelist, elder son of William Collins, the landscape painter, was born in London, in 1824. He was named after his godfather, Sir David Wilkie, a well-known artist. Collins was educated at a private school in Highburg, and then taken to Italy by his parents, where the family lived for three years. In his late teens his father placed him in the office of a tea merchant in London, but he used any free time for reading and writing. He later studied law and was admitted to the bar but had little interest in it as a career. In 1848 he wrote a life of his father, and in 1850 published his first novel, *Antonina*, which was inspired by his life in Italy. About this time Collins began his close association with Dickens and contributed stories and articles to Dickens' *Household Words*, where *After Dark* (1856) and *The Dead Secret* (1857) ran serially. Throughout the rest of their lives Collins and Dickens influenced each other's work and occasionally collaborated on a story. In his own time Wilkie Collins was regarded by many as the equal of Dickens and Thackery and his novels were enormously popular. Now he is best remembered for *The Woman in White*, a mystery novel, and *The Moonstone*, which has been called "the first, the longest, and the best of detective novels." He died in 1889.

EDGAR ALLAN POE, poet, short story writer, and critic, was born in Boston, in 1809, the child of itinerant actors. His mother died before he was three years old, and he was adopted by the John Allans of Richmond, Virginia. In 1815 his parents took him to England where he received a good education which was continued on his return to America. He published his first volume of poems in 1827 and his second two years later; by now he had spent one year at the University of Virginia, two in the U. S. Army, and was about to enter, and shortly afterward to be dismissed from, the Military Academy at West Point. In 1831 Poe's continued drinking and gambling led to total estrangement from John Allan. In the same year Poe published an enlarged edition of his poems, and in 1833 was successful in a competition for a prize tale and a prize poem, the tale being the "Ms. found in a Bottle," and the poem, "The Coliseum." The following year Poe was disinherited by John Allan's will and forced to support himself. He did so by becoming a contributor to various periodicals. In 1836 he married Virginia Clemm, who was devotedly attached to him until her death in 1847. *The*

Narrative of Arthur Gordon Pym was published in 1838, *Tales of the Grotesque and Arabesque*, in two volumes, in 1840, *Tales and The Raven and Other Poems* in 1845, and *Eureka* in 1848. He became famous in 1845 with the printing of "The Raven" in the *Evening Mirror* and the *Whig Review*. Although Poe's literary output was small he had great influence on world literature. He died in 1849.

SHERIDAN LE FANU, born in Dublin in 1814, was the son of the dean of the Irish Episcopal Church and a descendant of the famous Sheridans of Ireland. His grandmother was Alice Sheridan Le Fanu, poet and playwright, and sister of Richard Brinsley Sheridan, author of *The Rivals* and *The School for Scandal*. While a student at Trinity College, Dublin, Le Fanu contributed stories to the *Dublin University Magazine*, which he ultimately edited. Though trained as a lawyer, he decided on a literary career. Le Fanu became famous overnight with the publication of two ballads, "Shamus O'Brien" and "Phaudhrig Crohoors." He was fascinated by the occult and uncanny and wrote a number of horror and suspense stories which were enormously popular. He died in 1873.

RHODA BROUGHTON, novelist, was born near Denbigh in Wales, in 1840, the daughter of a clergyman. She was brought up in Staffordshire, but after her father's death lived in North Wales and later at Oxford. Her first two novels, published when she was twenty-seven, were *Not Wisely but Too Well* and *Cometh Up as a Flower*, both of which were considered very daring. Thereafter she wrote at the rate of about one novel every two years. Encouraged by her uncle, Sheridan Le Fanu, she tried her hand at the short story and wrote a number of excellent ghost stories. She died in 1920.

MARY WILKINS FREEMAN, American writer, was born in Randolph, Massachusetts, in 1852, of Puritan ancestry. Her early education, chiefly from reading and observation, was supplemented by a course at Mount Holyoke Seminary, South Hadley, Massachusetts. She then lived in Vermont until her marriage in 1902 to Dr. Charles M. Freeman of Metuchen, New Jersey. She contributed poems and stories to magazines and published several books for children, including *Young Lucretia and Other Stories* (1892) and *Once Upon a Time and Other Child Verses* (1887). *A Humble Romance and Other Stories* (1887) and *A New England Nun and Other Stories* (1891) gave her a prominent place among American short story writers. Her writing showed great skill in interpreting the psychological effect of the severe and frustrating life of rural New England. She died at Metuchen, New Jersey, in 1930.

WALTER DE LA MARE, English poet and novelist, was born in Kent, England, in 1873. He was educated at St. Paul's Cathedral Choir School, where he founded a school magazine. He worked for eighteen years for the Anglo-American Oil Company and, in 1908, was granted a Civil List pension which enabled him to devote himself to writing. His novels won many prizes, and his *The Listeners and Other Poems* (1912) established his reputation as a writer in the realms of childhood and dreamland. He died in 1956.

HENRY JAMES, novelist and short story writer, was born in New York, in 1843, son of a theological writer and brother of William James, the philosopher and psychologist. The elder James was wealthy and the sons were able to follow their inclinations. A long visit to Europe during his boyhood laid the foundation of the passion which Henry James had all his life for European culture. After an unsystematic education which included the study of law at Harvard, in 1865 he began contributing reviews, sketches, and short stories to various periodicals. In 1871 his first novel, *Watch and Ward*, appeared serially, and in 1875 his first volume of short stories was published. In the same year he moved to Europe, and in 1876 settled in London, where he lived for more than twenty years. His work falls roughly into three periods. In the first he was occupied with the impact of American life on the older European civilization. During the middle period he developed purely English themes, and finally in his third period he returned to his original theme of the contrast between American and European character. His works include *Roderick Hudson* (1875), *Daisy Miller* (1879), *The Bostonians* (1886), *The Spoils of Poynton* (1897), and *The Awkward Age* (1899). James also wrote over a hundred short stories. He had enormous influence on both American and British writers. Although he spent most of his life in England, he retained his American citizenship until July 1915, when he finally became a naturalized British subject, in protest against our failure to enter the First World War. He received the Order of Merit at the New Year Honors of 1916, and shortly afterward died at Chelsea.

O. HENRY was the pen name of William Sydney Porter, who was born in Greensboro, North Carolina, in 1862 and died in New York City in 1910. He worked as a drugstore clerk and cowboy and finally became a writer. He first laid eyes on New York City in 1902 and was in love with the city for the rest of his life. When he died he left over six hundred complete stories behind him, and the bulk of them are about New York City. His stories are mellow, humorous, ironic, ingenious, and shot through with that quality known as "human interest."

EDWARD JOHN MORETON DRAX PLUNKETT, eighteenth Baron Dunsany, poet and playwright, was born in London, in 1878. Educated at Eton and Sandhurst, he succeeded to the title on his father's death in 1899. He served in the Boer War and was wounded in World War I. In the Second World War he held the chair of Byron Professor of English Literature at Athens, and barely escaped capture by the Germans. By contrast with his work, which consists of delicate fantasies, he was an extremely athletic person; he once estimated that 97 per cent of his time was spent in sport and soldiering, the rest in writing. His first book was a novel, *The Gods of Pegana* (1905); other novels are *Time and the Gods* (1906), *The King of Elfland's Daughter* (1924), and *The Wise Woman* (1933). *The Sword of Welleran* (1908) is a volume of short stories. In 1909, on Yeats's invitation, he wrote a play, *The Glittering Gate*, for the Abbey Theater, and followed it with many others. He also published two volumes of verse and a series of autobiographies. He died in 1957.

M. R. JAMES was born in England in 1862. He was educated at Eton and King's College, Cambridge, where he was awarded many prizes and scholarships. In 1905 he was elected Provost of his old college, from 1913 to 1915 was Vice-Chancellor of Cambridge, and in 1918 became Provost of Eton. He published books on biblical, historical, and artistic subjects and had a special interest in archaeology. In more popular vein were his two collections of *Ghost Stories of an Antiquary*. He died in 1936.

H. P. LOVECRAFT was born in Providence, Rhode Island, in 1890 and was a lifelong resident of that city. Although only forty-seven when he died, he had reached the pinnacle of his creative power. He was an antiquarian by taste and a recluse by preference. His wide reading, backed by field explorations, gave him a scholar's authority on the colonization and history of New England. This knowledge provided him with the realistic detail and visual vitality that give conviction to his tales of supernatural horror. He died in 1937.

DAPHNE DU MAURIER, British novelist, born in London in 1907, is a daughter of Sir Gerald du Maurier, the famous actor, and granddaughter of George du Maurier, the artist and novelist. Two of her most interesting books are *Gerald, a Portrait* (1934), a study of her father, and *The du Mauriers* (1937), which relates the story of three generations. She was educated at home and in Paris. In 1932 she married Sir Frederick A. M. Browning of the Grenadier Guards, who became Comptroller of Princess Elizabeth's Household in 1947. *The Loving Spirit*, Lady Browning's first novel, was published in 1931. It was followed by *I'll Never Be Young Again* (1932) and *The Progress of Julius* (1933). She is a prolific and compelling story-teller. Her best-known work is *Rebecca*, which has been widely imitated since its publication in 1938. Among her other books are: *Jamaica Inn* (1936), *Frenchman's Creek* (1941), *Kiss Me Again, Stranger* (1952), *My Cousin Rachel* (1951), and *The Scapegoat* (1957). She was created a Dame Commander of the Order of the British Empire in 1969. Miss du Maurier lives in Cornwall.

RAY BRADBURY, science fiction writer and novelist, was born in Waukegan, Illinois, in 1920. His family moved to Arizona, and then to Los Angeles in 1934. In high school he founded and edited a mimeographed quarterly, *Futuria Fantasia*. Although he is now a successful writer, it took him quite a few years to become accepted. A prolific writer of short stories, he began his career with a collection of macabre fantasies entitled *Dark Carnival* (1947), some of which were reprinted in *The October Country* (1955). In twenty-five years he has published over three hundred stories and more than fourteen books including stories and novels. Bradbury now devotes much of his time to script writing. He wrote the screenplay for John Huston's *Moby Dick*, and his own novel, *Fahrenheit 451*. He has won many awards and honors.

SHIRLEY JACKSON was born in San Francisco in 1919 and spent most of her early life in California. She studied for a year at the University of Rochester, and then transferred to Syracuse University, where she took her B.A. degree in 1940. The same year she married a classmate, Stanley Edgar Hyman, the literary critic and author. Fame first came to her in 1948 for "The Lottery," a hair-raising intellectual horror story. Her last two novels were *The Haunting of Hill House* (1959), which was made into a motion picture, and *We Have Always Lived in the Castle* (1962). Her stories appeared regularly in *The New Yorker* magazine, and many were dramatized for television and radio. She died in 1965.

SEON MANLEY and GOGO LEWIS, who have worked together on many books, are sisters and have been collecting supernatural stories throughout their lives. Mrs. Manley lives in Greenwich, Connecticut, with her management consultant husband Robert, their daughter Shivaun, two dogs, and five supernatural cats.

Mrs. Lewis (Mrs. William Lewis) lives in Bellport, Long Island, where the mist comes in from the bay with all the atmosphere of a Dickens novel. Her daughters, Carol and Sara, are also devotees of the supernatural tale.